A ROOSTE
& OTHER SHO

C000083192

IVAN PHILLIPOWSKY

INDIA · SINGAPORE · MALAYSIA

Notion Press

Old No. 38, New No. 6
McNichols Road, Chetpet
Chennai - 600 031

First Published by Notion Press 2019
Copyright © Ivan Phillipowsky 2019
All Rights Reserved.

ISBN 978-1-64733-638-7

DEDICATION

This book is dedicated to Mrs Beatrice Therese Martyr, without whose constant encouragement and at times nagging I would never have had the courage nor the inspiration to carry this through to the end. Thank you, Aunty!

I also dedicate this book to all Ex-servicemen everywhere with special reference to my buddies of SSC-17. Here's to THE SUPERSONIC SEVENTEEN!!!

I dedicate this book to my two sons Push and Rakesh, whom I love more than life itself.

CONTENTS

Contents

DEFINITIONS

Quite a few of my tales refer to my having worked deep, deep under cover of our military establishment and quite often in my narration I have resorted to the patois of our brave men in uniform. I have also used some acronyms, as I deemed it necessary, in order not to distract the reader with some long-winded referral to what is essentially the designation of a very senior general or politician or a building or a conference or whatever. I have tried to explain it in the context of the narration. Here are a few:

1. **OFFICIAL SECRETS ACT**

   A must have for any government worth its salt. A gift (Trojan Horse more likely) from our colonial masters. The act prohibits any government servant (gs) from revealing to the public, the goings on in the government. For instance, if a gs were to reveal to the public that our honourable RM enjoyed spicy samosas for elevenses everyday it would be constituted as a violation of the act and you can expect a midnight knock on your door, as it is tantamount to helping the enemy, as vital information has been given to them, thereby enabling the enemy to do any number of things with this information, like spiking the samosa, to complete deprivation of his favourite snack thus causing mental anguish and turmoil to our poor RM. Now I am not saying anything, but I'm sure the ISI and likeminded well-wishers of ours are even now racking their brains and trying to figure out whether it is indeed the ubiquitous samosa or something else say Idli and Sambhar. Another example would be, the arrest of the two journalists from Burma, for reporting on Rohingya massacres.

2. BUREAUCRACY/BUREAUCRAT

Another beauty left behind by our erstwhile masters. This is a system of government designed to make sure nothing ever happens unless of course the Minister *really really really* wants it to happen. Ministers are political appointees, career, pure-bred bureaucrats sneer at them and talk in English whenever they are around them, knowing fully well of their limited powers of comprehension of this language, their attention spans or rather lack of one, is well known. Chickens have been known to have longer attention spans but then to be fair, chickens don't have to worry about sweeping railway platforms in their constituencies or espousing the cause on TV as to why rising fuel prices are actually good for the nation as it encourages thriftiness. The bureaucrats know all this and arrange their schedules accordingly, and then before you can say EVM it election time again and its back to the constituency, thus, it is rare for a policy to reach even the second *really* stage let alone the third. If by some miracle the third *really* stage is reached then said bureaucrat is bound to implement said policy, all the while selectively leaking to the press, juicy titbits of misinformation. See what happened to OROP (One Rank One Pension). In short, Bureaucracy epitomises the status quo.

3. **DIV HQ**

   Divisional Headquarters. We have plenty of these. These are fighting formations and are located in field areas. They have lots of tanks and big guns etc. each one is commanded by a General Officer Commanding (GOC) or GOD (General Officer Demanding) as we prefer to call him. The GOC's are normally crusty old farts who have ascended the 8 steps to success by sheer dint of their capacity to strictly follow the undermentioned few simple rules:

   a. **Kiss plenty of ass.**

      Always agree with your seniors until of course, you become a senior yourself, then you can screw anyone who disagrees with you. (this is a very rare phenomenon, but there are instances, lost in time, where juniors have been known to disagree with their seniors)

   b. Laugh at all his jokes, and I mean all, no matter how stupid or inane they maybe.

   c. Pass the buck,

   d. Sign only those financial documents where in another junior /senior officer can also be blamed

   e. Compliment their (Senior Officers') wives on how beautiful they look no matter if it is to the contrary.

   f. Parties, have plenty of parties but for only your seniors and if they are in a position to give you a good ACR,

g. Golf play plenty of golf, but only play well if you are partnering the GOC. If by chance the old coot is playing against you, then make sure you shoot plenty of bogies and aim for the sand traps, these are quite large and would be very difficult to miss. If possible, if there are woods, try and lose your ball in them.

h. Bridge play plenty of bridge. Same rules apply as for (g) above. If the GOC is your partner, play as per Culbertson (Kulbushan). If the Brits can anglicize our names, then we can Indianize theirs. If you are playing opposite the old man, then have a ball. Go for Grand Slams, overbid, miscount the suits, forget which side the queen is and screw up the finesse, when you are trying to make that extra trick, the world is your oyster and will guarantee your always being included in any foursome whenever the GOC is playing.

i. Strict adherence to these simple steps, if followed, is sure to ensure a rapid rise to the top, however if everyone were to follow these rules then we are back to where we started, hence the more ingenious resort to lying cheating and backstabbing to get ahead. Its Darwin's law all over again "Survival of the Fittest"

4. **ACR**

5. **Annual Confidential Report.** This is a formidable document designed to keep officers and soldiers in line. Indeed, so effective is this document that it has been exported to other government departments as well. The ACR is wielded in much

the same way as would a lion tamer wield his whip, a mere mention of it is likely to cause any officer or government servant to roll over on his back and beg to have his tummy tickled.

6. **OFFICERS' MESS**

This is a hallowed institute and to be entered with suitable awe and trepidation. As a Subaltern or Captain,one must consider oneself lucky just to be allowed ingress to its hallowed premises. In fact, this is the lair of the beast, the lion's den as it were. This is where, if you are in a field area, the GOC comes to relax. Of course, this place is also the place where officers come to relax supposedly. I say supposedly because it is impossible to relax with the GOC in the room. Say you are a wildebeest grazing on the Serengeti and you come across a lion sitting serenely and surveying the scene, even if he assures you that he's not hungry and you should carry on grazing, you would be an idiot if you believed him. The room is tense. Did the stupid barman pour the correct scotch, did the waiter serve it correctly, was there ice? Big problem in the field. That and Bitters Angostura. His every word is hung onto, as if the Oracle itself were speaking, those gathered at his feet and sitting around him gaze at him in wonder and awe, some take notes. The great man is looking around, not at those around him but looking for those NOT fawning. What's their problem he wonders, shall I haul them up tomorrow first light (day break)? maybe a 20 km route march would do the trick. But I digress, the officer's mess is the watering hole of the Division, it has a bar, billiards table, card room and a TV room. In a hard field area, sometime due to adverse conditions the card and billiard rooms are merged as also the bar and TV room. But these adverse conditions were known to everyone at the time of commission and officers have no choice but to accept them. They are not happy but they accept them. Oh yes! In field area there is no billiards marker so sometimes the barman has to do both jobs. It helps if he knows the game and is able to set the table properly for a game of Snooker or else the poor officer has to do it himself.

7. FIELD AREA

A field area denotes the absence of civilisation as we know it. In fact, these areas are so harsh, the government willingly gives us a field area allowance. This is a big thing as anyone familiar with how stingy governments can be when it comes to parting with the green stuff. How harsh? you ask well let's see; there are no air conditioners, we get only 8 to12 hours of electricity hence no ice can form in our refrigerators, so no ice in our Whiskey & Sodas, there are no showers, can you imagine? No geysers either, so its cold-water baths for everyone. There are no RO plants either, so the consumption of alcohol has gone up as it is a well-known fact that alcohol kills germs and one must take every precaution to remain healthy. There is always a shortage of Bitters Angostura, the few bottles there are, are hogged by Div HQ for their Officers' mess. Can you imagine having a Gimlet without bitters? That's how harsh.

8. **GENERAL STAFF OFFICER/ GSO1/GSO2/GSO3**
   often abbreviated to G1, G2 & G3

   They numbers denote the level of information needed by said officer, on a need to know basis. G3 would mean this staff officer need not know anything apart from the date and month on any given day. G2 level would indicate that this guy knows just enough to draft out letters to units down the chain which the G1 is too lazy to do himself. The G1 is normally a pompous, supercilious snob filled with his own importance. GOC's know this and often give their G1's a sound bollocking in front of his juniors at least once a week. This keeps everyone in their respective places.

9. **STATION HEADQUARTERS (STN HQ)**

   These are everywhere and are often a repository for re-employed officers... These organisations are mainly populated with re-employed officers barring one or two officers who are still on their way up the promotional ladder. These re-employed officers have an extensive knowledge and experience in all matters and their contribution to the organisation as a whole would be tremendous if any one were to only ask them but nobody really does and as a result they must confine themselves to mundane matters such as beautifying cantonments, running the CSD canteens, administrating army schools and so on. What a waste of talent.

10. 'Q'

11. He is the head of our nation's super super secret covert organisation. This organisation is so

secret that even RAW and NIA are unaware of its existence. Q is the 17th Director of this secret organisation, the first being A and so on, the next director after Q would be R. Not much is known about him, but being a super sleuth myself, I have managed to unearth the fact that he is a pahadi (generic term that refers to hill folk and not to be confused with the Gurkha who are from Nepal) he is short and curiously resembles a grumpy bulldog who thinks that you are about to swipe his porkchop. He is short tempered and prone to clipping one on the ear if provoked by any display of stupidity, when in conversation with him it is strongly urged that one keeps a minimum distance of 3 feet or more if possible. He swears I am his only agent but I know for a fact that there are more, at least one more and maybe hundreds. He has a goon squad of 6 to 8 hefty guys who seem to have sworn total loyalty to him alone and not to the uniform, and carry out his every command most zealously and literally. I am pretty sure that when Q kicks me out of his office, he doesn't mean that I should be literally hefted over one of these moron's shoulders, carried through the corridors and dumped on my ass in the carpark. Q also has 2 offices, one above and one below. One must go through the loo in the office above to access the one below, also known as The Labyrinth.

12. THE LOO

To access the labyrinth, one is required to go to the Loo. The loo, the first time I used it, it was a rickety hand operated lift of the old man OTIS era, but later on Q had it upgraded, so that now one merely sat on the commode (seat down) and pulled the chain. This started a process wherein one is catapulted downwards at a speed in excess of Mach 2 or 3. One is then slammed into a soft billowy cushiony sort of pillow. *Voila!* You are now in the lair of the beast (Q)

13. THE LABYRINTH

Built somewhere between 80 to 100 feet below Lutyens's Delhi its full extent is still not known but its area is rumoured to be about 100 acres at least and contains airconditioned bunkers, gymnasiums, heated indoor pool, multi cuisine restaurant, meditation hall, media centre and a host of other amenities to help Cabinet members weather a nuclear strike and remain underground for at least 6 months after that. Q has a media centre of his own and it is very sophisticated. With a click of his remote, Q can look into practically any office if he so desires, these include the PM, all Ministers including the Home Minister, the Defence Minister & the Supreme Commander! Q's audacity astounds me sometimes.

14. SAHAYAK. (ASSISSTANT)

The institution of Sahayaks, thank goodness has been phased out. Finally, albeit, reluctantly. I say reluctantly because it was a good thing, I mean, which officer worthy of a Sahayak, sometimes even two, would willingly abolish such a boon? Where else would he get a full time, well paid, well clothed and well-fed servant? And the beauty of the whole thing was that it did not cost him a cent. He had earned it. By virtue of his sheer hard work and by the sweat of his brow. (Read: by being a lickspittle and an ass kisser) It was one of the perks of getting promoted. Sahayaks were earlier called Orderlies (British Era) then came Batmen or Batty (Indian Era) then Sahayak (post 2000 AD era)

As soon as one reached the stage of being promoted to a rank which authorised one for the services of a Sahayak, two things happened; the first was that the officer threw a lavish party, the second was that the officer and his wife went into a huddle to discuss the selection of a suitable Sahayak. Now it is vital to point out here that this selection procedure would have started at least 6 months earlier, when the officer was first told that he is in the "promotion zone" and he, had blabbed it out to his wife while she washed the dishes or was doing laundry or some other domestic chore, "Don't worry darling" he would have said " you won't be doing that for long, after I put on the rank, we will be authorised a Sahayak only for us." He would say this in a tone of voice normally reserved for announcing something momentous, like winning a lottery. She would begin, by eyeing suitable candidates starting with the CO's Sahayaks and then the 2ic's and down the line. They would discuss names "what about X?" the officer would ask "No No, he is a drunkard, Adjutants wife told me, CO gave him 3 days RI for drunken behaviour in the lines "OK what about CO's earlier batman?" "No way" she would reply "CO's wife told me that he is lazy and doesn't do any work at all. That's why she changed him" "OK then what about Y?" "No, he is stupid! Quartermasters wife told me that he can't do proper *hisab* (account for money given to him by her to buy stuff from market) he is always 10/20 rupees less." By now the officer is getting worried that he may never get his coveted Sahayak if she kept vetoing his every suggestion so he says "I will speak to Adjutant, after all you are expecting soon and we need someone who is good with babies and stuff. Adjutant is a good guy and he knows that I'm on my way up so he will send someone good." I hope you have gotten the idea by now of the importance of this institution and its abolishment means just more hardship being thrust on our Braveheart's in uniform. And it's not as if the Sahayaks were cribbing either, they had it easy, excused PT and Parade, they were excused night duty (they have to go early in the morning so that sahib can get ready for PT, as madam sleeps till 9 am) they were a privileged class in the unit lines , plus they got to swipe sahibs liquor and were ready informers about misconduct in the unit. Most Sahayaks became *officer whisperers* (ability to make their officer do whatever they wanted them to do)

15. QUARTERMASTER. (QM)

This officer is a Principal Staff Officer (PSO) in the CO's cabinet. It is he who is responsible for the entire material requirement of the unit. Food, Clothing and Fuel for our vehicles as well as cooking. He is well aware of which side his bread is buttered and spares no effort to ensure that the CO and 2ic always get the best rations. Leg of lamb, rack of lamb, partridge or quail instead of chicken, ham bacon and sausages and oh yes fish and prawns if the CO is of the Bengali persuasion. These are just a few of the things that a competent QM must be able to do. Most QMs have come up the hard way (risen through the ranks) and know almost every trick in the book. So, COs, who are recipients of this bounty normally don't blink an eye and take it as par for the course.

16. ADJUTANT

He is CO's man! Pure and simple. Chosen for his bearing (Smartness) loyalty (to the CO) and how well he can follow orders (blindly). Although the 2ic is the 2nd in command in the unit, it is indeed the adjutant who is the de facto 2ic, for it is he and he alone who has CO's ear. He stands in for the CO whenever CO's wife needs to go into town for shopping or to the dentist or to MH or anywhere that the CO doesn't want to go. He will arrange the foursomes for bridge and golf as well as parties in the CO's house, ensuring that officers 'mess resources are utilized to the maximum. He will rope in the QM to look after the catering, a job that the QM is only too happy to do.

17. SECOND IN COMMAND (2IC)

This poor guy has nothing to do but stand in for the CO in his absence and be responsible for any fuck ups in the unit. He is known as the *Officiating CO* or half shitting CO.

18. RAKSHA MANTRI (RM)

He is a political appointee with little or no knowledge of any thing military though I must admit that some of them have really tried to learn on the job but rarely do they stay long enough to pick up anything useful. Their visits to our brothers in high altitude areas are really appreciated.

19. CHIEF OF ARMY STAFF (COAS)

He has done it all and survived every obstacle thrown at him. He is the role model and every Subaltern dreams of emulating him one day but such is our promotion system, only one subaltern among you can. My advice to all those with such aspirations is, be nice to everyone one your way up because you never know who may become the next Chief and you are going to regret it sorely if he is the very same person you belittled when you were the Camp Commandant and he was a GSO2 in the same division, by denying him a Sahayak on grounds of there being a shortage of manpower as all men were required to be on the golf course, that was being laid out, under the GOC's direct supervision. So be nice it pays to be nice to everyone.

Note for posterity. The above explanations are my perceptions and my perceptions alone. Much water would have passed under the bridge and with the passage of time and with hindsight I am sure that things would have changed now and I am positive they are not at all as I have described in this book.

A ROOSTER'S TALE

Surya was a mere egg (one of ten) when the very modern resort and Spa was inaugurated on a block of land adjacent to the small farm owned by the owner of said ten eggs, a childless widow, one Mrs Sonu Devi about 25 years of age. The inauguration of the Spa had been a grand affair, attended by elders of all the surrounding villages and politicians of course. There were sweet distribution and speeches ("Progress has come to Mainpuri district" said one well fed politician gleefully, "Now there will be jobs and plenty of tourists who will come to see our way of life") Sonu Devi had not attended the function that day, although the village *panch* (head man) had asked her to come. "See for yourself, Bhabiji (elder sister)" he had cajoled "So many little cottages and huts, just like ours but bigger and better quality and all modern amenities like AC, TV fridge Dish etc" But Sonu was in no mood for niceties, for one thing they (Spa owners) had built a huge wall alongside her property blocking out the early morning winter sun, forcing her to move further away from her house if she wanted to sit in the sun for warmth. She just went about her chores, one of them being taking her 10 eggs to the fowl house and finding a nice broody hen, not averse to sitting on them for 21 days or so. Having done this, she went to her vegetable garden for some fresh vegetables to prepare for the mid-day meal.

In due course the eggs hatched and ten fluffy little yellow chicks made their first appearance into this strange new world. Now these were desi chicks, laid by desi hens and fertilised by a desi cockerel. (Desi means local as opposed to the foreign white leghorns that were now bred in India and were the backbone of the poultry industry. Desi birds are brown in colour as are their eggs and are Free range birds) Desi eggs were in high demand in the city and because of their high nutritional content, they fetched a premium over the normal eggs produced by the white leghorns which were locked up in small coops for their entire lives and fed on a staple diet of factory produced poultry feed. In a few weeks it became obvious to Sonu that she had nine hens and one cockerel. She was overjoyed as her last cockerel had fallen prey to a fox just a few days ago, who had made off with him leaving nary a feather behind. So, she singled him out and called him Surya, and fed him grain and corn and green scraps. He blossomed into a beautiful rooster and his crows echoed around the neighbourhood.

Surya did his job well. He strutted around the yard and kept his harem of more than 35 hens content. Every morning he would announce the arrival of the sun in clear and resounding tones. Sonu Devi was very proud of his crow and so also seemed Surya for he would carry on and on and on till she threw an old potato at him, and he, suitably distracted would cheese it, and strut off to investigate it or scratch at the ground looking for the early worm. Sonu Devi prospered, as did the village and the surrounding villages. Jobs in the Spa were plenty, in fact there wasn't a family in her village that did not have somebody working there. Needless to say, the Spa also prospered. In winter months (November to March) the Spa was totally booked with people from all the metros flocking to its bucolic surroundings for a taste of the rural life but with all the comforts of modern life and without the hardships. And every single wintry morning Surya was there, faithfully greeting the sun with his resounding CUKARUKOO! every 20 seconds or so, he would let out his morning greeting to his namesake CUKARUKOO! CUKARUKOO!

Now the sun in winter, in Mainpuri, invariably rose at 545 AM and it was at 545 AM that Surya began his chorus. 545 AM was the normal awakening time for the villagers of her village but it was an ungodly hour for the residents of the Spa. And rumblings soon began to be heard. "Bucolic life should start after 9 AM" said a red-faced IT General Manager from Bengaluru "Yes!" echoed a bleary-eyed socialite from Mumbai "Who on earth gets up at 545 AM? I only went to bed at 2 AM damnit! We are on a holiday". Vikram, the manager, a young English speaking high flyer from Delhi who had never seen a farm bird or farm animal in his life before (except in the form of his daily breakfast of bacon and eggs and a glass of milk to wash it all down) was at a loss for what to do. "What is that noise"? he asked a Housekeeping Executive (roomboy) who happened to be a local from that very village "Oh Sir! that's Surya! He is very popular in our village" But the manager wasn't listening anymore, he was busy trying to contact the village panch, Gajadhar, Gajjo to his friends and supporters, who was shown on the company payroll as a *consultant*, but was in fact a troubleshooter with a dubious background, hired to sort out problems precisely like this. Now Gajjo harboured political ambitions (this was normal, most Mainpuri District residents of dubious distinction, harboured political ambitions, it was a sort of USP for the modern-day wannabe politicians) and he hoped someday to be his districts' (Mainpuri) representative in parliament. He also harboured a distinct affinity for the good life and the Spa looked after him in every way, not only by way of a pretty handsome monthly retainer, but also by way of weekend getaways with his *setting* (mistress) of the day and a highly subsidised food and bar bill. (Blender's Pride Whiskey and Butter Chicken) So when Vikram called him he was all ears. He listened and then flipped his phone shut. Surya! He loved that rooster, his early morning ruckus always woke him up, giving him enough time to slip out of his mistress' bed, do the 10-minute walk of shame and slip unnoticed into his own. His wife hadn't a clue because he was always in bed when she woke up, but Sonu Devi was another kettle of fish, quite the feisty little thing. She always had something handy (bricks, scrap iron old rotting vegetables meant for her compost pit and broken plastic chairs) to throw at any visitor who tried any funny stuff, thinking that she, being a young widow, must be lonely and in need of male companionship. Two of his friends had found out the hard way that this was not the case at all and still had the scars to show for it.   Anyway, he had a job to do and he was if anything, a man of action and a man of his word (whenever convenient)

Gajjo and two of his henchmen reached the gate of Sonu Devi by 8 AM the next day. Surya was in fine fettle and his CUKARUKOO's resonated across the yard. On seeing the visitors, he puffed out his chest and let out a series of crows that caused birds perched in the surrounding trees to rise as one and head for more sylvan surroundings. As usual Sonu Devi came out of her house, potato in hand, which she flung at the bird with unerring accuracy, thus subdued, the bird hurried off to pester a few hens pecking lackadaisically at the ground hoping for a juicy worm or insect or two. The silence was deafening and Gajjo taking advantage of it folded his hands in traditional greeting "Namaste Bhabiji" he said She did likewise but eyed him suspiciously "What do you want?" and she moved closer to the stack of bricks. "No, No Bhabiji we want to talk about Surya" said Gajjo nervously "What about him" she asked "he is making too much noise in the neighbourhood and disturbing all the residents of the village. They have asked me to speak to you." "You're a liar Gajjo" she flashed fiercely "what is it? What is the real reason you have come? Speak!" So Gajjo spoke. He decided to tell her the truth. He told her about the Spa and its residents complaining about the racket Surya made so early in the morning "What do you want me to do?" she asked "he is a bird. It is his nature, and roosters will crow at sunrise. Tell the Spa people to make the sun rise at 9 AM and then Surya will crow at 9 AM." Now being one of the rural folks himself Gajjo fully understood the way of life of the simple villager. The sun rose and people arose with it, less those with hangovers and the like. People bathed performed puja at the temple and got ready for a hard day's work in their fields or if they had no fields of their own in somebody else's fields or they looked for daily work in the many home handloom factories that had sprung up in the village. In the evening they had their dinner, watched some TV or some porn on their mobiles and then prepared for bed. All temple events, *Melas* and *Bhandaras* were enthusiastically attended by everyone as were births and deaths. *(**Mela** – village fair complete with roundabouts, hurdy gurdys and competitions also cotton candy and balloons. **Bhandara** – free meal distributed to everyone in the community on happy or sad occasions. Usually but not necessarily conducted on the temple premises)*

Gajjo went to the Spa and was warmly welcomed by Vikram who came straight to the point "have you done something about that stupid bird?" he asked "My guests are in an uproar about the noise. And did you hear him today? He seemed extra loud! Mrs Chatterjee, she is a prominent socialite from Mumbai and here as a guest of one of the partners of this property, has threatened to call him and complain about me! Can you imagine? What did I do?" he sat down, out of breath and perspiring slightly. Gajjo looked at him sympathetically "I understand "he murmured "but this is natural, a rooster will crow at dawn" "that may be true" said Vikram sullenly "but do something about it. Its why we hired you." Gajjo went back to the village and held a meeting with his trusted henchmen (none of whom except Ravinder, who was a graduate, had progressed beyond the 5thgrade in school) "Let us kidnap the bird Boss!" said Kalia, a grade III dropout, "Then we can then chop it up and have butter chicken tonight!" Gajjo gave him a withering stare "You're an idiot Kalia! Sonu Devi will chop us all up before we get anywhere close to the bird" "Let us offer to buy him, offer her so much money she won't be able to refuse to sell him" said Ravinder quietly "how much?" asked Gajjo "Twenty Thousand!" said Ravinder "we can go higher if need be" "who will pay this amount?" asked Gajjo "I don't have so much money with me" "Let the Spa people pay, in fact we should ask for Thirty Thousand so that we make a nice profit as well" said Ravinder. The idea seemed a good one and they decided to act on it.

"Let us go and meet Sonu Devi" said Gajjo decisively "but only Ravinder should come with me, she gets nervous if a crowd gathers and starts to throw things, and I'm going to start by offering her Two Thousand, we will see from there"

The two-man delegation reached Sonu's yard and stood outside the gate nervously. Sonu was sitting in a plastic chair soaking up the sun and Surya too, was close by pecking distractedly at a line of ants who had now broken formation and were scurrying helter skelter trying to avoid his sharp beak. "what now?" asked Sonu Devi peevishly, "Sorry Bhabiji" said Gajjo apologetically "we have come about the bird" "What about him?" she asked fiercely. "We want to buy him" said Gajjo nervously "We are offering you Two Thousand rupees. That's a lot of money." It was but she shook her head "What will you do with him?" she asked "You and your drunken friends will eat him. The Spa people have ordered you to silence Surya isn't it? How much have they offered to pay you?" "No! No! Bhabiji we could never eat him; we will just take him to a farm faraway from here where he can crow to his heart's content."

"then what will I do?" she asked angrily "selling eggs earns me more than 10,000 rupees per month. Do you want me to starve to death so that you can steal my land?" she asked emotionally "we will offer you 20,000 rupees for the bird!" blurted Ravinder, deeply moved by her outburst "Never! Never!" she cried "I will never, ever sell Surya! You go tell your Spa masters that this is natural, this is what roosters do they will crow every morning they can't stop it!" Gajjo noticed that as she spoke, she had moved closer to the stack of bricks near the house and he and Ravinder backed slowly towards the gate. He folded his hands politely and said "Sorry to upset you Bhabiji. Namaste!" the two of them made a hasty exit and almost ran back to their house, expecting a well thrown brick to clobber them at any moment. Once they were out of range they slowed down to a walk and discussed the matter. There was only one thing to do and that was to tell Vikram that they had failed.

Vikram didn't take it well. Gajjo and Ravinder listened patiently to his rant and sipped their cold drinks sympathetically. When Vikram had finished with his taunts about their manhood and his leadership, he fell silent, but only for a minute he then picked up his expensive Galaxy 10+ mobile and called Corporate HQ. he explained the situation in clear precise terms to his boss and then listened attentively as the boss told him what to do. He clicked off his phone and faced Gajjo and in a triumphant voice said "we will take that bitch and her bird to court. We will sue her for lost business and damages worth crores and make sure she is thrown of her land and has nowhere to go. Then she will come begging. I will show her! Now go! I have to discuss this case with the corporate lawyer who is flying in at this very moment to deal with the matter.

It was a very dejected and disheartened Gajjo who returned to the village. What had he done? Because of him this poor widow was going to lose her land and livelihood. Surely, he could think of something to save her. It was Ravinder who came up with the idea to save her, he didn't tell Gajjo his plan initially but just told him that they were going to Agra today to meet a guy.

A week later Sonu Devi was served with a notice that she was being sued for 5 crore rupees (500 lakhs) for lost business and damages to the Spa's reputation due to her rooster's constant crowing so early in the morning. A high school teacher had translated the letter for her. She was at a loss and didn't know what to do, what could she do? She was poor and this was a huge corporation with hundreds of crores of rupees at their disposal. And though she didn't have any, she knew the awesome power of money.

A day later, early in the morning, while she was sitting in her plastic chair, in the shadow of the spa wall which earlier had seemed a nuisance but now appeared to be ominous, she heard the gate being opened, she looked up and saw Gajjo, Ravinder and a third person who was hefting what looked to be a video camera on his shoulder "what do you want Gajjo? You have ruined me." She said moving swiftly towards her bricks "Bhabiji listen please! I am on your side. This is Damodar, he works for a local TV station in Agra. Tell him your side of the story and we will make sure all the TV networks know about this Spa. Just calm down I want to help you; we want to help you"

So Sonu Devi calmed down and tearfully narrated her story to Damodar. She told him about her widowhood and the living she made selling eggs and how now the Spa people wanted her rooster to stop crowing at daybreak. She told him of her efforts to soundproof the coop where she kept her fowls at night but it made no difference to the volume of Surya's crowing. As if on cue Surya strutted up to her and let fly a resounding CUKARUKOO! CUKARUKOO! This too, Damodar captured on camera. After about an hour or so the trio departed and Sonu Devi resumed her chores but still kept a sharp eye out for Gajjo or any of his henchmen for that matter, she still didn't trust him completely.

Gajjo was like a reformed man. Ravinder had explained to him as to how he should use this issue to catapult him into prominence for the coming Lok Sabha elections. Gajjo began touring every village in his constituency drumming up support for Sonu Devi and Surya. He went from village to village denouncing the Spa and its high handedness. "What's next?" he would bellow into the microphones "first they want to silence our Roosters, then they will try to stop the birds from flying and singing and the insects from chirping. When we visit the city, do we tell the city people to stop the vehicles from blowing their horns? Do we tell them to remove traffic lights so that we can move without stopping for red lights?" and every time "No!" was the resounding chorus.

Meanwhile Damodar was quite the busy videographer himself. he had shown his clip to the station head who heartily approved of the project. Prominent news networks were contacted and enormous fees were negotiated. Three days after the recording most major networks were reporting the high handedness of the Spa and the bravery of the poor widow who stood up against them. Surya became an icon immediately. Posters stickers and memes sprang up literally from nowhere. He even had his own Facebook page!

Sonu Devi who never watched the news or TV for that matter was blissfully unaware of the ruckus and turmoil her plight was causing. Until a cavalcade of cars and SUVs pulled up outside her house and a very important looking man stepped out. She knew he was a politician because he had a small army of SPG men with him and an even larger army of his followers with him but they were kept at bay and only he and a familiar face alongside him entered. The familiar face was that of Damodar the videographer who was day by day, becoming ever increasingly enamoured of her. He introduced the VIP as the State Minister for Animal

Husbandry, she hurriedly went inside her house and pulled out another plastic chair and gestured for him to sit down "What is this?" She asked Damodar fiercely "He wants to talk to you" said Damodar calmly "I won't give up Surya" she said in a fierce whisper "Just listen to him please" said Damodar so she listened as did the several hundred people who had gathered around them. The minister had his audience and began to speak. He spoke in the local dialect and he spoke for a long time widely cheered at short intervals even Sonu Devi felt heartened. In essence he had announced that with immediate effect the State Government was declaring the Rooster as its state bird. He also announced that from now on it would be illegal to kill Roosters for their meat but hens who had stopped laying could be killed for meat. Also, he had spoken to the postal department and they had agreed to print postage stamps of 50 rupees value of Surya, the brave rooster.

Surya, meanwhile was totally unfazed by the crowd, decided to mount one of hens who was staring vacantly into space, this action of his caught the minister's and Damodar's eye. The minister spoke and Damodar recorded simultaneously "This is rural life!" said the minister nostalgically, "just mount the female whenever the male wants, no fuss, no drama, no rape reports just like in nature." His last act before he left was to present Sonu Devi a cheque for One Lakh Rupees.

Vikram oblivious to all that was happening in the surrounding villages prepared assiduously for his case that was scheduled for hearing in two days. At the Allahabad High Court. A chartered plane was hired to take him and his ace team of high-priced lawyers from the Safai air strip. That evening, he switched on to a popular national news channel and was horrified to see that the penniless widow had one of country's top Supreme Court lawyers representing her and the rooster, *Pro Bono* it seems. "We are going to file a counter case against the Spa, demanding that it be shut down and the entire campus be handed over to the neighbouring villages under the Prime Ministers Housing Scheme. How dare they try to interfere with our rural way of life!" Vikram switched channels, on this one, the new Animal Husbandry minister (the old one had had to resign due to his insensitive remarks about the Surya coupling incident, was speaking in to the cameras directly "the rooster has been declared a state bird and is protected by law. We will be taking legal action against the owners of the Spa and their partners. We will prosecute them under IPC and seek NBWs (Non Bailable Warrants) against them to prevent them from leaving the country and fleeing justice." His legs turned to jelly and he sat down. His door flew open; it was the lead lawyer "switch off the damn TV! these damn people don't know anything about the law! We will win in court. Don't worry about it. Have a drink and get some rest we are flying out to Allahabad tomorrow!"

Gajjo and his team plus Damodar were in his house planning his election strategy. He had done phenomenally well in his campaign to save Surya and his getting the party ticket was a sure shot. He was assured of this by no less than the assistant to the Party Supremo's private secretary. Damodar was there because he was interested in seeing Sonu Devi again but didn't know how to go about it. Because of his success in bringing the Surya episode to the national stage he was flooded with offers from major TV networks, and he was spoiled for choice in picking one. Gajjo had an inkling as to the real reason Damodar was becoming such a frequent visitor to their village and told Ravinder to speak to Sonu Devi about Damodar.

The case was fought in the courts as well as on all Major TV channels. Experts were called in to testify about the fact of their crowing and whether it was only at dawn that they would crow or throughout the whole day. The religious aspect was also discussed and one expert hogged the floor with his thesis that roosters were worshipped by the Persians from 2000 BC to as late as 700 BC. He regaled his audiences with tales of how even to this day in prominent South East Asian tribes in the Philippines and Indonesia the bird is still worshipped. He blessed the state government for its sagacity of declaring the Rooster a state bird and making it's killing illegal. Needless to say, his every word was hung onto and he received a rousing ovation at the end of his summation.

Vikram and his team were faring badly. The honourable judge had been scathing with his remarks about frivolous cases and that he wanted the case to be wrapped up one way or another before the week end. He too, had received a phone call from someone very high up in the PMO's office, that his name was being considered favourably for a seat on the Supreme Court bench and everything depended upon how he rules on this case. "how do you want me to rule?" he asked in a quavering voice "that depends on you "said the voice "this case has evoked tremendous populist emotions and should be handled as such. Give the people what they want. Elections are around the corner!" "I was going to do that anyway" said the honourable judge but he was speaking into a dead phone, the caller had disconnected.

Ravinder came alone to Sonu Devi's house that evening, he explained that he had come with a proposal for her marriage to Damodar and that she should give it some thought. He was still standing outside her gate ready to run if she moved towards the brick stack but she smiled shyly and opened the gate and asked him to come in. Over a cup of sweet tea, he told her that if she agreed the whole thing can be formally done in the morning. She agreed.

The honourable judge threw the book at the plaintiffs. He ordered the two partners and the entire board of directors (Five of them) and the Spa manager to personally visit the defendant and get her to drop filing of counter charges against them. He gave them one week. He further directed that they pay her the same amount of compensation that they were suing her for. He further directed that they pay the entire legal counsel fees of the defendant, and that the legal counsel should be paid at the same rate as they were paying their own lawyers none of this *pro bono* stuff. He further warned them that if they ever tried to interfere again with the culture of the people of where ever their numerous Spas were located they would have him to contend with.

Gajjo got elected with the biggest margin of victory ever and was now a honourable member of parliament (MP) his loyal henchmen were comfortably placed in various positions of authority and of course whenever Gajjo was required to be in the national capital, they accompanied him. Ravinder realised his childhood dream of becoming a principal of the village primary school, thanks to a little bit of arm twisting by Gajjo. Ravinder promised to do his B Ed privately.

The High Court judge became a Supreme Court Judge and a few years later CJI.

Vikram, for his failure to silence Surya, was banished to a remote Spa in the Andaman and Nicobar Islands, where he had to contend with a sizeable population of man-eating natives.

Damodar and Sonu Devi got married in the village with great pomp and show. Sonu Devi would be moving to her husband's village in Lodhi where they had bought a couple of acres of land with their new found money, so that she could continue with her poultry farming. In due course they had a child and they named him Surya! And of Surya? Well he lived to a ripe old age of 15 years way beyond the average lifespan of ordinary roosters, but then Surya was no ordinary rooster, was he?

AN ENCOUNTER WITH JUG SURAIYA

I saw Jug Suraiya today. It was an awesome moment. He was to address a gathering in the gambanquet hall of a run down 5-starred hotel. It so happened that I happened to be Senior Steward in that very same hotel and hence it was my privilege to walk onto the small dais with great dignity, in full glare of TV cameras and argon lights, proudly bearing aloft the hotels best silver salver, three tall glasses perched precariously on it filled almost to their brims with chilled sparkling water. I bowed to Jug making sure that my better profile was inclined towards the cameramen crouching hardly 10 feet away, and offered him a frosty glass, but so engrossed was he in the introductory speech of the gentleman at the mike, and so well versed was he in the rituals of functions like these that without even seeming to notice me; he just flicked two of his elegant fingers in my direction. What a graceful flick it was, never before had I been fobbed off so elegantly by anyone. Here was man, I thought, who had done this a million times before and was able to convey so effectively to me and to the audience in general, that water was for the plebes and that I would have to do a whole lot better than that if I were to get his full attention.

Duly chastened I turned my attention to the heavily perspiring gentleman on his left and proffered my salver in his direction. He scooped up a glass drained it and returned it to its place in one swift motion. So rapidly was this manoeuvre executed that I was caught unawares.

I had just returned my full attention back to Jug and was drinking in his visage to the fullest extent, his closely-knit brows, his beady eyes and his prominent proboscis; this was a face capable of achieving almost anything I thought reverently. Now I must admit that when I had swivelled on my heel to gaze once more on Jug after serving the sweaty gentleman, I was expecting a time lag of at least forty-five seconds, that being the average time it took for a guest to fully consume a glass of sparkling water. There was plenty of time for me to study this celebrity at close quarters once more and turn back to retrieve the empty glass from my thirsty guest. My tray therefore had also swivelled slightly with me and was thus no longer in front of said guest nor was my grip on it as firm as before and the guest, perhaps being out of breath from drinking a whole glass in one go failed to notice that the tray was no longer available as a final resting place for the empty glass. As a result of this fluid motion the glass failed to contactwith the tray and continued downwards towards a speedy rendezvous with the parquet flooring.

Now I must add here that hotel policy stipulated that any breakage s that occurred were to be paid for by the steward concerned unless the management was confronted with irrefutable evidence that the guest was to blame. Knowing that no such evidence was available, and that the statistical data of drinking water, was a result of my own observations and hence not official, I reacted instinctively. These were expensive glasses specially brought out for the occasion and normally kept locked away in a glass case; any breakage would set me back a pretty hefty amount.

The dive I executed was reminiscent of Jhonty Rhodes fielding at slip. I caught the glass before it made contact and shattered with my left hand my right still holding onto the tray but the two other glasses on the tray were launched into simultaneous orbits. I could only watch in horror as they headed towards Jug. "Incoming" I called out feebly. Time froze and morphed into a slow motion dream I watched in horror as they reached their apex hovering in the void and then tumbling downward spinning on its axis then beginning its descent towards the table on the dais. Jugs I must say reacted marvellously to my call. Like a panther on a deer, he pounced on the nearest glass and plucked it out of the air and then with the agility and lissomness of a 15-year-old ballerina executed a half pirouette and neatly caught the last of the airborne duo. Sadly, the contents of the glasses did not remain in them and proceeded to spray the dais, Jug and his sweaty companion were drenched in sparkling water. There was pin drop silence for a few seconds, only the cameras continued their relentless recording, the audience were staring at the frozen tableau on the dais, I was where I had fallen my left profile fully exposed to the spectators and my hand still clutching the errant glass, the sweaty companion was looking like a guppy fish that had just ingested a smaller guppy fish and the speaker was frozen at the mike caught unawares by the icy deluge that had descended on him, Jug crouched magnificently like a Ninja warrior ready for more incoming objects that maybe hurled towards him. Then the moment vanished and a mob of people rushed the dais to render aid to the guests and unwarranted abuse at me.

Anyways all's well that ends well. Hotel re-enforcements had arrived and while a houseboy mopped up the spillage, the manager was busy soothing soggy egos, the sweaty companion could be heard muttering

"BluddyPhool, BluddyPhool" continuously to himself as he was blow dried. I looked with trepidation at my Hero, tears of remorse in my eyes and silently begged his forgiveness but all he did was flick two of his elegant fingers in my direction and I faded quietly back into oblivion. My fifteen seconds of fame were over. I have the CD though.

A CUT BELOW THE REST

The overhead light in the makeshift Operation Theatre gleamed brightly onto the shiny instrument tray. Bright light reflected off the scalpels, saws and forceps that were laid out in neat rows, in order of their proposed use. The rest of his staff waited expectantly, eager to begin. The patient already prepped and suitably anesthetized lay unconscious on the table directly under the light. A green sheet covered his whole body except for his head and the infected limb. Wires snaked out from under the sheets, connecting the patient to various monitors. An Oxygen cylinder was propped up nearby, in case it was required, though he doubted it, the patient was young and as healthy as a horse and all of twelve years old. It was almost time for him to make the first incision and he knew that as soon as he made that fateful cut, his life would never be the same again. There would be no looking back. His heart told him that it was not too late and that there was still time for him to walk away but somehow, he knew, even as he washed his hands and forearms for the third time in 5 minutes, that he would not, the money was just too damn good, besides if he didn't do it, he knew of at least two other surgeons who were waiting in the wings for just such an opportunity. He had memorized the procedure and knew exactly what and how to perform the operation. All precautions had been taken and every eventuality anticipated and now all that was left was for him to begin. .

He bent over the exposed leg and probed the infected area, called for a scalpel and decisively made a deep incision just above the left knee. The amputation went like clockwork, and lasted three hours. All the patient's vital signs were normal and the oxygen cylinder had not been used, it would be another hour for the anaesthetic to wear off and for the patient to regain consciousness. By that time the limb would have been disposed of and he would have collected his fee. The paper trail was impeccable and no aspersions or doubts could ever be cast his way by nosy NGO's or social workers.

He went back to his office, turned the A/C on full, then leaned back in his swivel chair and mulled over the strange turn his life had taken over the last 15 days. Two weeks earlier he had been sitting in his shabby little office, regretting his decision to take up the appointment of Orthopaedic Specialist in a small government hospital in a mofussil town, but things had been different when he had applied for the job and was selected 10 years ago, he had been filled with an altruism that befalls all young professionals at the start of their careers, a desire to help and heal those not so fortunate as he was. At that time the Hippocratic Oath rang loudly in his ears. The passage of time dimmed the resonance of the oath and subdued his altruistic urge, replacing it with cynicism coupled with a desire to help oneself rather than his fellow man.

It was not long before he had fallen in line with the other government doctors and started his own surreptitious practice using the ample verandah of his spacious government accommodation. Pharmacists worked out a suitable commission for medicines he prescribed and that his patients bought from them. The money wasn't much but added to the healthy salary he drew as Senior Specialist in the hospital and it was enough for his small family to live on comfortably.

Then his mother broke her leg while pottering about the house, he raced home when he got the news, and in a trice had set the bone and had her in traction and propped up in bed. His wife scurried along to make her famous bone soup, a vegetarian broth guaranteed to fix the most stubborn of broken bones. Unfortunately, his mother had diabetes, and none in the family knew it, before remedial measures could be taken gangrene had set in and the infection spread rapidly upwards. The wound would not heal and when they finally did figure out why, it was too late. Too much time had elapsed. Septicaemia quickly followed and his mother's heart, unable to take the strain, finally stopped beating after 70 years of loyal unblemished service. He was inconsolable, not so much at her death, but at his inability to do anything about it. One day he had vowed, as he watched the last of the smouldering embers of her pyre, he would make a state of the artOrthopaedic Centre, so that no one would ever have to undergo the trauma of losing a loved one.

One day, about 15 days ago, he had been sitting in his dinghy office, watching the wall clock and willing it to reach 2 PM. His official lunch break started then and he could go for lunch. He would not return, after a nap, he would attend to the rush of patients who were no doubt already beginning to queue up outside his gate, waiting for him to attend to them and prescribe suitable treatments for their broken bones and fractured limbs. A shabbily dressed man, entered his office, closed the door, and sat down uninvited. "My name is Pyare Lal, that's all you need to know." He said "My friends and I have a business offer for you, which I want you to consider very carefully." Half dazed and utterly taken aback, he listened as Pyare Lal spoke, what he proposed was so outrageous and so abhorrent that at it outraged his senses and violated every rule, code and all that was decent. It was inhumane, diabolical and evil. But like a rabbit trapped by the gaze of the deadly Cobra, he could not say a word, although every nerve and every muscle in his body wanted to throw this monster out of his office he was paralyzed, he could not move, all he could do was listen with his mouth half open. What Pyare Lal was proposing was that he amputate and mutilate the healthy limbs of homeless people, so that their helplessness evoked the pity of whichever town's citizenry, and they gave generous amounts to these beggars. He had just been introduced to the Beggar Mafia.

As Pyare Lal spoke his mind flashed back to the numerous beggars he had met at traffic crossings and outside the temple gates and everywhere else. They were ubiquitous, ever present on streets, bus depots, railway stations, markets even hospitals. And he remembered that on every occasion that he had given them money, it was always to one who was missing a hand or leg, sometimes two legs and he would wonder what great tragedy had befallen this poor man that he had to lose *both* of his legs. He remembered that his heart would always go out to the plight of the little children who would hobble after him missing an arm or a leg or both asking him for alms in the name of God. Now he was being asked to help create them. He shifted his mind back to what Pyare Lal was saying, by now he was rattling of the names of several eminent doctor who were thriving on his business and he recognized a few of his batch mates' names as well. It was evident that Pyare Lal had his speech well-rehearsed and had the answers for all the frequently asked questions down pat and he covered them meticulously, one by one. Finally, Pyare Lal wound up his spiel with one last comment "Don't worry Doctor Sahib, you will not be cutting of healthy limbs, we will infect them first and then bring them to you. You will be covered. Just don't try to save them. We will pay you handsomely for this, besides these are homeless people, nobody cares for them. In today's world each man must look out for himself, besides these people also will benefit, nobody will give money to an able bodied person but they will feel sorry for someone who has lost his legs or arms" Speech slowly returned to the doctor, but all he could say was "I don't know...." "There is no rush" said Pyare Lal generously "I'll return in 3 days, you must give me your answer by then, there are 2 other orthopaedic specialists here, but you were our first choice. This is your chance"

For three long days he wrestled with his conscious but on the third day he gave in. The money was the decider. When Pyare Lal came again, he happily agreed to his terms and even shook hands with him as if they were old friends. He had sent in his resignation and it would take a month to be accepted. He contacted his bank manager friend and negotiated a personal loan, enough for him to buy the necessary equipment required for such operations. Pyare Lal would be sending him his first case within 7 days; he was ready with 2 days to spare.

His new friends had promised him a steady stream of such patients and at 40k a pop, his dream of opening an Orthopaedic Research Centre in his mother's name was that much nearer to fruition. She would be so proud of him, God rest her soul.

EXAMINATION FEES

Dharamveer, Rakesh and Pawan had been friends for as long as they could remember. They had studied up to the eighth grade together until Dharamveer and Rakesh had dropped out as their parents could no longer afford the fees for their education. Pawan's father had a government job so he was luckier and carried on with his studies. Rakesh and Dharamveer both got part time jobs, first as vendors in nearby tea stalls then as time elapsed as assistants in shops until now, at the time of writing this story, Rakesh, aged 15, was an assistant for a local building contractor and Dharamveer, aged 15, was the head mechanic in an auto repair workshop close by and their friendship continued to flourish. As wage earners Rakesh and Dharamveer shared their earnings with Pawan, soft drinks, snacks, popcorn movie tickets were paid for by them and Pawan never felt that he was scrounging or that he was not contributing, they all knew that if it were the other way around, he would do the same for them.

Their friendship and the antics they got up to in the colony were legendary. Any mischief was immediately attributed to them until proved otherwise. Missing potted plants, bed sheets hung up to dry being imprinted with saffron stained palm prints, doorbells ringing mysteriously, cycles falling off their stands and of course the evergreen 'ghost that haunted the by lanes after midnight'. It was all good clean fun and the worst trouble they ever got into was getting a sound thrashing, ably administered by their respective fathers whenever the other residents' complaints would get too frequent or too high pitched.

Their worst critics would never go so far as to even think of accusing them of any real crime; like stealing or eve teasing or selling drugs.

When Rakesh and Dharamveer dropped out of school, the frequency of their getting together naturally dropped, but they tried to meet as often as possible and have as much fun as they could.

Then, one day Pawan's father had a heart attack and died before they could get him to a hospital for treatment. This was a huge blow for Pawan. Rakesh and Dharamveer never left his side in the days that followed. They took time off from their jobs and would spend the day outside Pawan's house ready to do any odd job that was required by the bereaved family. This was the first time that they were encountering death from such close quarters and it had shaken them.

Pawan's father had been the sole earning member of their family and he was still a few years short before he could qualify for a government pension. In short, they had no real money and could no longer afford to send Pawan to school; both he and his mother would have to look for work if they had to survive and continue to send their other three children to school. This was a big blow to Pawan who was preparing for his board exams. His fees were due in a month as also exam fees for several other competitive examinations. He had needed a total of 19000 Rupees and his father, who had great faith in him promised to make the arrangements. Now all that had changed, his mother, who was not very educated herself, refused to give him such a large amount, especially when there was no guarantee that he would even qualify for any college, and how would they afford the fees for those expensive colleges if he got admitted?

Now it seemed that all Pawan's dreams of ever becoming a doctor or engineer or Army Officer had come crashing down into the dust.

Rakesh and Dharamveer talked out Pawan's problem; between the two of them they were now earning about 6000 rupees a month however both were supporting their respective families so it wasn't really so much; they hardly had a few hundred rupees left over for themselves once all the expenses had been paid. They would never be able to borrow such a large amount and in any case the interest that the local money lenders charged was exorbitant, so that route was out. Their bosses would never give them an advance as they did not believe they would ever get it back; they had burned their fingers too many times before to take a sympathetic view of Pawan's all too familiar situation. It seemed that Pawan was destined to give up his dream of graduating and making something of himself in life.

Late one evening Dharamveer came to meet Rakesh at the contractor's office "Come with me" he ordered Rakesh mysteriously. Rakesh excused himself, it was quitting time anyway. They walked for some time quietly, in the direction of their favourite tea stall; Dharamveer had not said a word since then. Once they reached and were seated as far away from the other customers as possible, Dharamveer spoke in a whisper "I have an idea about how to get Pawan his money." "What are you talking about?" Rakesh whispered back heatedly "We have discussed this and there is no way we can raise so much money in such a short time. The money lenders charge too much interest, our bosses don't trust us and if we don't give money home our parents will kill us so what way have you figured out? Unless you want to steal it!" Dharamveer's eyes lit up and he said excitedly "That's exactly what we are going to do! I have a fool proof plan!" Rakesh could not believe his ears. He was as eager as the next person to make a lot of money quickly, but he had never seriously considered stealing it. His favoured route was more in the line of lotteries and other gambling devices. A large percentage of his earnings used to go towards the purchase of lottery tickets but ever since the state government had banned the sale of lottery tickets that dream also gradually faded away. Now his best friend was rekindling the flame albeit cleverly masking the true intent by linking it with an altruistic ideal of helping Pawan.

Rakesh decided to hear his friend out first, "So what is this plan of yours and how can I be sure that I won't be spending the next 10 years of my life in jail?" "No, it's fool proof I tell you. Look I've been talking to some guys who come to the garage for repair work. They buy and sell stolen bikes" Dharamveer dropped his voice even lower and continued; "They buy stolen bikes cheap then grind out the engine and chassis numbers and etch in new fictitious ones. Then they take them to a different state and make fake papers for them with the help of corrupt transport authorities and sell them cheap to anyone who is willing, especially the villagers, who are looking for motorcycles to give in the dowry demand. They even gave me a master key! We can get about 7000 for each new bike we steal. Just think, if we steal three bikes, that's 21000. 19000 we give Pawan and the rest we split between us. 1000 each." "But what if we get caught" asked Rakesh uneasily, "we could both go to jail, what will our parents think of us, what will the locality think of us?" "That's the best part; we are both underage and at most we will go to a juvenile home and be out when we are 18. It won't even be shown on our record. By that time Pawan will be finishing his studies and then he can help us to get better jobs. Maybe even set up a business together."

Rakesh thought about what his friend had suggested. It was a good idea especially if what he said about not going to jail was true. He really wanted to help Pawan and felt that the risk was worth it if Pawan could get a chance to realize his dream. "I'll think about it, meet me here tomorrow at the same time and I'll let you know."

That whole night, Rakesh lay in his bed, tossing and turning. He thought about their friendship and what this chance would mean for Pawan, he recalled the many movies they had seen together where their favourite heroes had made great sacrifices for the sake of their friendship and every time they came out of the theatre they had marvelled at the great sacrifice they made for each other, and although they had never made any pledge or taken any oath, the three of them knew that under similar circumstances they would also do the same for one another. This was the acid test of their friendship, he knew that if he refused, Dharamveer would think that he had failed him and wouldn't help him out either. It would be the start of the breakup of a friendship that spanned 12 years and Rakesh could not bear the thought of it.

The next evening Rakesh met Dharamveer at the tea stall "Let's do it!" he said in reply to Dharamveer's questioning look "But it must be well planned and we'll only do three bikes OK?" Dharamveer was overjoyed "I knew you wouldn't let us down, let's go to your place, I have a plan, you tell me how you can improve it." With that the two friends began a journey that could only end in disaster.

The plan was simple enough; Steal only new unregistered bikes, no upscale models, and only popular brands i.e.; relatively cheap and good average per litre. Most importantly they must steal them from areas where they were unknown. The best places would be cinema halls and busy shopping areas.

The next few days were spent scouting out the areas; they would meet briefly in the morning and mark out the areas each should visit and then in the evening they would meet again and discuss the best place each had seen. After 3 days they had drawn up a list of the best possible places from where to steal a bike from. It was time for the action.

The first two bikes they stole were easy, Rakesh would walk up to the bike they had selected, check his pockets and shout to Dharamveer "I don't have the keys, they must be with you!" People standing around would admire the new bike and Dharamveer would walk casually up insert his master key, kick start the bike revv it up a few times and the two would drive off. It was all in the open and nobody suspected a thing. The stolen bikes were promptly handed over to the contact man who paid the money willingly. They now had 14000 rupees, they had given Pawan his money and the look in his eyes more than made up for the effort or guilt that they may have felt in committing the crimes. Pawan of course never knew and both decided to tell him at a much later date.

Since they had a contract with the gang for stealing three motorbikes they decided to steal one last bike and then call it quits. The tension of being caught was getting to be a bit too much and they just prayed for the whole thing to be over as soon as possible.

They planned their third job as meticulously as the previous two, but they had not taken into their calculations the police's tenacity and determination to act when under pressure. Stung by public outrage and local media criticism the Police Commissioner had summoned his station heads and warned them of disciplinary action including transfer from their present stations if the thieves were not caught. No station head relished the idea of giving up their lucrative posts for some obscure and more importantly, non-financially rewarding far flung village outpost. So, they renewed their efforts, extra men were put on the job, known car and bike thieves were "vigorously" questioned and plainclothes men were placed in parking lots of cinemas and shopping centres.

This was not a good time for our two friends to steal another bike, but since they were unaware of these extra precautions and since they were so eager to finish off their obligation to Pawan, they just went ahead with their plan.

The bike they chose for their final job was also a mistake. Firstly, it was a high-end bike; secondly, it belonged to the son of the Police Commissioner and was known to the two plainclothes men sitting close by. Everything was predictable after that. They went into their routine and the police went into theirs. As luck would have it, a national TV channel was in town covering a story about corruption in the municipal department and was being escorted by the local TV channel, while driving by the reporter saw this commotion in a car park and sensing a story drove in and started filming.

The sudden appearance of a TV crew, probably saved Rakesh and Dharamveer from receiving the soundest public thrashing of their entire lives; instead they found themselves staring bewilderingly into a TV camera too dumbfounded to speak. Meanwhile a huge crowd had built up and the lot was crawling with uniformed policemen, police officials began arriving in droves and as word spread more TV crews began to set up their cameras. It was as if some dreaded underworld criminal had been caught after a huge gun battle instead of two scruffy looking urchins. The Station Officer in whose area the crime had been committed was pompously talking into the small forest of microphones that had sprung up under his nose. By the time he had finished, Rakesh and Dharamveer were being blamed for every bike that had been stolen in the city for the last two years.

The police commissioner finally arrived, in a freshly pressed uniform. Car doors slammed as he got out, six or eight hefty policemen formed a cordon around him and he walked solemnly towards a tight knot of people crowding around our two heroes. He arrived in time to hear the national reporter quiz Rakesh as to why he had committed this crime. Rakesh began to stutter something about how he was innocent and was just passing by when one of the plainclothesmen who had arrested him gave him a sharp clip on the side of his head and said "Tell the truth." So Rakesh thought "Why not?"

In the full glare of the TV cameras, flash bulbs and reporters, not to mention a few hundred onlookers, a battalion of policemen and the Police Commissioner himself, Rakesh narrated the full story; the friendship, Pawan's shattered dreams and their pledge to help their friend. Now the Police Commissioner was a wise and wily old man, (you don't make it to the highest rank by not seizing an opportunity when it presents itself on a platter) watching the boy tell his story it took him seconds to realize that they were not actual criminals and that this was not a very big arrest but it was a wonderful human interest story and he saw that this would be the angle that the media would play on, he saw at once how he could garner some really favourable publicity for himself in particular and the police force in general. He pushed a few inspectors aside and faced the cameras, "This is a truly heart-warming story, and since the bike in question belongs to my son I will advise him not to press charges." There were loud cheers from everyone, including a "No probs Dad!" from his son who was standing to one side hoping that no one would question him too much about what he had been doing in an area known for its pubs, pool halls and other venues of questionable entertainment. "Furthermore, since I believe their story, if they co-operate and lead us to the gang, no charges for the stealing of the other two bikes will be framed either and lastly I will personally see that these three friends finish their education and get decent jobs so that they can look after their families. Such friendship, devotion and loyalty deserve to be rewarded." There was tremendous cheering and handshaking all around, Rakesh and Dharamveer had been transformed from petty thieves to heroes and posed for photographs with the Commissioner and sundry lesser police officials with great gusto, a lot of sweets and samosas were passed around. Since none of this was being broadcast live, there was plenty of time for the police to round up key members of the auto lifter gang and by evening Rakesh and Dharamveer were back at their homes quite excited at the prospect of seeing themselves on TV during the evening news.

When the news broke and the people of the colony found out, a huge crowd gathered outside Rakesh's house to congratulate him, so once again he was saved a thrashing from his father who was furious but could do little in front of so many people. Then he saw Pawan pushing his way through the crowd until he was face to face with him, Rakesh could see that he was crying and realized to his dismay that there were tears in his own eyes too, highly embarrassed, he hugged Pawan, suddenly they both were being hugged by an equally tearful Dharamveer. Their tears were soon replaced with laughter and they sat around till the crowd thinned out recounting their exploits to Pawan who was amazed at their daring then angry at being left out of the fun.

With a bright future to look forward to our three friends went to their respective homes firmly convinced that sometimes Crime DOES Pay!!!

LOVE STORY

Rohit and Chetna were in love. And what a love that was. Sadly, it was a forbidden love, as she belonged to a higher caste (highest) and he to a lower one. This,is a story of inter caste marriage. It's a twisted tale but ends well even though the means were not justified, or were they? You decide.

Anyway, they were a passionate couple and as is wont for all young passionate couples, they indulged in making passionate love whenever and wherever they got a chance. Since they were neighbours, many chances presented themselves and they availed themselves of each and every one of them. The fact that their love had to be clandestine did not bother them a whit, natural urges needed to be satisfied on the spot and to hell with the consequences. They were naïve young things, and the harsh reality of social disapproval and caste distinctions had not yet thrown its ugly shadow over their lives, but surely as the Pope is Catholic it was bound to.

It's not as if their romance was all plain sailing, No Sir! they fought and threw things at each other, whatever was handy, mainly their mobile phones but also hair brushes, water bottles and pomegranates. She loved that fruit and took great pleasure in watching him peel the fruit and separate the arils and lovingly feed the red juicy morsels to her, the tips of his fingers stained bright red with the juice, brushing sensuously against her lips. These were the type of fights that Rohit looked forward to as they invariably ended up making wild passionate love afterward, with teary promises that this would be their last fight.

All these encounters took place in moderately priced hotel rooms in Taj Ganj, an area in Agra adjacent to the Taj Mahal, and favoured by the not so well-heeled tourist. Rohit's job as a small debt collector for a big ass finance company ensured that he was always in touch with a host of hotel managers, waiters, bell boys and catering staff, who were not averse to turning a blind eye to mysterious activity in 'unoccupied' honeymoon or Deluxe suites in return for a nudge and a wink on a delayed EMI repayment or two. They went to movies, to restaurants, and to hotel rooms they even went 'outstation' to romantic getaways and hideaways always ensuring they were back the same day. When they saw each other from the confines of their respective houses, it was as if they had never met or even knew each other and that made their romance even spicier. Their families never mixed socially so meeting friends of each other's friends was not a problem. Nobody knew. Well almost nobody, Chetna's sister knew and was justifiably both outraged and mortified and Rohit's best friend Saiz, he also knew, and would thump him on his back enthusiastically and encourage him to share all the details, but nobody else. As in the case of all love stories like this (forbidden love type) dark clouds has begun to loom ominously on the horizon. If either one of them had taken the trouble to consult a respectable cartomancer, she (the cartomancer) would have told them that the 13th card of the major arcana figured prominently in all their readings. This card features an armoured skeleton riding a horse carrying a black flag with people in its path dying or begging for salvation, quite the scary card to repeatedly keep popping up. But since the did not do this they had no idea of the pitfalls that awaited them.

Then when Chetna turned 18 and Rohit 21, talk began in their respective households, of marriage. He to a suitable girl and she to a suitable boy. Things became sticky and the shadow descended. On one of their clandestine meetings she disclosed that she was finding it harder and harder to resist her parents' cajoling and sometimes threatening pleas to agree to a suitable match. She merely sniffed sorrowfully at Rohit's suggestion that she tell them about him. He was more than miffed when she scoffed at his suggestion that they elope and get married in court. What will my parents say she said what will society say, she asked? My family will be outcasts, we will be ostracised in our community. My parents could never live down the shame. Rohit knew that these were cogent arguments but his heart couldn't, wouldn't believe that his Chetna was actually beginning to even consider the fact that they would not be together for eternity.

Things got worse when eligible suitor's families or emissaries began turning up with proposals, to meet her parents. He watched all this from his window across the road from behind a strategically drawn curtain. He grew sullen and morose and wept in front of Saiz his loyal friend who would often come over and just sit quietly with him, saying nothing. For his part he refused every proposal outright saying he wanted to get a proper job first.

Every night at a fixed time he would text her messages filled with love and passion begging her to come out of the house and meet him, sometimes she came and sometimes she didn't. Most times she didn't. when she did come, they would kiss passionately and he would smother her body with kisses and his hands would be all over her. She would even allow him to enter her briefly, looking around anxiously lest anyone see their furtive coupling.

Then she blocked his phone number, this infuriated Rohit and he would rant and rave to his friend Saiz about what a bitch she was and how she had just strung him along for whatever she could get out of him. He would show her! From his window, he watched as she got engaged, he watched as the 'Bharat' arrived and though he was not on the guest list he was there at the reception held at a marriage hall not far from where they lived. He never went inside, but since the marriage hall entrance was on the main road he could easily enough, merge with other bystanders to try and catch a glimpse of the bride and groom as they arrived. She resplendent in red and gold and He in a sherwani that looked as if could do with a bit of ironing. He looked like an idiot (groom) and chewed paan. "Oh God!" Rohit said to himself "is he going to kiss her with that mouth?" He continued looking, craning his neck trying to watch her for as long as he could before she was finally lost in the melee.

Somebody grasped him firmly by the elbow, it was Saiz, loyal faithful Saiz. "come with me" he said. Saiz took him to a beer bar and Rohit got thoroughly pissed that night. Somehow, he got him home and into bed. The next few days Saiz never left his side and continuously coaxed him into getting on with his life and with Saiz's help he did, relapsing only when she came home for holidays and festivals.

Gradually he became his cheerful self again, he started going to the gym and grew a light beard (designer stubble) he discovered the joys of being single as also the joys of massage parlours and the happy endings they offered.

He plunged himself into his work and found that he was actually making a decent amount of money. With Chetna, he never had enough money for himself, for he was spending it all on her, now, with her out of the picture he could finally spend some on himself and still had some left to spare.

Throughout all this time, Rohit continued to love Chetna with a dark passion that he managed to conceal from all his friends even Saiz. Whenever he thought abought her his blood, usually bright red and highly oxygenated would turn to dark molten lava, and burn its way through his veins, all the time murmuring Betrayal! Betrayal! Betrayal!

Then Chetna came back, this time for good. Her marriage had collapsed and her husband kicked her out. It was at about this time also that she discovered that her mother had breast cancer. Breast cancer is curable but in an economically backward community such as hers it was dire news. The best cancer hospitals were in Mumbai, Delhi and Jaipur. Since Jaipur was the closest, they took her for treatment there.

Saiz was dismayed at Chetna's return, he knew the effect she had on Rohit and feared Rohit might relapse into his old ways. His fears were well founded and Rohit again became besotted. But this time he had a plan. Blackmail! During their frequent trysts in hotel rooms and honeymoon suites Rohit would record their activities on his mobile phone even their fake marriage ceremony. Chetna knew about these recordings but didn't think much of it, after all it was her Rohit and he wouldn't harm her in any way, would he? He loved her and she loved him, what could go wrong? Plenty apparently.

The truth is that Chetna loved Rohit with all her heart and soul, but she was more afraid of her parents and sister and brother in law. When her idiot husband kicked her out, she was relieved but she had not catered for her parent's anger. Anger not because their daughter was unhappy or could not make her husband happy but anger because of all the shame and social stigma that accompanied an errant daughter's return from her husband's house. This is the worst sort of anger.

When Rohit began to blackmail her, she was dismayed. How could he even think of doing this, let alone do it? She submitted to him but with a heavy heart, every lunge, every thrust was like a dagger into her heart and she knew that this could not go on forever. It was time to let the women take over. She had a plan. Her uncle from her father's side, was the Pradhan of her village block. Quite important too, for there were several villages within their panchayat. Regular meetings would be held and important social and political matters would be decided on. Once decided everyone had to abide by their decision or risk being ostracised. Begging him to secrecy, she told him everything. Now all that was left was to implement the plan she and her Uncle had hatched.

The next time Rohit sent a pathetic message begging her to meet him outside she texted him to come to her house at midnight, she would leave the door open and he should walk right in. he was there in a flash, he had done this before, her room was second from the left and he entered eagerly. He quietly closed the door and groped his was towards her bed, she met him halfway and whispered "tear my nighty off, quick!" Rohit obeyed happily and proceeded further to disrobe himself but she stopped him

"No, take me with your clothes on" once more he was her obedient servant. What happened next hit him like a bolt out of the blue. She began to scream incoherently; 'Help! Help! he is attacking me! Save me save me! 'Within seconds her sister and her husband barged in and turned on the light and took in the spectacle before them. Rohit was still inside her and she was struggling in his arms, it looked like her nighty was wrapped around her neck as if he was trying to choke her into silence. Within minutes, as is wont in all Indian mohallas, the whole Mohalla had gathered outside the house. Rohit got soundly thrashed by a few residents, who were more irritated at being woken up in the middle of the night than anything else., the police came in due time, made a few inquiries and carted Rohit off to the police outpost nearby.

The next few days were a whirlwind of activity for the village, Chetna's parents said that he should go to jail for raping their daughter and wanted to lodge an official complaint (FIR), now no one would marry her they lamented. Saiz informed any and everyone who would listen that they were in love. The police kept hanging around waiting for someone to file charges. Saiz showed everyone that she called (texted) him to come over. Such confusion. Chetna refused to talk to anyone and Rohit as well, even though the police thumped him on the head several times in a half-hearted attempt to get him to confess. But their heart wasn't in it, Rape cases, in areas under their jurisdiction, didn't go down well with head office, and in this case, rape was doubtful and highly unlikely.

Finally, a panchayat meeting was set up. Both the aggrieved parties were present and because of the scandalous nature of the case, several hundred busybodies attended as well.

The meeting had been called by the Secretary of the panchayat, a government appointed official, who kept records and minutes and who was also a friend of Chetna's uncle, Babu Lal. Chetna's side insisted that rape had been committed whereas Rohit's side insisted it was consensual, (neither Chetna nor Rohit was present. She being confined to her room and he confined to the jail cell of the police thana) "in any case" Chetna's father wailed dramatically "my daughter's life has been ruined who will marry her now?" He asked plaintively. There was considerable agreement among the on lookers who were impressed with the oratory skills of the poor father. The meeting then broke up into smaller groups for 45 minutes, for a discussion as to what was to be done on this very vexed and divisive issue. Babu Lal got to work. He visited each group and gave his suggestion to each one. At the end of 45 minutes the meeting assembled again. Now only the panch members were allowed to speak. No one else. One by one each member got up and gave his opinion. The first speaker, a staunch friend of Chetna's father, said that this was clearly a case of rape and that a First Information Report (FIR) should be registered against the accused. This verdict was greeted with sporadic applause by a few family friends. What followed next, from panch No 2 to panch No 9, was nothing short of astounding and mind blowing. Each and every one of these panches supported the view that the two should be married immediately despite the difference in their castes. Some had doubted whether it was indeed 'rape' in the first place. Others had said even if it were rape, the couple had a history, which couldn't be denied. Young blood was the consensus boys will be boys!

There was an uproar, as the crowd voiced their approval, a few scuffles broke out but were hastily broken up by the police, a few well-placed blows with their lathis put an end to that. The Sarpanch importantly called the meeting to order, and he gave his verdict, he ordered that the intercaste marriage of Rohit and Chetna should take place immediately and that the groom should be released from police custody as no charges were going to be filed. The panch of Chetna's village was told to make all necessary arrangements at the village temple and that all would meet again at 2 pm to witness the marriage ceremony. Funds from his discretionary fund were to be allocated for a grand feast and a plot of land was to be allocated to the young couple for starting a new life.

Chetna's family took the decision well, the father was a bit miffed but the fact that her second marriage was not going to cost him an arm and a leg offered him some consolation, plus the fact that their marriage was socially approved by the panchayat meant that they were no longer in fear of ostracization and every one could get on with their lives again.

As for Rohit and Chetna, well they lived happily ever after, well at least she did, once she had told him the full story, he realised that she was the real brains in the house they decided on a division of labour. He would decide the major issues concerning their lives, who to vote for and which government policies to support, whether Article 370 really integrated Kashmir with the rest of the country or not, should there be another demonetisation or not and were surgical strikes good for us vis a vis our relations with Pakistan or not. She in turn was happy to be left alone to decide the minor issue, when to build their house, when to have kids, how many kids and which school to send them to, she was also allowed to decide the household budget and other such petty issues. The system worked fine, is working fine in fact and today to this day Rohit knows that whenever he comes back late from a night out with the boys, he needn't bother going to the bedroom to snuggle up to her. He automatically goes to the guest room, flops down on the bed and has a dreamless sleep for the next 4 to six hours. He would make it up to her tomorrow.

FAMILY HONOUR

Shaheen stood by the window and looked out at the familiar dusty barren landscape that shimmered in the scorching desert heat. He knew every contour of the land outside like the back of his hand and had been exploring every ravine, wadi and dry well in the area from the time he could crawl. Continuous exposure to the sun and the elements had bronzed his skin which now had the texture of leather. His nose was sharp, aquiline and resembled the beak of the desert falcon, after which he had been so aptly named. But it was his hands that immediately drew one's attention, large in proportion to rest of his slender body, broad, rough and calloused, his habit of continuously cracking his knuckles over the years had made his fingers broader and more spatulate. He brought them together again and cracked them subconsciously.

He was considering his next course of action. Whatever had to be done, had to be done quickly, in the next hour or so, before the rumours circulated amongst the other clansmen and the family was irredeemably shamed. The honour of the family was at stake and he wished with all his heart and soul that he didn't have to be the one to decide the course that needed to be taken in order to retrieve it. If it had been someone outside the family who had shamed them so, it would have been a simple matter, one that could be easily set right in a manly and honourable manner and everyone would applaud his valour and courage.

They lived outside the rules of whichever government was in power, in this vast wilderness tribal law was paramount, and no government or lackey sent by the government, dared to interfere or even consider imposing a different value system on them.Over the last two centuries they had successfully resisted and overcome any attempt to impose one. The ruthlessness of the British, the tanks and helicopter gunships of the Soviet army and now even the Cruise and Tomahawk missiles of the technologically advanced Americans were all resisted and overcome, with a tenacity that was secretly admired by their adversaries and wished for in their own armies

They had no interest in the affairs of the rest of the nation and couldn't care less for the rulers provided they were left alone. In the past, a few tentative military incursions had occurred in an attempt to bring the area under one central authority, these ended with such disastrous results for the intruders that a consensus was quickly reached wherein it was decided to leave them to themselves and they became virtually an autonomous region; paying only lip service to the flag content to be left alone to follow their own laws and values. In their book Family Honour was second only to their religion and must be upheld at all costs.

Traditionally the decision of how to uphold the family honour would have been taken by the head of the family; in this case, it would have been his father, had he been alive. Now as the eldest in a family of three brothers and an only sister, the mantle fell on his shoulders and the three brothers all looked to him as he stood by the window dreading to articulate what was already on every one's mind. The women had retreated earlier as they had no say in the decision making, his mother was in the huge kitchen, her refuge in times of inner turmoil, and his sister had each gone to her heavily curtained room to await the outcome in semi darkness. No lamps would be lit today for the family was in mourning.

He turned away from the window and drew a heavy curtain across it, this kept the bright afternoon sunlight at bay, and the room was suffused in a soft glow. He faced his brothers, each seated on a stool at the table their hands nervously picking at stray flecks of dirt or drumming nervously on its ruff hewn surface. None dared to look him in the eye. A year each separated the youngest to the eldest and then came their sister Amal; their beautiful loving and talented sister all of 16 years old, in her prime and pledged in marriage to Sheikh Abu Masood, the 65-year-oldpatriarch of a powerful desert tribe.

The suitor's family had visited their house a few months ago and the Sheikh had formally requested for Amal to be his bride, and he, as head of the house along with his mother had given their approval to this union, a princely sum was agreed on as Mehr and the Shabka agreed upon reflected the high social status that the Sheikh enjoyed. All arrangements were proceeding smoothly and the engagement party was barely a fortnight away. Now tragedy had befallen this household. Now throughout the entire negotiations Amal's opinion was never considered. The fact that she was only 16 and her fiancé was 65 was never a factor in the negotiations.

Shaheen had been thrilled at the prospect of forging an alliance with such a powerful family and often imagined uniting the two clans into one really mighty entity under his leadership. His sister's happiness was not even considered after all she was just a girl and the Holy Book demanded her obedience and compliance to her husbands every demand. From her early childhood the concepts of 'Eib' and 'Sharaf' which means 'Shame' and 'Honour' had been drilled into her head. This concept was further reinforced repeatedly for it was written"As to those women on whose part ye fear disloyalty and ill - conduct, admonish them, refuse to share their beds, beat them" Yet she had shamed their family in so brazen a manner that merely beating her would not suffice, his senses reeled at the consequences and served to strengthen his resolve about what he must do. There was no shortage of precedent, Family Honour had been avenged in countless instances before and would continue to be avenged thus in the future as well. It was the only way.

This morning he had come upon his sister and Ali, a stable boy employed to feed and water and feed the numerous horses and camels that they owned, he was not even allowed to enter the house. It was clear that Ali was raping the girl, her struggles and groans bore out this fact, in fact so engrossed was Ali in his task that he didn't even notice Shaheen standing there. In a rage he drew his dagger and in one vicious motion slit Ali's throat as he groaned with lust while still on top of his sister. Amal screamed with terror and wriggled out from under the gasping and wheezing Ali and ran into the house and Shaheen had gone straight to his mother. It was obvious that Amal was now no longer a virgin, the Sheikh had insisted that she be pure and had paid a handsome amount for her purity. Now she had brought dishonour to the family name. His mother well versed in the high traditions of their family history, simply told him "This is a subject for the family council, our honourmust be retrieved somehow, and the decision must be unanimous. Call your brothers and do as you think your father would have done had he been here. May God grant you wisdom"

So Shaheen sat down at the table, in the only chair strategically placed at the head and looked at his brother's "Do you agree then my brothers that our family's honour must be restored and that this is the only way to do so?" Each brother nodded his agreement. Shaheen got up and walked towards his sister's room "Each one will play his part, Rafeek you are the youngest fetch the Book and read from it, Aslam you will hold her legs, Sajid hold her arms, I will do the rest."

The four brothers trooped into Amal's room and stood around while Shaheen sat on the bed by her side, she was crying and shivering "It is not my fault brother; I had gone to feed my pony I didn't know Ali was also there. Please forgive me" Shaheen's rough hands smoothed her brow "Hush little sister all will be well soon. Close your eyes and go to sleep" He nodded to Rafeek who began to recite from the Book, as the brothers held onto her arms and legs, Shaheen's rough calloused hand moved to her throat, instinctively found the spot and closed over her slender neck and closed choking her air supply. As his grip tightened she opened her eyes once and looked at Shaheen but his own were shut tight as he fought back tears of regret and remorse. She did not struggle at all, she had accepted her fate. At the end her body twitched involuntarily and then was still forever. Shaheen never relaxed his grip on her throat until Aslam bent forward and pried his hands apart. The brothers trooped out of the room as silently as they had entered, the muzzenein could be heard in the distance, calling out to the faithful, it was time for the evening prayer. The brothers fetched their prayer mats. The Family Honour had been avenged.

GUESS WHO I SAW TODAY?

We were huddled together for the final briefing, one excited soggy mass, sixty in all; I was the oldest at 22 years of age everyone else was younger, there were thirty boys and thirty girls. The girls were all dressed in skimpy pastel shaded tops, ten each of pink, lime green and sky blue and frayed denim mini shorts that stopped well short of the mid-thigh area. We, the boys that is, were more conservatively dressed; denim jeans frayed and cut off at the knee and nothing else. We were soggy because all of us had been forced to stand under the open showers used by the prop department for shots that called for heavy rain and stormy weather. Our bodies had just been oiled and our chests gleamed under the lights.

You see, we were on the sets of the BR studios, another Salman Khan starrer and musical blockbuster was in the making and we were the backup dance ensemble. It had no name as yet but was sure to incorporate the letter Kay. The director was some big shot's son and could be seen in the background fussing about with the props, lights, and making good use of his megaphone as he barked instructions to spot boys hidden high in the rafters, to adjust the orange light on row B just the teensiest.

Our choreographer dragged up his stool, stood on it and clapped his hands for our attention "Boys and Girls" he said in a voice that oozed false pep and joviality "We have rehearsed this sequence a hundred times, in about an hour we will be shooting the first 4 stanzas of the theme song. Everybody knows what to do so don't worry, you all will be great. Stay together. Do this one for me! You and You!" he said pointing at me and my friend Rocky "The hero will be coming onto the set shortly; I want you both to rehearse with him and show him the moves. Don't worry He is a fabulous dancer and will pick up the steps fast."

One of the reasons that the two of us had been chosen was not because we were the best dancers but because of our physiques, or rather lack of them, of the 30, ours were decidedly the puniest and hence represented no threat to the star who undoubtedly had the Muscles from Brussels sort of body but still didn't want any competition from the extras. Stardom was so fickle, "Today's star was yesterday's extra!" and most stars knew this adage only too well. It was this mantra that kept us from chucking it all up and going home, back to forgotten families and becoming accountants or truck drivers as our parents had wished in the first place.

I was absolutely thrilled. This was my big shot at fame; if I played my cards correctly I stood a good chance of actually being in the same frame as Sallu Bhai for more than the 6 seconds it took for the cameraman to lose interest in us and pan to close up shots of our female counterparts who unfortunately were also required to gyrate in a similarly lewd and suggestive manner. Plus, their tops would be wet. Sallu had just made his entrance, trailed by makeup men, script holders and his very own PA; he was immediately surrounded by the director, three anxious producers and a medley of minor actors, guests and a tea boy who was thrusting a cup of scalding hot tea at him through the throng. Sallu accepted the cup and sipped it meditatively as the director and script writer explained to him how exactly he was to deliver his dialogues, where he was to stand, which camera he was to face and at what moment in the delivery of his lines. The fight director was catching forty winks as this was one of those rare occasions in a Salman movie where he was not required. The choreographer caught up with us as we stood nervously on the periphery watching our idol's every movement and mannerism and making them our very own. This was a star whose mannerisms were worthy of emulation. Just look at the cool way he sipped hot tea, the way he snaps his fingers at his PA, who whips out his special brand of cigarette and offers it to him. The way he inhales the smoke, savouring it as if it were the most precious thing on earth and then the exhalation; smoke bellows out of him like an overworked steam engine. He flicks the remainder of the cigarette towards an ash can but misses by a mile and a flunkey duly runs to stub it out, glancing backwards coyly to see if this noble action of his has caught the eye of the great man himself. Alas for him! Who had caught his eye was our choreographer who elbows his way into the circle, grabs his hand and pulls him towards where we were standing. "Sallu Bhai" he gushes "These are my boys, they will show you, it is a basic step movement, 3 to the left, then sit, then up then overhead clap, turn right and same, turn left and same. Then repeat. Okay Bhai? See my boys! They will show you then you do with them. Music" he yells offstage and at once a melody with a very catchy tune belts out from dozens of speakers lying around. The crowd had now gathered around us and as we moved into our routine I felt a moment of great joy and pride surely all the pain and heartache that I had undergone was worth it after all. I thrust my hips out at the camera as suggestively as I could; we were required to smile perpetually but my smile doubled when Sallu joined in, his body swaying to the rhythm and then the full routine, just as if he had been practicing with us for weeks. What a guy! "Cut" shouted the choreographer "On set 5 minutes!" "Makeup shouted Sallu's PA importantly as the great man flopped down into his chair. A dozen things were thrust into his face, tea, cigarettes, mikes and make up brushes. We stood not more than 5 feet away still in shock and Sallu noticed this and called us over offered us tea and a cigarette each, although we didn't smoke, we both took one and lit up like veterans. The choreographer hurried over to shoo us away from his presence but as we retreated I heard Salman telling him "See that those two are always behind me for this song, no one else understand? They make me look good!"

That's how it happened, go and see the movie. My song is after the fight Sallu has with the drug smugglers, then he goes to a bar to see his girlfriend who is a bar dancer and he gets drunk, we are also there I am drinking beer straight from the bottle, then it starts to rain, Sallu runs out into the rain and onto a football field, we run with him after one stanza we are joined by his girlfriend and all her friends. I'm there always to the left of Sallu and Rocky is there on the right, I have an earring which dangles as I dance and Rocky wears a Spiderman tattoo on his right bicep. The song is already a big hit and soon all the publicity will start but first they have to figure out a name. It should start with the letter Kay.

LADIES COMPARTMENT

Shalini Sirsikar waited patiently besides Mrs. Kamini Deshpande on the crowded Platform Number 3 at Bandra Station. They were waiting for their local train to arrive; the arrival time was 8.04 AM and Kamini had assured her that it was an express train and was never late. She glanced nervously at the digital clock that hung midway between the exit sign and the sign indicating where the Station Master's Office was located. 8.02 it read "It will come, it will come!" said Mrs Deshpande patiently perhaps sensing Shalini's nervousness "Now pay attention! Always stand under this sign. When the train stops walk quickly to the entrance and take the first seats you get to your left, I always sit there, they all know it." she indicated a small marker over their heads which read LADIES COMPARTMENT, and in smaller letters underneath '1st Class' "Have you got your ticket? Good! Keep it handy the ticket inspector can ask to see it anytime" Shalini nodded her head and clutched her voluminous handbag tighter to her. This was her first time on the subway system and she felt lucky that Mrs Deshpande in her officious manner, and perhaps feeling sorry for this newcomer, had decided to adopt her and become her guide and friend as well. There were plenty of other ladies; some stood aloof, some chatting in groups some in pairs, all of them old traveling companions and veterans of the subway system.

The train arrived with a whoosh, silently and suddenly, as if from out of nowhere. Shalini who was looking elsewhere at that time was jerked forward by Mrs Deshpande who had attached herself to her forearm firmly and was ploughing through the crowd like an ocean liner, scattering those in her path with Shalini stumbling behind in her wake. The crowd of ladies surged through the narrow entrance to the compartment and dissipated once inside as each group found their own favourite spot. Mrs Deshpande found her place and seated herself regally as befitted her stature and size. Extra space was found for Shalini as people reluctantly adjusted themselves to make place for her.

With a soft toot the train began to move forward gliding silently past the seething mass of office goers who were waiting impatiently for their train to arrive. The train accelerated rapidly and though they had not yet cleared the platform it had already reached its top speed. The rest of the platform vanished into a white blur as the train broke into the bright sunshine and the clickity clack of the train changing tracks drowned out the high-pitched voices in the compartment. Soon the train was on the main line and people settled down to their routines. Some had opened up tiffin boxes and were having breakfast, some took out their cell phones and rang friends or loved ones, the majority gossiped amongst themselves. Handbags, lunch boxes and shopping bags had been stored in overhead luggage racks or under the seats. Shalini had stored her bag under the seat.

It was obvious that Mrs Deshpande liked to gossip but today she took it upon herself to also familiarize Shalini about her co passengers. "See that one in the green sari; that's Mrs Joshi she has two children, her husband left her 6 months ago, now the poor thing has to work to support herself and children." Shalini glanced sympathetically at Mrs Joshi, who was gazing out of the window, a far off look in her eyes. What was she thinking about thought Shalini to herself; perhaps wondering where her husband was, what he was doing, maybe he was also sitting similarly in a train thinking about her. Mahim station flashed by in a whirl and flurry of white and before her mind could even register the fact, it had passed and they were clattering again between the decrepit buildings which loomed above on either side. These buildings, abandoned long ago by their owners, had now been taken over by the homeless and wretched of this great metropolis. Shreds of tattered cloth hung over openings in the walls, filthy naked children played or sat perilously close to the track scarcely noticing the monstrosity that thundered by. She turned her attention back to Mrs Deshpande who was discussing an absentee member of their group with the lady sitting opposite. "I'm telling you Vimlaji; she is now going by bus but won't tell us. It is all these bomb blasts and hoax calls we've been having lately." The lady in front, Mrs Kale (she had diabetes but still ate sweets on the sly Mrs Deshpande had told her later) spoke in a loud brassy voice "No! No! Kamini! Her husband wants her to stay at home, his mother is very ill and she has to look after her. So, she has taken long leave."

Matunga Road flashed by, there was no let-up in the decibel level inside the compartment, Mrs Deshpande was engaged in an animated conversation with a lady three rows away and Shalini tuned in "So Kantabhen, how was last night?" She giggled lewdly and the rolls of fat around her waist shivered in unison with her bosom. In an aside meant for Shalini's ears alone but picked up most of the other passengers she explained "It was their 14th anniversary yesterday and her mister took her to the Bandstand and then for a late-night movie." Kantabhen laughed good naturedly and replied "Oh Kamini! You know my mister! Every day is our anniversary for him but yesterday I also had prawn curry and ice cream." Shalini didn't get the joke but the rest of them did and they all laughed simultaneously. What happy and simple people they were she thought to herself. She felt sorry for them, if they only knew what was in their future perhaps they would all have stayed home today, like that wise lady who had begun to avoid traveling by train.

Their arrival at Dadar Junction was heralded with a loud screeching of brakes as the fast-moving train jerked to an abrupt halt. The noise on the platform was chaotic; the public address system was also announcing their arrival along with imminent arrivals and departures of a host of other trains standing on their respective platforms, their powerful diesel engines humming with pent up energy waiting impatiently for the green signal. A colourful mass of oily squawking womenfolk surged into their already overcrowded compartment. "Keep sitting" Mrs Deshpande ordered her young charge as she glared ferociously at any intruder daring to even think of attempting to sit inside their little circle. There was no room to even stand and the air was stifling. A variety of odours assailed her nostrils, at times a cloyingly sweet sticky perfume which made her want to retch and at times the stench of Bombay Duck was so powerful and overbearing that she was sure that she would surely suffocate. An old woman hobbled by and Shalini stood up and offered her the seat before Mrs Deshpande could react. She smiled reassuringly at her as the old crone slid effortlessly into the vacant space. Shalini clutched the overhead handrail and swayed in time with the motion of the train.

As she stood in the aisle she eyed her large handbag guiltily, it sat under the seat barely visible, black, ugly and squat, like a toad on a rock by the lake near her house. But this was no harmless amphibian, it was filled with death. Her instructors, fervent holy men had drilled it repeatedly into her head; "At Dadar station you must prepare, get up and move towards the door, it will be crowded, but just keep on moving till you get to an exit, then get off at Mahalaxmi, walk away as fast as you can but don't run once outside the station we will contact you." She looked sadly at Mrs Deshpande one last time; the kindly lady was busy talking to her immediate neighbour about something very juicy apparently for they both had their heads so close to each other it was as if they had been glued together. She moved slowly away further and further until she stood almost at the entrance. In two minutes, they would reach Mahalaxmi Station. It would be over in five. They were at the outer signal and Shalini knew at once that something was amiss; they were going too fast; the train was not going to stop. Sure enough, within seconds they were hurtling through and past the station, everything was a blur of white. This was an express train and the next major halt was Mumbai Central, a good ten minutes away. Somebody had made a serious mistake – or had they?

At that very moment she saw Mrs Deshpande calling out to her gesticulating wildly. She glanced away ignoring her, with all the noise and confusion in the compartment no one would even notice that it was she who was being hailed. "Shalini! Shalini! You forgot your bag!" To Shalini's horror she saw that the lady was now holding the bag aloft in one hand and frantically signalling her with the other; moreover, she began to move towards her end of the compartment. Shalini cringed and continued to ignore her, praying that the end would come quickly for she realized now that her kindly instructors had never meant for her to survive. "Are you Shalini?" a young college girl asked her "That lady has your handbag; I think you left it under your seat." Shalini looked directly into the young girls' eyes and simply said "My name is Zubaiya and I don't have any hand bag." Those were her last words. The explosion ripped through the crowded compartment mowing down every one in its path. The compartment itself seemed to surge towards the sky and Zubaiya's final thoughts before she was torn limb from limb were "I have been betrayed!"

PERIPHERAL

Hi! My name is not important but I'm sure that my face is familiar to you; you must have seen me on television dozens of times. I have been interviewed on several occasions, I'm sure you may have noticed the calm and collected way in which I addressed the larger audience. Did you notice my teeth? Pearly white! Sometimes I'm just part of the crowd surrounding the reporter, trying hard but failing to catch his or her eye so that I could give my version of the event. I have waved out frantically and smiled cheerfully at them but sometimes these reporters have their own agenda and ignore those with meaningful things to say and instead interview some loudmouth gutkachewing moron, who has no idea of how to behave when being interviewed for national television.

Several times I have been edited out just because I knew the answer and the reporter was trying to say that most of those she interviewed did not know the answer. For instance once this cute young reporter with a terribly screechy voice went around our campus asking us the formula for *steam,* I knew the answer and said so but she just brushed past me and collared somebody else. This guy wasn't even from our college but the moment he gave her a dumb look she excitedly began squawking about how low our levels of intelligence are. Same was for the *National Song;* I sang it word for word and in the exact tune but the reporter was keen to tell his viewers that the youth don't know it so he ignored me. I tell you had my rendition been aired on national television I am sure some famous composer would have heard it and contacted me and my life would have changed.

The same thing happens when a tragedy takes place. During the recent floods when the water entered our town, I was among the first to begin helping in the evacuation of the old, infirm and those children who were in danger of being drowned due to the rapid current and rising levels of the floodwater. The whole morning was spent in ferrying people and their possessions to higher and safer levels. The reporters arrived many hours later and began interviewing survivors and displaced persons. Finally one of them approached our little group but unfortunately at that precise moment some overweight woman stumbled in the current, which began to carry her off in a swirl of arms, legs and umbrellas. I rushed in to save her and dragged her to safety; the cameraman was also capturing all this and broadcasting it live to the nation. This is it, I thought to myself as I dragged the soggy mess ashore, I would be a national hero by this evening. Imagine my consternation when I saw the footage; Of my heroics there was not a frame, all that the cameraman captured were scenes of this grossly obese lady being swept downstream arms and legs flailing wildly, my dramatic rescue was edited out and all that remained was a 3 second shot of my scrawny arms pulling her out of the water. I think the crew were disappointed that she did not drown as it would have made the news that much more dramatic.

Then there was that sensational case where the professor was beaten to death by the other students union's members and political leaders. I was there, I saw the whole thing. You would think that at least one of the reporters would think of interviewing me. I made the rounds; there were at least half a dozen TV crews clustered around the scene of the incident and at least half a dozen reporters talking excitedly to the cameras, every now and then she would turn to a spectator standing there and quiz him about what exactly happened. What does he know? He wasn't even there! But as soon as the camera was trained on him his chest puffs out and he begins to give a completely garbled version of what actually happened. Why don't they ask me? Remember the clip where the Police Chief is interviewed? If you look carefully I can be made out trying to push my way to the fore but his bulk thwarts me and he keeps edging me with his broad back and I'm quite obscured by it. I'm wearing a bright yellow and green checked shirt and jeans. I have noticed that yellow and green show up well on colour television.

Are you remembering me now? Let me jog your memory with a few more instances. Did you watch the coverage of the recent bomb blasts? No, not the train blast, though I was there as well, I'm talking about the town where the minority is in a majority. Anyways I was right there at the exit at the time of the blast. I was among the first to help in pulling the dead and wounded out of the way of the stampeding hordes. In fact I was covered in so much blood that people thought I was one of the wounded and wanted to evacuate *me.* I fought them off furiously when I spotted an eager young reporter threaded her way through the throng towards me, microphone held aloft like a banner. I thought it would look more heroic if I was holding a wounded child in my arms and turned around and grabbed the first child I could lay my hands on and hoisted it onto my hip unfortunately the child was hale and hearty and put up a frantic struggle to get out of my grasp.

It kicked and screamed and shouted for its mother lustily. The burkha clad mother pounced on me like a lioness and snatched the child from my grip abusing me in chaste Urdu. When I turned back to face my interviewer I saw that she had been side-tracked by a bearded gentleman who was talking about brotherhood and secularism. I tried to worm my way into the circle hoping that after he finished I would get a chance but he just rambled on and on and on. Then the time was up, the reporter had gotten her sound bite and she was packing up for the day. If you look carefully at the footage you can get a glimpse of me peeking into the camera from the reporter's side, I'm wearing glasses, you can't miss it, at times my head covers half of the reporter's chest.

Then surely you remember the anti-reservation agitation every news channel reported on it for days on end. I was there but on the other side; I was pro-reservation and we got hardly any coverage at all. Every TV camera and journalist was busy recording statements and threats of the anti-reservationists and our voices were once again drowned out. At one stage of the agitation the coordinator selected me for the *self-immolation bid,* and solemnly swore to have half a dozen people ready to douse the flames. I would have to be prepared to spend a few nights in hospital/jail he told me, but if I went through with it he guaranteed that my face would be famous the next day and my place in medical agitation history assured. I agreed albeit reluctantly. The number of pro reservation agitators were as numerous as those of the anti-reservationists but because of the angles of the cameras and other photographic sleights of hand the anti-reservationists were depicted as gathering in massive crowds and we were shown to be a rather sparse hastily organized rally. Luckily as we marched towards Jantar-Mantar, we were dispersed with water cannon. The TV crew duly showed up and I was pushed forward and a can of gasoline was thrust in my hand for me to douse myself with. The cameraman took his time to set up his equipment and just as he was preparing to get me exclusively in is focus, the cops broke us up with a cane charge. In the footage that was aired you can see the reporter chattering in the foreground while the cops chase us helter skelter, waving their huge canes. If you scrutinize the footage closely, I can be seen running for my life, as a burly cop chases me and smacks me twice in rapid succession on the seat of my paper thin pajamas. If you use sound filters and eliminate all the other sounds I can be heard loud and clear yelling, and cursing the organizers and the ministers who had assured us that the policemen would leave us alone.

Have you been able to figure out who I am? I am the one who is never asked, whose opinion never counts, whose version of events is never recorded. No microphone will ever be stuck in my face and my opinion sought and no camera will ever focus exclusively on me. I am always the face that will end up on the cutting room floor my voice will always be part of the background noise drowned out by the shrill vacuous pubescent screech of teeny boppers masquerading as serious journalists. What a joke it has all become.

THE ALCHEMIST

The deadly fever made its first appearance within the narrow confines of the walled city. The area was suffocating and congested, with narrow roads, a high population density, cattle and sewage spilling ankle deep onto the sidewalk, it was an open invitation to the virus to cast its deadly spell; it was not long after, that the first case was admitted in the General Hospital but ignored by the doctors who were in any case too busy running their own private practices or going on flash strikes, to be overly concerned about the fate of one mysteriously sick patient, especially one who was so poor that he would never be able to afford their fees. Nobody took note when he died three days later and nobody took note when six more mysteriously sick people, all from the walled city were admitted over the next two days.

Mukesh Sharma sat fat and smug in the chemist shop that he owned. He had reason to be smug; his son had cleared the CAT examination with a 98 % *percentile* and IIM's were lining up with offers. Marriage proposals had increased severalfold and he was having a happy time evaluating each proposal in terms of how much each was worth in terms of money, prestige and material gain.

The Chemist shop sat in the middle of the busiest lane in the walled city, it was in fact five shops in a row, bought long ago, when property was cheap, by Mukesh's father who had great foresight and some money to spare. The property was now worth *crores* of rupees and Mukesh, when he inherited the shop over the heads of his two sisters and younger brother, (whom he had declared mentally challenged with the help of obliging doctors and psychiatrists) had spared little to make it the most up-to-date shop in the area. Medical representatives sought him out and offered him all manner of incentives in order that he place huge orders for their products with them. The shop had a virtual monopoly in the walled city and other chemist shops had long ago converted to other businesses.

Mukesh's son Amit, the CAT prodigy, threaded his way through the crowded street with great dexterity, after all, he had grown up in these lanes and knew every twist and turn like the back of his hand. He was feeling on top of the world, his new bike, an immediate gift from a proud father, handled well, he was wearing the latest in designer clothing and he knew that he looked good, so it was with a flourish that he parked the bike in front of the chemist shop and looked up at his beaming father who was leaning over the counter and said "Hey Dad! I have a great idea for you!"

Meanwhile, the myriad TV news channels that had mushroomed post cable TV revolution, were just beginning to break the news, that several people were admitted from the walled city with a mysterious viral infection, that seemed to affect the brain, although three people had died, health officials, were telling reporters that it was not uncommon for the summer and that *they were looking into it and that an inquiry would be held shortly.*

Amit sat his father down and turned on the portable TV set, the newsreader was now reporting 5 deaths and 55 admitted in hospitals and private clinics, all the patients were from the walled city but as yet nobody could pinpoint the cure or recommend an antidote or vaccine. "I'm telling you Dad, this is a money spinner we can make a killing!" said Amit excitedly. "It's all a question of supply and demand. I was talking to a pharma guy and he tells me that his company has identified the disease as well as the vaccine. His company has limited stock of the vaccine and it will take time to produce fresh batches. He wants us to place an order for 47000 vials which is their entire stock, by the time the government reacts it would have become a full-blown epidemic and the demand would shoot through the roof. People would pay premium prices for a vial; I reckon we can make at least 1k profit on each vial."

Once Mukesh had figured out that *1k* translated into *one thousand rupees* his eyes shone greedily and it was with great emotion that he told his son "Amit I'm so proud of you, I don't know why you want to bother going to a business school, you are a genius!" Amit blushed and said "Oh Dad, whatever I have learned I have learnt from you."

Sadly, things occurred exactly as Amit had predicted, and by the time a full-blown epidemic had been declared, and the demand for the vaccines had sky-rocketed there was none available except with the Chemist Shop in the walled city and huge queues snaked their way down the lane to the shop.

Amit who was handling the sale had discretely sold most of his stock to other chemists outside the walled city as the disease had long since breached its confines and now spared no locality, posh or slum. It was a highly contagious disease and could be spread by coming into contact with body fluids, oral or nasal; sneeze droplets, sweat or saliva. Amit removed four vials from his last container and put them in the shop's refrigerator, these were for his father, mother, brother and himself, just in case. The remaining eight he sold to a shifty looking person who put them in a thermacool box filled with ice. That afternoon Amit breezed out he called to his father from the road; "Dad, don't sell those vials, they are for us, the stock is over and there are no more vaccines left in the city." But Mukesh never got the whole message as a neighbouring shop was pulling down its iron shutters and the noise and racket that it made drowned out most of his words, Mukesh waved dreamily after his genius of a son.

That afternoon Mukesh sat in his shop once more, fat, smug and satisfied, they had sold all the vials for a premium of one thousand rupees and the profit was enormous, he once more thanked God for blessing him with a son as clever as Amit. When he came out of his reverie he saw that a very distinguished old man was standing in front of him, leaning over the counter and looking very agitated, "Do you have the vaccine?" he asked desperately, "I need 4 desperately" Mukesh looked into the refrigerator and said "I have 4 vials left, but my son told me something about them that I can't recall now" "Let me have them, I will pay you good money." "How much?" asked Mukesh greedily "We are charging 1500 for a vial now." "I'll pay you 5000 for each vial, that's 20000 rupees for four vials." The old man reached into his coat pocket and took out a wad of 1000 rupee notes, much more than twenty there noted Mukesh to himself, "I don't know" said Mukesh "My son said something about not selling these, I think I'll ring him." Mukesh looked around for his cell phone, "I'll pay you forty thousand for four vials, I have to protect my family, money is not important." The offer was too much; Mukesh saw the bunch of notes in the old man's hand and opened the refrigerator door, and took out the vials "Here you are." He said as he handed over the vaccines in exchange for forty thousand rupees. The old man thanked him profusely and hurried away, but Mukesh was too busy counting his money to acknowledge him.

That evening Amit returned quite late, he was not his normal cheerful and ebullient self. His mother worriedly took his temperature; 103 degrees, he was burning up, "Dad" said Amit hoarsely "I think I may have been infected with the virus, but don't worry give me a vial and I'll go to the doctor and get myself inoculated, it's not serious. It would have been if we didn't have those four vials as the manufacturers can't keep up with the demand and promise to resume supply after a month. I would be dead by then." Mukesh looked in horror at his son, even as Amit sneezed several times in succession. Amit looked at his father who had a strangulated look on his face, no one spoke, and only the deadly hum of the air conditioner could be heard as it cycled and recycled the deadly droplets of virus until everyone in the room had inhaled and re-inhaled and were well and truly infected with the disease. Such is the nature of greed.

That evening four more infected people were admitted to the General Hospital, they too were from the walled city.

7344 people died before the epidemic could be brought under control. Mukesh's mentally challenged brother (suddenly declared sane by the same doctors) inherited the Chemist shop which he promptly sold for an enormous amount of money which he wisely invested in government bonds and now lives quite comfortably off the interest.

THE LAST 1000 RUPEE NOTE

March 31 2017 was the last day to deposit 1000 & 500 rupee notes in banks.

On 01 April 2017, Rakesh was walking hurriedly through the hot, humid, dark & dirty corridors of the District Hospital towards the exit, his mind was far too preoccupied with his day to day problems than to be bothered about deadlines about depositing money. Such large notes, he could onlydream about laying his hands on. His little brother lay on a dirty hospital bed struggling to breathe, the doctor had scribbled the name of some drugs that were to be administered within the next three to four hours otherwise it would be too late. Rakesh was not worried though although the doctor had warned him that these medicines were expensive and could cost as much as One Thousand rupees his Seth (Master) owed him money from jobs done earlier and he would just ask him for it, He threaded his way through the teeming crowds outside clutching the prescription in his hand, and finally was out of the ramshackle main gate of the hospital. He was all of twelve years old and the burden of looking after his mother and younger brother had fallen onto his narrow shoulders.

Its not as if he had no father, but his father was of no help and more of a burden, when he did work, it was as a daily wager and he invariably returned home via the local country liquor shop and an illegal gambling den which were side by side of each other. He was not concerned if his children ate   that day or not. Some days he would throw a small pile of notes on the bed, a portion of his winnings at three card poker, but this was not often. He had become immune to his wife's shrill abuse. Whenever this happened Rakesh would take his little brother Jitu by the hand to a nearby chow mein stall on the main road, and   buy him a plate of the stuff, whatever his little brother couldn't finish he finished for him.

Rakesh himself worked as a loader, and filled tractor trolleys with sand, an essential cog of the building boom that was enveloping the city. He was never short of work but because of his age and size the contractor, knowing his desperation, never paid him full wages. It was this money that sustained the family and Rakesh took his responsibility seriously and visited several building material sites looking for work. His Seth was a miserly man and would sooner part with his mother than lose an extra rupee, he liked Rakesh because he paid Rakesh only 50% of what he had to pay the other workers.

Rakesh reached his Seth's shop and explained his circumstances to the contractor, who listed quietly, his mouth working tirelessly as he chewed that disgusting Gutka, his lips glistening red as he spat out a mouthful and then a gleam came into his eyes and he spoke "You are like my Son, how much do I owe you,"? "Three Thousand sir" the contractor dug into his pajama pocket and pulled out a roll of 1000 rupee notes, he peeled off 3 and handed them over to Rakesh, who took them eagerly, thrusting them into his pocket.

He went to the chemist's shop and thrust the crumpled prescription across counter and asked the helper who was not much older than him "how much for these medicines?" The kid scanned the list briefly then showed the list to the owner's son who merely glanced at the list then said "Rs One Thousand Rupees".

Rakesh dug his hand deep inside his pants pocket and pulled out a crumpled note. He smoothed it out on the counter and pushed it forward "here is the money, please give me the medicine" but the helper made no move "yeh note jaali hai " (this note is fake) he said on hearing this the owners son come over and glanced at the note lying on the counter "he is right, this note is not legal anymore." "Since When?" asked Rakesh aggressively "Since today! Don't you read the newspapers? You should have deposited this money in the bank yesterday" "but Seth ji only gave this to me today!" Rakesh wailed suddenly realizing the import of what had happened. He had no money for the medicines for his brother "Please Sir lend me the money I will pay you back as soon as I can." But the owner's son would have none of it and chased him away

By the time Rakesh reached the hospital it was too late, Jitu had died and the hospital had hurriedly vacated the bed and shifted the body to the morgue. There was a huge crowd at the morgue, and at first Rakesh thought some bigshot had died but it was not so, but a lot of little people had died instead.

Every single post mortem report read the same "died of natural causes"

Tell me, is it natural for a government to take such a momentous decision, and not think it through, past the elite, past the vast middle class and down to your daily wager, who has no access to debit and credit cards and no knowledge of lapsed deadlines and crooked contractors.? It is clear that the person who took this decision had never worked a day in his life, he probably did not know the consequences of missing a day's work or not having any work when there is a strike or a bandh.

Rakesh went back to the contractors later that night, the contractor was alone and having a drink before closing the shop. He welcomed Rakesh guiltily and bade him sit down "how is your brother Jitu?" he asked "Oh! He is at peace now" said Rakesh quietly, "Good! Good! Listen if you need more money I can lend it to you, how much do you need? 5000? 10000? You can pay me back later." The contractor had pulled out a wad of notes from his pocket again and Rakesh could see the yellowy notes as well as pink notes. These were the notes that he should have been given! he saw that the contractor was counting out the yellow notes, on seeing this something inside Rakesh seemed to snap, "one minute sethji," Rakesh moved behind the contractors desk and directly to the row of heavy iron shovels lined up neatly ready for the next day's work, the contractor reached to pour himself another drink as Rakesh brought the heavy shovel down upon his head... again and again and again.

THE MODEL

She sat upright in the straight-backed Louis XIV Bergere imitation chair, staring out of the window; her tired eyes drooped, as if reluctant to see beyond the sill. Her back ached already from sitting upright, but the half hour session had just begun and she would have to maintain this pose for another 20 minutes at least.

The bright sunlight accentuated her pale freckled skin exposing its flaccidity and wrinkles for all to see; she cringed inwardly with shame, but continued to gaze stoically out of the window, focusing on the bustling, crowded market scene down below. How the mighty had fallen.

She gazed once more at the semi-circle of easels that around her and at the would be artists behind each one, a motley crew of if ever there was one, all dressed for the part in khadi kurta pajamas, chappals and of course the mandatory designer stubble, they stared at her from all angles, pencils raised to get a sense of proportion of the various heights and lengths of her exposed body and she sucked in her belly involuntarily; did any of these people feel her need or her desperation? She wondered, and how many of them would do as she was doing? Not many she knew, but was there enough for her to justify what she was doing? Probably not she concluded and turned her attention back to the semi-circle of people grouped in front of her., she wished she could pull up her breasts in similar manner. Alas! They sagged terribly, the sexuality they had once exuded had long since evaporated, and she prayed inwardly that no adolescent would peek in on his way to a class, his first encounter with the female form, would probably be his last and likely to scar him for life. She imagined, that at one time there would have been quite a few of these intrusions, but that was when the models were her granddaughters age now these young girls felt ashamed to be undressed in front of males although it was belied by what they wore nowadays; they had dried up as a source of inspiration for the modern day Van Gogh and Rembrandt.

She felt for the young male students in her group; having to gaze for hours on the unclothed female form would have been the prime motivator in their enrolling in the arts class in the first place. Quite a few would have felt short changed after seeing her unclothed. She chuckled inwardly at the thought, glad that she had still not lost her sense of humour. A student walked around his easel, sighing with exasperation, he approached her and adjusted the flimsy red georgette dupatta that had been strategically placed and ran from left shoulder to right bony knee, blurring her genital area on its downward journey it had slipped from its place but she had not even noticed it and she mumbled something inaudible to the boy as if apologizing for having submitted him to such a horrendous experience. He resumed his place and she her reverie. There was still five minutes to go.

The ArtSchool was older than she was, that means they would have been a need for models even then when she was a teen. If she had known, that she would be posing in the nude 60 years later, she would have surely sat for budding artists when she was in her prime and perhaps made immortal like a modern-day Mona Lisa. She had been proud of her body with its firm perky breasts,perfect thighs and translucent skin. She had been a beauty in her youth, and even in middle and late middle age. She was still of noble stature and regal bearing but with every decade that went by an additional layer of clothing was added or new areas of her body were discovered that required to be hidden from public view. In her younger days she couldn't remember a social occasion when she was not surrounded by ardent young men, pretty much as she was surrounded now but then they had held tokens in their hands for claiming her favours not pencils and bits of charcoal, the smiles she got were always winning smiles not frowns from brows furrowed in concentration. Oh Well!

The alarm sounded and she slouched immediately, her ancient body crying out in relief, soon she would be too old, it was taking her longer and longer to recuperate from each half hour sitting and she would have to look for new means to supplement her daughter's and her measly income; perhaps her daughter, who was 37 years and no spring chicken, could take over her job. She would have to speak to the College Administrator, but first she would have to find a way to tell her daughter, who was under the impression that the money she brought home was from her wages earned by tutoring pre-nursery children.

She stepped into the busy market, her days' wages safely distributed among the three pockets of her handbag. The money she put in each pocket was for a specific purpose. The biggest pocket, which had a zip, held the largest portion of her earnings and was earmarked for her daughter, as her share towards household expenses. Money was put into it on a daily basis but removed from it only once a month and handed over quietly to her daughter whilst they shared a cup of tea. Her daughter was always teary eyed with gratitude on these visits and it would be an occasion for both of them to open up the waterworks and have a good cry. The money in the second pocket was for her son-in-law and the grandchildren, it was the second largest amount earmarked and was used to buy gifts and birthday presents or for emergencies, also added to every day and removed only on birthdays and festivals sometimes no money was removed for months. The last pocket was also the smallest and got the least amount, but it was the most important pocket of all; for that pocket contained money set aside only for her. It was her *mad money* pocket. With this money she could do as she pleased, give it away if she chose to, or spend it on some outrageous trinket or splurge it on some spicy food or a cold ice cream sundae.

She smiled at the people whose eye she caught and they were quite a few, for when dressed, the crone disappeared and she was once more the gracious matriarch, her patchy wrinkled skin, sagging breasts and flabby arms and thighs once more cosseted below layers of the finest silk and the softest cotton. She threaded her way through the maze of shoppers and vendors, delicately picking her path through slush, filth and the plastic bags that lay strewn everywhere. She would buy some mangoes for her daughter and drop them off on her way home. With her purchases firmly in one hand and her handbag in the other she hailed a three-wheeler gave him the instructions and sat back against the back rest and closed her eyes for a moment of solitude.

She saw a toy shop and signalled the driver to stop; she bought her 3 grandchildren toys appropriate for their age and sex, an adjacent shop had a nice blue shirt for her son-in-law who was a manager in a small factory and for her daughter a nice bead purse, very dressy and sparkly.

The three-wheeler driver who had co-opted himself, into the role of valet meekly carried her purchases back to the vehicle while she paid off the storekeeper

On her way out she picked up a day old newspaper of the counter absentmindedly and seated herself once more in the vehicle, she unfolded the paper and scanned through the larger printed headlines not wanting to use her reading glasses, but an advertisement caught her eye that had her fumbling for her glasses excitedly. She made the driver pull up to the side of the road as the 3-wheeler was vibrating furiously, and read the ad again. The ad simply read:

WANTED A MOTHER! CAN YOU BE THE MOTHER OF OUR CHILD?

We are an educated, well off childless couple who cannot have children of our own. We are looking for an educated lady not more than 40 years of age with kids of her own who will be willing to be a surrogate mother to ours. All expenses will be borne by us. Handsome remuneration assured. Apply in strict confidence.

A phone number was also given alongside the address which she hastily dialled on her mobile (a mad money purchase). She spoke briefly into it and then clicked off, a soft smile on her lips. She had just the job for her daughter. She had found just the right supplement for their income.

THE PICKPOCKET

Rakesh always started his work in the same way; with the careful selection of his mark. This was the main part of his job, if he was lucky and he found a target quickly he could get down to the much easier part of his job which was relieving the mark of his wallet or if the mark was a woman, her purse or handbag. An early start meant that he stood a fair chance of earning some easy money well before lunch.

Rakesh was a pickpocket and one of the best in the city. He was so by choice having arrived at this decision after careful consideration of the alternatives confronting him on his successfully passing his Board Examination. Further studies were options that was briefly considered and then quickly cast aside as were the options of being a shopkeeper's assistant, a busboy in the local eatery and several similar such jobs. Manual labour was similarly discarded on the grounds that it was demeaning and degrading. For a brief period, he became an active member of a political party but it was too strenuous. He had participated in a vociferous 'sit in' outside the residence of the Police Commissioner and had chanted slogans lustily with all the rest, then just as they were getting ready to burn an effigy of the gentleman, the police, who, until now were standing around in groups and ignoring them, decided to move in. They moved swiftly and suddenly, canes swinging wildly. After receiving three or four sharp whacks on the seat of his pants, he had high tailed it out of there, never to return.

A life of crime now stared him in the face as being one of the few options left and was to be considered carefully before discarding. Since he was slightly built, violent crime, assault and battery, mugging and auto theft were deemed to be too dangerous as they all involved a certain degree of musculature and strength along with an aggressive streak that sadly, he lacked. He needed something less strenuous and more suited to his nonviolent nature.

And then Gopi bumped into him, quite literally, there was a flurry of apologies, an energetic dust off and then Gopi shuffled off on his way down the crowded street. By the time he realized that his pocket had been picked, Gopi's head could just about be discerned as it bobbed up and down a good 30 yards down the busy street and gaining momentum by the second. Rakesh could move fast when he wanted to and in no time at all he had swooped down on the unsuspecting felon before he could empty the wallet of its meagre contents and dispose of the incriminating evidence. Seeing the curious glances, they were attracting, Rakesh hustled Gopi into an alley and confronted him meaning to get in a few quick blows and teach the little fellow a lesson.

It was this chance encounter with the young vagabond that set him on his chosen path. Gopi turned out to be a silver-tongued orator; he got into his spiel before Rakesh could start with his own, and in no time at all he had convinced Rakesh of the merits of the noble art of pick pocketing, by the time the two walked out of the alley they were partners in crime. Gopi became his mentor initially, but Rakesh was a fast learner and it wasn't long before he was teaching Gopi a trick or two. They practiced on each other and soon Rakesh had perfected the *art of the bump and lift.* Gopi became his accomplice and was happy to play second fiddle and quite satisfied with his share of the pickings since even a third of what he now earned was more than what he was able to earn on his own. Besides when they worked as a team it was always faster, quicker, easier and safer to confuse or divert their mark. Their work places were bus stations, railway stations, market places and cinema halls in fact any place that attracted crowds or where people queued up and were in a hurry to get on with their lives. Distraction was the key to a successful lift. Crowded places drew them as would a bee to honey.

Then one day an incident happened which changed their lives forever and it happened something like this;

It was Gopi who had pointed out the mark; he was a young man, well off, well dressed in a light summer suit. He had slung his coat over his left shoulder in a debonair almost cavalier fashion quite similar to those in the suiting advertisements that one sees so often on TV, a compact slim line leather folder stuck out of the coat pocket provocatively. From experience they knew that this folder would contain at least the following items: a diary, a scratch pad, pens, a calculator, ATM and credit cards and if their luck was in – some hard cash stashed away in one of the pockets. He was walking determinedly towards the Chemist shop nearby and Rakesh silently signalled Gopi to go into the bump and lift routine. Rakesh merged with the shoppers in front of the mark and Gopi slid into position immediately behind him, within a few seconds the mark was neatly sandwiched between the two. So, it was perfectly natural for the mark to trip over Rakesh as he suddenly stopped and bent over to tie the laces of one of his trainers which had mysteriously become undone. As they spluttered apologies to one another Gopi's deft hand expertly removed the folder from the coat pocket and he was gone in a flash. Rakesh sauntered on down the street, without looking back or sparing a thought for their latest victim. He was to meet Gopi in a predetermined restaurant in fifteen minutes and he quickened his pace. It was a fine day and the restaurant was not far off so he decided to walk for a change.

In the restaurant, an excited Gopi was waiting for him in their booth; he had already ordered soft drinks and samosas and was puffing inexpertly on a cigarette, not inhaling the smoke but blowing it out in huge clouds a sure sign that they had hit it big. The lighting in the booth was dimmed but could be adjusted by the little regulator on the wall. Gopi turned it up to the fullest extent and the folder was at once illuminated like some prized exhibit in a display. Rakesh sat down opposite Gopi and fingered the gleaming leather not speaking but his heartbeat began to race. It was obvious that Gopi had seen the contents and judging by his excitement the folder contained a handsome reward for their efforts but since a tradition had gradually grown between the two of them that the contents of wallets, purses, handbags or briefcases would either be revealed together or if one were to find out earlier, he would not reveal the contents till the other had seen the contents for himself. Like a gift that one received on one's birthday, it added to the excitement Rakesh had tried to explain this to an impatient Gopi. Today the tables were turned; Gopi looked at him with sparkling eyes and said simply "Happy Birthday Boss!"

Without further delay Rakesh unzipped the folder and saw two white envelopes inside where the scratch pad should have been. The left-hand flap had slits for holding ATM cards and credit cards from which a VISA credit card and an ICICI debit card shyly peeked out, two pens lay horizontally firmly held in place by leather straps. The Company name and address was embossed in golden letters as was also the folder's owner's name. ROHIT AGARWAL it read proudly and in smaller letters DY MANAGER, theright-hand flap had a deep pocket into which Rakesh delved his hand and came up with five crisps 1000-rupee notes. A bit disappointed Rakesh turned his attention to the two white envelopes. One was addressed in firm neat handwriting to a MRS ANJALI AGARWAL the address was a local one; in fact the colony in which she stayed was not too far from where they were at the moment. The letter was extremely bulky and heavy and unsealed, it had no postage stamp. The other was slim and was addressed TO WHOMSOEVER IT MAY CONCERN. It was also unsealed and the flap was tucked inside neatly. The letter read as follows:

I, Rohit Kumar Agarwal, do hereby declare that I am 25 years old and don't trust anyone anymore. I have been under a lot of stress lately and I have started to rely on medication to keep me happy enough to stay alive. I am sick of taking pills just to fight this depression that seems to engulf me completely and plunge me down into such depths of despair. There is no use in fighting against such odds. The pressures of work are too much, my boss always wants more and more. I made a mistake today and I will surely lose my job and be sent to jail because of it.

Anita of Accounts Section is a bitch and a whore. We have been friendly for more than a year and six months now and used to meet outside work quite regularly, we have spent many glorious nights and week-ends in the Radiant Hotel in each other's' arms. I was in love with her and treated her like a lady but two weeks ago I told her of my medical problems and she immediately began to behave differently, then last week she was with Nikhil from Sales department and I saw them hugging near the coffee machine. When I confronted her she just laughed. Now she was told everyone in the office that I was not a man and has cast doubts on my sexuality, she of all people should know that it is a lie. People began to look at me suspiciously. Early this morning I confronted her in her cubicle and begged her not to say such horrible and mean things about me but she shouted even louder that I was useless to a woman. Luckily no one else had arrived as yet so only I could hear her shrill screeching. In a fit of rage I hit her across the face, repeatedly. I picked up a glass paperweight and struck her across the head several times till she began to bleed. I think I killed her. Her safe was open and in a panic, I grabbed whatever I could lay my hands on and ran away before I could be seen. I know in my heart that I have brought shame and dishonour to my family and soon the world will know of my shameful deed and rather than bring any further disgrace to our name I chose to end my life. If anyone is to be blamed it is Anita.

I have booked a room in the Hotel Radiant; room number 212, for it is in this very room that I have spent the happiest times of my life; in the arms of my Anita but she has betrayed me. She never loved me.

I'm not even afraid of dying. I'm not afraid of pain. I just want to leave this world. Please pray for me. I'm tired of trying.

Rakesh was amazed at what he had just read; this was a suicide letter that he held in his hands. He and Gopi had picked the pocket of a man just about to commit suicide. He handed the letter absentmindedly to Gopi but Gopi handed it back for he was illiterate and barely knew how to sign his name. Rakesh quietly explained the contents but his mind was racing as to what should be done. In an effort to stall for time he opened the letter addressed to the mother. A flurry of crisp new 1000-rupee notes tumbled onto the table Gopi at once gathered them together and began to count them. A neatly folded sheet of heavy bond paper slid out as well. Rakesh unfolded it and began to read –

Dear Mom,

I love you with all my heart but I have brought shame on our family name. After what has happened today I will only be an additional burden on you. I just wasn't meant for this world and day by day the hope that I can find a place of peace and happiness gets dimmer – I am in search of a place where I am child enough to live, yet man enough to survive sadly that place does not seem to be in this world. I love you! I hope you can truly believe me. Maybe on my journey I'll find the peace I want so badly. Pray for me, pray I will find happiness. I hurt so bad inside! I really loved her but it is over now and I want it all to just go away. I want a new beginning. I am not afraid to die I'm just so afraid of tomorrow.

Your loving son

Rohit

Rakesh knew that he had to act fast; about thirty minutes had elapsed since the lift and if they moved quickly maybe they could still save his life but what was bothering him was that if they did reach him they would have to return the folder and all its contents. Gopi had counted the notes by now and the total cash from the folder was about twenty seven thousand rupees, this was no small amount of money by any standard and in their line of work, especially with the advent of plastic money, such opportunities were extremely rare and it would be foolish to even think of returning it plus he had Gopi to think of. In any case the guy was a loser, if they intervened and he didn't commit suicide today what was to stop him from doing so the next time a girl dumped him? Also, Rohit was a self-confessed murderer and if he returned the folder to him it would be stolen by the corrupt cops who were always on the lookout for easy money. Rohit in any case would go to jail for Anita's murder.

If she really was dead. Everything depended on whether Anita really was dead. Rakesh in his 21 short years had received several thrashings when he was still a novice pick pocket for he had been caught on a few occasions and he knew from experience that the thrashings he got by the bystanders often looked and sounded more violent than they actually were, the loud shouting of the crowd coupled with his screams of pain and fright, ironically seemed to have a soothing effect and mob fury was quickly slaked at the first appearance of blood. He was thus able to slink away with relatively few injuries but it was his ego that was bruised the most. Also head wounds bled profusely especially the shallow ones and it was likely that Rohit on seeing so much blood had assumed the worst and fled in panic.

Rakesh explained to Gopi that they were going to try and save Rohit's life and maybe keep the money as well. Gopi was to go the offices where Rohit worked and find out for himself what was going on there. By now Anita's dead body would have been discovered and the police would be all over the place. He was to ring Rakesh immediately he found out anything and then come straight to the Radiant Hotel and wait for him outside. Rakesh would himself go to the hotel with the folder and all its contents except for the money of course.

The Radiant Hotel was a fairly decent hotel, fully air conditioned with potted plants in the lobby and soft music playing through hidden speakers. There was a heavily moustachioed doorman who courteously opened the heavy door for Rakesh as he entered. He walked confidently to the reception counter and asked for a room, he glanced at the keyboard and saw that room 211 was vacant and requested for that room as he was born on 2nd November he explained to the receptionist. Smilingly the clerk handed over the keys, this was the 'off season' and they were not too choosy about their guests and most of the rooms were vacant. He pushed the register towards Rakesh for him to enter in his details. Rakesh was an old hand at filling in hotel registers and did so with a flourish. He paid for a day in advance with a crisp 1000 rupee note which he extracted from a wallet crammed with many more, making sure that the clerk got a good look as well. He took the stairs to the second floor and soon found himself outside 212 which was opposite his own room. The door was locked but the TV was on and from the sounds of it the channels were being changed rapidly. Rohit was still alive, but for how much longer? And where was Gopi? He should have phoned him by now.

He paced up and down the corridor outside, trying to figure out the best way to go about this intervention. At any moment now Rohit would take the plunge, probably pills of some sort or would he try the traditional and popular method of hanging himself? Gopi had still not phoned and without his vital input he could not formulate a plan. Time was of the essence. At that moment the TV was switched off and there was total silence on their floor. Rakesh knocked on the door of 212.

Rohit opened the door slightly "Who is it?" he asked in an abrupt manner "What do you want?" Rohit was in a vest and had a hotel towel wrapped around his waist Rakesh introduced himself and told him that he was a fellow guest in the hotel and that he needed to talk to him. "May I come in?" he asked politely "I need to talk to someone, anyone. I know you are busy but I will only take a few minutes." "Sure" said Rohit pleasantly "I have all the time in the world. Grab a seat I will just change." Rohit disappeared into the bathroom and Rakesh seated himself in the conversation area and looked around. A bottle of premium whiskey still sealed stood on the coffee table, a glass, an ice bucket and a bowl of peanuts were placed discreetly to one side. On the night stand beside the bed was a bottle of pills placed carefully next to a jug of water. From where he sat he could not decipher the name but he was pretty certain of their purpose. At that moment his cell vibrated noiselessly in his pocket. It was Gopi! "Boss" he shouted "She is alright! Most of the hits were on her hair which was tied in a knot at the back. Only one shot got her on the forehead. I was there when she told the police that she couldn't identify her assailant. The description of the assailant that she has given to the police does not match that of Rohit's at all. "What else?" asked Rakesh curtly, anxious not to say more than was required in case Rohit overheard him. "She is reporting a sum of 5 lakhs missing from the safe. Rohit must have hidden the rest of the money somewhere else.

Try and find out where before he kills himself. Where are you?"

Rohit came out wearing the same outfit as had worn earlier, less the coat and tie and Rakesh snapped his cell phone shut and turned his attention back to Rohit. "I have a confession to make and I hope that you will forgive me. All I ask is that you hear me out. This morning while I was walking down the Main Street on my way to a meeting with some friends of mine, I happened to glance inside a dustbin and saw a beautiful leather folder lying right on top. Wondering who could have thrown away such a beautiful thing I picked it up and carried on my walk. Curious to see what was inside I unzipped it and saw that it was not empty. I must confess to thinking that this was my lucky day but sadly when I checked it thoroughly all I found were two envelopes and some credit and debit cards which as u know are of no use to anyone without the PIN numbers. I entered a sidewalk café and read the letters. I know that I should not have but I'm still glad that I did so, for I have wonderful news for you." Rakesh took a breath and reached inside his shirt and pulled out the slim folder which he handed over to Rohit "This I believe belongs to you"

Rohit had all this time been alistening silently while Rakesh spoke but he was getting angrier by the minute. He snatched the folder from Rakesh and hastily checked the contents. "All the money is missing, even the money I was sending to my mother. What have you done with it? Tell me you rascal or I will thrash you" Rohit was older, taller and much heavier than Rakesh and he towered over him threateningly "I don't know about the money; I came here to help you if I had stolen anything why would

I return? I would have let you kill yourself and need not have bothered. Everyday dozens of people kill themselves, does anybody care about them? But I cared about you, you, a total stranger, I saw that you needed help and I came here to try and stop you" Rakesh had spoken these last few lines with great passion and his earnestness got through to Rohit. "I suppose you are right, I'm sorry but can't you see the fix I'm in? You can't help me now, I'm a murderer and a thief, my reputation as a man is ruined. I have no option but to end my life. Sorry that your good intentions have come to zero. I must do the honourable thing or my father's name will be forever disgraced."

Buoyed by the thought that the money was no longer an issue Rakesh pressed on with his good news. "When I read your letter, I was really upset and I told a friend of mine about it. He also offered to help and we made a plan; he would go to your office and see what was happening while I was to come here and try and persuade you not take such a drastic step. He phoned me while you were in the bathroom. Anita is alive and well!" Rohit looked stunned "Impossible!" he sputtered "I killed her! I saw the blood! I hit her several times on the head with a paperweight! I saw her slumped on the floor. Either your friend must be mistaken or this is a trick on your part to get me to change my mind. But my mind is made up, thanks for trying but I must do what honour demands be done."   Rakesh was taken unawares by this unexpected turn of events and his mind raced furiously for some idea to convince Rohit that he was telling the truth "No! Please! I beg of you. Believe me! What can I do to convince you that I'm telling the truth? Anita has given a description to the police of the man who assaulted her and it does not match yours. Tell me one thing; how much money did you steal from the safe?" Rohit was standing by the bed the bottle of pills in his hands. "About Thirty thousand" he said "Why?" Rakesh wanted to give him the exact amount but he refrained from doing so instead he simply said "Anita is reporting a theft of 5 lac rupees" Rohit looked dazed "That's impossible! I saw all those stacks of notes but I just took the loose ones in the bottom shelf. Something is wrong!" By this time Rakesh had switched on the TV and flicked through the channels till he came to their local news channel. Anita's face was shown talking animatedly to the reporter describing her harrowing tale in great detail. Rohit stared for a moment then as realization dawned he burst out laughing "What an opportunist that woman is! I think she provoked me deliberately. It's the perfect crime and I almost killed myself because of her. Thanks friend I don't know how to repay you but I will find a way." Rakesh stood up "Glad I was able to help" he said and moved towards the door "Wait" called Rohit behind him, he emptied the folder of the credit and debit cards and handed it to Rakesh "Keep this as a token of what happened today. You saved my life and I will be forever in your debt. Just call me if you need me and I will come running to you as you came to me." They embraced briefly and soon Rakesh was back on the busy street. Gopi was lounging outside looking quite the urchin. Before Rakesh could say anything, Gopi gave a silent signal and indicated a likely mark. The target was a harried middle-aged man carrying a burgundy leather briefcase in one hand and a large envelope in the other. He had stopped in front of a juice vendor and ordered a juice. He had placed the briefcase on the sidewalk and was sipping his drink and taking in the sights. Rakesh just laughed and called out to Gopi just as he was preparing to snatch the case "Hey Gopi! Your sister is on the phone" The mark was startled, he hurriedly finished his juice, picked up his briefcase and continued down the street unaware of how close he had come to being relieved of his property. The cache of sparkling diamonds nestled cosily in their velvet environment beneath the false bottom of the briefcase clinking together, rubbing shoulders, prepared to dazzle the world with their astonishing beauty. Rakesh and Gopi strolled down the road without a care in the world; it was 4 PM just the right time for a cup of hot sweet tea and some spicy samosas.

THE VACANT PLOT

No one knows for sure why the plot had remained vacant for so long. The colony was over ten years old and all the other plots had been developed. It was a large plot, over 1500 sq meters and was worth a lot of money to whoever owned it. Yet it remained a plot.

The people of the colony were very proud of their vacant plot. For many it was the last open space in their cramped-upneighbourhood, to the children it was a safe playground for their various games including a modified version of cricket, for the teenagers it became a badminton court or volleyball court, on hot summer nights makeshift lights were put up and badminton or volleyball was played with great gusto. For the neighbours on three sides of the plot, it was a rubbish dump where almost everyone in the colony dumped their rubbish, but the kids always cleaned it up burning all the plastic in a bonfire every other day.

Rakesh and his friends played here daily, for many of his friends, this was the only playground they knew. A Gulmohar and Jamun tree obligingly provided them shade when the sun was at its hottest and kindly neighbours provided them with icy cold water whenever they asked. In winter there was enough space for all to bask in the sun's warmth, colony dogs included.

Then one day a shiny car drove up, Rakesh couldn't tell the make as he had no knowledge of these things but it looked huge and very expensive. A very distinguished looking old man was sitting at the back and he motioned for Rakesh to come to the car.

Now though Rakesh had dropped out of school a year ago, he was not stupid and he instantly summed up the situation during the short walk to the car; the plot's owner had finally decided to either sell it or build on it; either way they would lose their playground. He had to do something, but what?

As it turned out the old man wanted to buy the plot and construct a lavish house, as a wedding gift for his son-in-law to be. Since Rakesh had grown up here, he knew everyone in the whole area so he easily directed the old man to a man who knew who the owner was and where he lived. Once the car had driven away in a cloud of dust Rakesh called his friends and they sat down in the shade of the Gulmohar tree while he explained what was about to happen.

Everybody was upset about this turn of events, but nobody had a clue as to what should be done to prevent it. It was a very glum and disconsolate group of kids that huddled in the shade of the tree as they contemplated a future without their playground until Aunty Vimla who lived opposite the plot called out to them to come over and have some chilled Rasna that she had made. As they thirstily drank her Rasna she asked them what was making them so sad and Rakesh explained the whole thing.

Aunty Vimla liked these kids a lot and enjoyed the noise and racket they made while playing, very often she was the arbitrator to the many disputes they had while playing and though her knowledge of the rules of cricket, Kho- Kho or catch was rusty she did her best and the kids accepted her decisions which made her feel good. She was childless herself and her husband spent long hours in the small factory he had started. If the kids lost the playground they would drift away and she would be terribly alone all day. As the kids trooped out through her gate she called out after them "I'm going to the temple to pray to the Goddess, it helps me get relief and maybe she'll help". Rakesh heard these simple words in a daze. The mention of the word 'Temple' had triggered a memory at the back of his mind, of something he had read in a newspaper a few years ago. It had occurred in a different town but the uniqueness of the whole thing stuck in his mind and as he walked slowly out of the gate he struggled to remember the whole episode.

Once he had recalled the whole incident, the idea to save the playground came automatically to him, the problem was that he needed an accomplice and it should not be anyone from the colony, even his best friends could not be told of his plan if it was to succeed.

The accomplice took the form of his former teacher one Mr Albert who used to teach Science in Rakesh's former school. Mr Albert was quite fond of Rakesh and was very upset when Rakesh's father had withdrawn him as he could no longer afford to send him there. Mr Albert had since gotten a better job and had moved to the other end of town and they rarely met though Rakesh had been to the school where Mr Albert now worked and had been very impressed with it and he had often imagined himself studying there.

That was neither here nor there however and as he stood outside the massive gates of the school trying to spot his former mentor he thought of how best he should put the problem to Mr Albert. Fortunately, Mr Albert spotted Rakesh standing outside and as he called out and hurried towards him Rakesh decided to tell Mr Albert the whole story including his plan to save the playground.

Mr Albert did not approve of the plan but he did say that it was feasible in theory and that he did suppose that such an occurrence would be cause for astonishment, and to the uninitiated some sort of miracle. He felt bound to warn Rakesh of the dire consequences of his actions if people found out that it was a gimmick. He however sympathized with his reasons and made a list of all the items required including a short description of how he should go about doing the whole thing. He even gave Rakesh enough money to buy the few items required but from now on Rakesh would be working alone.

A bag of wheat, a few feet of plastic pipe and a black stone Shiv Ling, that completed the list. These items were carefully hidden away, Rakesh impatiently awaited nightfall. He told his friends that he had some work at home and disappeared from the plot. One by one the others too dissipated, the teenagers played their last game of Badminton and drifted off, the grownups also were winding up their after-dinner walks and chats and by 11 PM it was quiet and dark except for the light from Aunty Vimla's porch.

Rakesh crept back to the plot as stealthily as a thief in the night. He recovered his things from his secret hiding place and looked around for a good place to dig. The place must be easily visible from the road and at the same time not interfere with the space required for their games and other activities. The left forward corner seemed perfect and Rakesh began to dig like he had never dug before always making sure that he kept as quiet as possible. After about two hours he took a break, the hole was about 4 feet deep and about a foot in diameter. He carefully poured the wheat into the hole leaving about one and a half feet till the top. He had also buried the pipe in such a manner that he could pour water onto the wheat from the surface of the ground. He then placed a layer of soil over the wheat and on that he placed his muddied-up Shiv ling, he then covered the remaining hole with soil and scattered rubbish and plastic waste around the site, by morning it would look like any other part of the plot. He carefully scattered the leftover soil to other parts of the plot and his final act was to carefully soak the wheat with water through the pipe.

Every night for the next 3 nights Rakesh watered the wheat just as Mr Albert told him to. On the third night he gave it a final watering and then carefully removed the pipe cut it up into pieces and threw the bits away.Now came the hardest part, waiting for something to happen

For 3 days after that Rakesh watched the plot, waiting for something to happen. Nothing did and he began to doubt that maybe he had done something wrong, maybe Mr Albert had made a mistake in telling him how long he should water the spot. Maybe the huge rats that roamed around had eaten all the grain. So many things could go wrong. Rakesh eventually decided to wait a few days longer.

The next day Rakesh was back at the plot and waited impatiently. He was convinced that something had gone wrong and he resigned himself that they would surely lose their plot. As if on cue the big black shiny new car drove up and the old man got out of the car to have a closer look at his prospective new property. Aunty Vimla, ever the friendly neighbour came out to greet him and they stood around talking about native places and relations of theirs that the other might have met. The owner was also expected and the deal was about to be struck. Rakesh, who was hanging around in the background had decided that nothing more could be done, wandered off despondently towards the main road to have an ice lolly. From there he strolled over to the nearby theatre to see which new movies were expected and if any of his favourite stars were in them.

As he headed back towards his home, he heard a slight commotion, people were running into the lane that led to his little colony, he picked up his pace and began to run along with the crowd. Chants of "Jai Bholenath" were heard and people were crying "It's a Miracle, it's a Miracle!" His heart pounding Rakesh sprinted towards the plot. A huge crowd had gathered and were milling around talking excitedly, every now and then a chant of "Jai Bholenath" rent the air and Rakesh could now see that people were crowding around the spot that Rakesh had worked on so assiduously. He spotted Aunty Vimla who seemed to be at the centre of things. "What has happened Aunty?" Rakesh asked her as he tugged on her arm to get her attention, "Oh son, it's a miracle, the God Shiva has blessed us. He has miraculously appeared in the form of a Shiv Ling, go see for yourself and receive his blessings." Rakesh pushed his way through the crowd and finally was able to admire his handiwork. The ground around had been pushed up and the soil was turned, the statue had risen majestically to the full extent of its 18 inches and lay tilted at a slight angle. Already incense sticks by the dozen were burning along with smoky candles, garlands of marigold were strewn reverently around the site and people were prostrating themselves before the deity. Rakesh did the same then got to his feet in a hurry and headed towards the black car. The seller and the buyer were in conference discussing what was to be done next, one thing was obvious, this was sacred land there was not going to be a sale. Aunty Vimla had also joined them so Rakesh also pushed forward and joined her. The two old men were talking of building a temple dedicated to the God along with a *pujari* to manage it.

This alarmed Rakesh as they would still lose their playground and all his effort would have been in vain. He whispered to Aunty Vimla "Where will we go then Aunty?" The kindly lady thought a moment and then addressed the two gentlemen; "Brothers, instead of that why don't you just mark out that exact spot with marble and mount the Shiv ling so that passers-by can worship, if you build a temple it will be a lot of trouble getting the permissions to build one from so many different agencies." The two men thought it over, "It's a good idea" said the owner "but what about the rest of the land?" Aunty Vimla thought for a minute then said "Why don't you make a park and dedicate it to your late mother, that way everyone benefits."

So, it came to pass, the colony got a brand-new little temple, about 4 feet by 4 feet by 4 feet in the left-hand corner of the plot and also a little park with lights and swings and see-saws. Mr Albert read about it in the local newspaper and smiled to himself. The next day he paid a visit to the colony and gave Rakesh one last piece of advice, weed the entire area around the spot to catch sprouting wheat plants and remove them before anyone became suspicious, a task that Rakesh did with great enthusiasm. In the evenings, during the weeks that followed Rakesh and his friends would sit on one of the benches and marvel at the miracle that saved their playground. Rakesh never ever mentioned his role in this and although it seemed a shame that his good work would go unrecognized and unrewarded, Rakesh felt that in this case it was well worth it.

The next day as Rakesh was playing with his friends in the park, a black Scorpio ATV drove up, and Mr Albert stepped out and called to Rakesh. Rakesh ran towards the vehicle greeting Mr Albert cheerfully. Mr Albert opened the door of the vehicle and motioned to a man sitting inside "Rakesh, this is Father Mathew; he is the principal of the school where I work." Rakesh folded his hands and gave a respectful greeting. The priest spoke, he had a rich melodious voice and each word really was like music to Rakesh's ears "Hello young man, Mr Albert has told me a lot about you and I really admire your initiative and resourcefulness, how would you like to study in my school on a scholarship?" Rakesh blushed and mumbled about fees and the school being too far, but Mr Albert interrupted "No, No! It's a full scholarship, if your parents agree you can stay in the hostel and visit them on holidays or they can come and visit you whenever they wish." Aunty Vimla who had joined the group, added her bit "Say yes Rakesh it's a golden opportunity, don't worry I'll speak to your parents, they always listen to me!" With that she walked off to tell his parents. "There's one more thing" said Mr Albert "What you did, though for a good cause was not correct, and you have caused Mr MotichandLalchand Agarwal a big loss of money. I want you to come with us and meet him and tell him what you did, and apologize and accept whatever punishment he may or may not give you." "I'll apologize" said Rakesh and got into the car.

Mr MotichandLalchand Agarwal was one of the city's richest men. He had made his money in the shoe industry and had several factories, shops hotels and property all over the city. He was also an old boy of the school where Father Mathew was principal.

As they drove through the imposing gates and up a very impressive driveway, Rakesh got a glimpse of the palatial house and as they parked in the huge porch he stared in awe at the huge brass and teakwood door. Mr Albert got out and pressed a doorbell, Rakesh marvelled as the sonorous chimes filled the house. A servant appeared at once and gestured for them to enter. Rakesh was dumbstruck by the luxury and magnificent surroundings and stared around; he didn't even see Mr MotichandLalchand Agarwal as he entered. Father Mathew introduced himself and began talking in a low voice to him. Rakesh turned around at the sound of voices, for the first time he felt afraid and he sat down on a sofa cautiously. The old man listened to Father Mathew and then to Mr Albert, since they spoke in English and in low voices, he could not understand what they were saying; Rakesh got even more afraid, by the time the old man turned to Rakesh he was petrified and having trouble breathing. "So young man, what is your story?" Rakesh began his story falteringly at first but soon he gained confidence and he explained everything, he ended by apologizing and asked for forgiveness. "I will go back to the colony and tell them it was a trick that I played and accept their punishment Sir, you will get your plot back." "No, No, people must have faith, it will do more harm to tell them, it is good that they believe, you did a good thing, you restored the faith of hundreds of people, for that I'm grateful to you, I don't really need that plot, as for punishment, Father Mathew tells me you will be joining his school from the new term, it's my old school also, so your punishment will be for you to visit me once a week and give all the news about what is happening there, My daughter has gotten married and moved out, this house gets lonely, so you and four or five of your friends will come for lunch once a week okay?"

So, Rakesh went to his dream school, he played all the games, the school had a stadium and he played cricket on an actual sized pitch with real cricket ball and bat and pads and gloves! Once a week he went to the old man's house with a few friends and while they played he sat with him in the sun or shade depending on the season, and told him about his studies and the great cricket match they had played and won against a rival school, or about a play he was acting in and the old man listened eyes closed nodding his head and sometimes dozing off while he talked. Rakesh knew this, but he never stopped talking, he was happy at last.

TWO FUNERALS

Two people died that scorching summer afternoon, under normal circumstances neither should have died, but then times were not normal, the heat that summer was unprecedented and people were behaving strangely, the normally meek and mildly mannered, began displaying traits similar to those displayed by pit bull pups, and the more aggressive personalities showed an increased propensity to settle disputes physically.

So, when Karan Bokade walked up the driveway of his brother's house, no one could possibly foresee the tragic turn of events, that would result in Karan pumping several bullets into the sleek, well-watered and well-fed body of his elder brother Kunal leading to his demise after a heroic battle lasting 11 days. Certainly not Kunal, he had been reading the newspaper, his brother had greeted him and he had grunted in reply, his brother had asked him something and he had grunted in reply. It was not as if Kunal was incapable of speech; this was how he always spoke to Karan. Karan was the weak link in the family, meek and mild mannered, incapable of deceit or guile. He had failed in every business venture and the now the loser was back again asking for God knows what. Well he could wait a few minutes he thought as he absentmindedly scratched the big black mole on his cheek and noisily turned the page of his paper, looking for more articles about himself. BANG BANGBANG. Karan had been ignored by Kunal for the last time.

Ram Kumar's tryst with death also began 11 days earlier, when he was evicted from his ramshackle hut for failure to pay his rent and the arrears of several months as well. The slumlord, cantankerous at the best of times, lost no time in mustering the necessary number of goons required for an eviction of this nature, ignoring the fact that the cost of the thugs so hired far exceeded the total amount due. Ram Kumar, now homeless, had wandered the city's busy thoroughfares seeking respite from the scorching sun beneath the few shade producing trees that had not yet fallen to the woodsman's axe as boulevards and avenues made way for expressways and six lane carriageways.

This afternoon was no different and as he sat in the sparse shade of the under nourished Gul Mohar tree, his mind went back to his favourite memory this summer, when he had been called into an air conditioned sweet shop, and fed royally by a generous middle aged man, sweets and snacks generally taste the same and were forgettable, but what he would never forget was the cool air that wafted around his burning cheeks and bare legs, the continuous draft of breeze surged around him and he actually began to feel cold. His stainless-steel bowl had misted over with condensate. His last memory, before the SUV climbed the pavement and crushed his skull, was the memory of cold air swirling around his inner thighs, his bare arms and his burning face. As the heavy radial tires actually crushed his skull, he once again glimpsed the face of the kind man who had given him this memory, the black mole prominent on his cheek.

The funeral cortege of Kunal was several kilometres long, and traffic was stopped on the route to the burning ghat, thousands of mourners lined the road and beat their breasts and wailed at their loss. At the ghat, hundreds of kilograms of sandalwood logs were burnt aided by several kilograms of pure ghee. Priests chanted and conch shells blew. Ram Kumar's funeral arrangements were slightly different, his cortege consisted of the dilapidated old municipal van, his body bloodied and clumsily bandaged, bounced around at the back, along with the few planks of wood, a packing case and the withered branch of a tree, this was all the wood that had been spared for his cremation. The van was unloaded at the entrance to the ghat by the caretaker, "I don't know when I can do this one" he said importantly "I have a big one about to start" "Do it fast' he's beginning to smell" Replied the driver as he drove away hurriedly.

And so, the two cremations took place, one on the grassy banks of the sacred river, the flower bedecked pyre, burnt mightily, a sweet fragrance wafted over the area filling all those with their fragrance. Hundreds of people watched the spectacle; millions more saw it on TV. The other took place in a far corner of the ghat, the fire sputtered fitfully; coaxed along by the caretaker, there was no ghee to aid in the burning, a rusty tin, half filled with diesel would have to suffice, a half-burnt log, still smouldering, from a previous pyre was added here, some cardboard cartons there. A few stray dogs waited patiently a discreet distance away. In both cases, the smoke spiralledupwards, both being equally acceptable.

On the other side of the big divide, Ram Kumar waited patiently for Kunal to tear himself away from his mortal remains, and when he had done so he saw a radiant Ram Kumar extending a welcoming hand to him. He instinctively knew who he was, and grasped his hand as a drowning man would a straw. There were no black moles, bullet holes or crushed skulls to disfigure their bodies. Just peace and a diffused light and oh yes, a cool breeze that swirled around and between their legs, and brushed against their cheeks and enveloped their bodies in icy cool cocoons. It truly felt like Heaven.

THE STORY OF ADAM & EVE

It's not easy you know; being God. Ask anyone. This creation thing was a big mistake. Okay the stars, planets and galaxies – the whole universe thing - that was pretty cool. I mean it took real brains to work the whole thing out...an ever-expanding universe, black holes, quasars and pulsars and my piece-de- resistance Dark Matter... pretty cool I think, Mankind is still grappling with that one. It all goes to show that I had a keen scientific mind. In retrospect I think I screwed up at the micro level. All I can say in my defence is that I got a bit too creative and that I got carried away. So sue me.

Creating man in my own image was cool, I even made him this little garden wherein he could play and maybe sing my praises a bit, if he felt like it, after all I was his creator and he should be a little grateful that I had made him possible. In the beginning he did, but lately all that the idiot did was to brood and mope around my beautiful garden drowning out the chatter of birds and the chirrup of insects with his incessantly long and loud sighs of longing and wistfulness. After sometime it became unbearable, I would run and hide in some other star system but his sighs like a mighty cosmic wind would reverberate across the ether and I would get no peace there either. "What bothers you this time Adam?" I would ask him grumpily, from behind a low-lying cloud "What is it this time?" "I feel so lonely" he would whine "I need someone to talk too, someone to share my feelings with. You are never here anymore. Earlier you were always talking to me, telling me jokes and bragging about your other achievements but nowadays you seem to be avoiding me. Have you made another in your own image? Tell me, have you got another Adam stashed away in a cozy garden somewhere else?"

Of course, I hadn't! One Adam was enough, look how he turned out! Of course, I had tried my hand at creating life and got quite creative at it if I may say so. But Adam was my only attempt to really create someone in my own image but I think I screwed up when I gave him a brain. Why did I give him a brain you ask? Well what else was I to put inside the head I had made for him? I couldn't very well make his skull solid bone, could I? Well I could have and judging by how the whole thing has turned out, maybe I should have but at that time that just didn't make sense. Anyway I had one and I reckoned that my image should have one too, after all people would take a look at him and say "So this is what God looks like" In retrospect, for a guy who made the whole universe in 5 days, to devote a whole day simply to creating just one guy was a bit too much. Overkill. But at that time, it was different, making someone in my own image was a project that I took to as does a fish to water. Since I did not know what I looked like it did seem challenging. What did I look like? I don't know for sure, since mirrors hadn't been invented as yet and, in any case, where would I find one big enough to reflect me in my entirety. So, I felt around, I had a head, two eyes, nose, ears hair two hands two feet ten fingers and ten toes and of course a belly button. I devised an incredibly intricate nervous system with a very low pain threshold, so that he didn't destroy himself the first time I took my eye off him. I gave him a heart and a circulatory system to match the nervous system. I even gave him lungs! But my crowning glory was the reproductive system that I devised for him, penis, gonads and sperm, and of course erectile tissue! Wow that erectile tissue sure created a fuss in my little Garden of Eden didn't it? Velcro gets the same response today. Of course, Adam had no immediate use for it but I suspect that as time passed, he discovered the joys of playing with himself and the supreme delights of ejaculation. There I said it! Why did I make ejaculation so pleasurable? Beats me, I mean I have never played with myself so I wouldn't know, would I? I know the rest of my creations only do it to procreate, and they have a fixed time etc I naturally assumed it would be the same for Adam, blame Mother Nature for that one.

Back to Adam's cosmic sighing. He wanted a mate. "Everybody's doing it!" he explained. "Everywhere I go in that beautiful garden of yours, they're doing it. The birds are doing it, the animals are doing it even those stupid bees are doing it. What did you create bees for? They keep stinging me. They're even doing it under the forbidden tree.

Where's my mate? Did you screw up? Get me a mate" "Adam" I cajoled him, "Believe me you don't want a mate. I am your God, your Creator, would I lie to you? To you and to you alone did I give the ability to pleasure yourself, go and enjoy. Have fun! A mate would only screw up your head; she will have you doing chores within no time. Now I have to go to another galaxy, go to bed when it gets dark and don't eat the fruit of the forbidden tree." But Adam didn't go to bed, he howled at the moon and stars and scared Joey's clean out of their mother's pouches within no time, the whole garden had taken up his song and the racket that they made was awesome.

Such was the relationship between Adam and I that his whining and whining reached my ears even as I was trying to relax in one of the alternate universes I had created, under a beautiful triple moon on a beach strewn with jewels and Passion fruit. I put down my book and whizzed down to him. "OK Adam, you win, go to sleep now and when you get up in the morning you will find a mate beside you. Remember you asked for this. Once I create something I cannot uncreate it so you will be stuck with her forever unless you hunt it to death and make it extinct. This is your last chance to change your mind." Adam did not change his mind, but at least he did stop his yowling and lay down beside a sheep and went to sleep. Seeing how he had snuggled up to the animal, maybe my creating a mate for him wasn't a moment too soon. Anyway, while he slept I swiped a rib from him and created a long haired, long legged, blonde bombshell for him and just to prove me right I made her biologically, genetically and mentally superior to him. That would teach him to ignore my warnings and advice. Did I mention to you that I am also a mean and vindictive God?

I couldn't wait for Adam to wake the next day and see his face when he saw this beauty sleeping beside him, but he continued to sleep! The one day when he should have risen with the lark, he oversleeps! Impatiently I sent down a bolt of lightning followed by a thunderous clap of thunder, thereby scaring the crap out of him, but it worked and he jumped for the sky. On his way down, he saw this gorgeous blonde fast asleep at his feet and for once he looked up to me and said "Thank you Lord, truly you are a wondrous and great God. In honour of this day I shall sing your praises all day. What's her name by the way?" "Her name is Eve and please don't sing to me you have a terrible voice, take the day off show her around, introduce her to your furry friends. Lay down some rules; show her where you want the kitchen, make sure she knows who the boss is. Tell her about me, what a great guy I am, warn her about the forbidden tree and the fruit you are forbidden to eat." With that I whizzed off back to my book leaving Adam to play with his new playmate.

Now apart from the tree of knowledge that I had planted in Eden I had also planted the Tree of Life (another no-no for Adam). Anyone eating the fruit of this tree would live forever and never die. The Tree of Knowledge I had planted in the midst of Eden, but I had kept the Tree of Life's location secret. Whosoever had eaten of the Tree of Knowledge would know and recognize the Tree of Life. Adam being a simple soul avoided the Tree of Knowledge like the plague but Eve was a different kettle of fish altogether. She was the nosy one, and questioned Adam relentlessly about all the birds, plants and animals that she saw. Adam poor guy, he didn't know the names of half the things although I had specifically told him to give a name for everything that he saw. So, she took it on herself to name my creations. She also renamed plenty, thank goodness or else the cow would be a Moo Moo and the zebra would be Stripey!

Adam preferred to frolic by the river bank, playing with the river dolphins, who I might add ran circles round him. His typical day after that would be for him to stuff himself with every type of fruit and berry that he could lay his paws on. A quick nap, followed by perhaps some more frolicking with maybe lions or lambs and then at sundown he would say his prayers to me (Eve would have come back by this time from her naming spree, she was giving them Latin names and classifying them into *Phyllums*) curl up beside her and go to sleep. Quite idyllic really. One day all that changed.

Enter the Serpent. I'm not even sure why I created this creature; I mean have you seen one? There must be some perverse streak in me. In my defence when I created the serpent, it had 4 cute chubby little legs and hardly ever bit anyone. Adam was too dense to understand its subtle enticements regarding the fruit of the Tree of Knowledge but that Eve.....she fell for the serpents smooth talk hook, line and sinker, and took a big bite out of the juicy apple, pronounced it delicious and then forced Adam to take a bite as well. The rest is history. I blew my top and cursed the hell out of them, as for the serpent, I took away his legs so that he had to slither along the ground and has been hated by man ever since. Poor Adam, I really didn't want to kick him out of my garden, but I had given him free choice, and he chose to listen to the floozy. What was I to do? Anyway, I kicked them both out and barred them from coming back and just to make sure that they didn't sneak back in when I wasn't looking, I put one of my cherubim to stand guard. He stood East of Eden with a flaming sword in his hand, guarding the way to the Tree of Life. After that fiasco, fat chance that I was going to allow them to live forever. Poor Adam was forced to till the soil in order to eat, no more freebies.

CAIN & ABEL

Cain and Abel; Wow! What a handful *they* were. Having tossed their parents out on their ear from my beautiful garden, they were forced to work the land order to eat. Like a good general, Adam delegated responsibility, to Cain he allotted the task of tilling the soil, and to Abel that of looking after the sheep and stuff. For a while things were quiet, Adam lolled around the house ruing the day he had ever met Eve, Eve roamed around the desert naming everything in sight. She had already named every type of cacti, insect and animal that she had come across and was now categorizing rocks and naming dunes. For fun I would shift the dunes around in the night and chuckle mightily at her perplexed look, as she consulted her maps, scratched her head now lousy with lice and sat down to redraw yesterday's sketches. The boys tilled the soil and tended to their herd of sheep and cattle.

One day Cain, after a good harvest, brought me an offering of the fruit of his efforts; not much, just some dates, a handful of wheat, a few ears of corn and maybe an onion or two. Abel not to be outdone also brought me an offering of the fruit of *his*labours; veal cutlets, lamb chops and a nice thick juicy steak if there was more I did not notice it, I was already salivating at the prospect of a hearty lunch. It was no contest, I mean which offering would *you* have preferred? Cain's? Just because he was the eldest and made the offering first? You're kidding! Naturally I accepted Abel's offering and left Cain's stuff lying there on his pathetic little altar. Cain was miffed to say the least and his countenance fell. "Why are you miffed Cain?" I asked conversationally, through mouthfuls of juicy steak "Why has your countenance fallen?" but he just glared in the direction of his brother who was doing a little jig with his favourite ewe. Big mistake I now realize, like an idiot I carried on with my little spiel, trying to let him down gently "If you had tilled the soil a little harder" I continued, unaware that a Shakespearean tragedy had just been triggered "Maybe used proper fertilizer, watered the crops more often and put up a few scarecrows, varied your crop, perhaps your harvest would have been better. I don't see any fruit, the least you could have done was throw in a few Passion Fruit, you know how much I like them, and what about a few tangerines or maybe a bunch of grapes. I'll be frank Cain, you screwed up. Did you see your brother's offering? Did you notice the cute, frilly paper panties he dressed the lamb chops with? It's all in the presentation." Cain stomped off muttering into his beard but I was too satiated to notice.

The next thing I knew Cain killed Abel and buried his body hurriedly. When I looked in on them, hoping for another juicy offering, I noticed that although Cain was busy in the field, Abel was nowhere to be seen. "Hey Cain" I called out chummily hoping to patch things up with him "Where is your brother?" "How should I know?" he shot right back "Am I my brother's keeper?" Now I'm a keen observer of human nature and I noticed that Cain's eyes which were shifty to start with kept darting in the direction of a fresh mound of earth nearby, under a few dry gorse bushes. "What have you done?" I roared at him realizing in a flash just exactly what he had done "You killed your brother! Don't deny it! I can see his pinky sticking out of that mound of earth, you moron!" And I began to curse him right properly. I cursed the land he tilled and vowed to make it barren, he would be a fugitive and vagabond for the rest of his life. I had to relent a bit when he protested that if he was in perpetual hiding with all those hordes of bounty hunters after him, I would not be able to see *his* face. Big deal! I don't think he was aware of how pissed off I was at him or for that matter how stupid he looked, why on earth or anywhere else would I want to see his face? Anyways I relented and put a mark on him so that whosoever found him and killed him would himself be smitten seven times over. We smote a lot in those early days. That was enough to call off the bounty hunters and Cain was free to go about his vagabonding but he set up a city instead just east of Eden and called it Nod. As for Eve, Adam bless his soul, knocked her up for the third time and she bore him a son, and called him Seth, Eve said that I had given her this child as a replacement for Abel, maybe but Seth could never dress lamb chops up the way my Abel could.

THE FLOOD

Did I mention earlier that Being God is not easy? You bet it's not. I was never very good at spying on people; I firmly believe that everyone is entitled to some privacy, especially from someone like me, who can see all, hear all and who knew about everything before it even happened. To avoid barging in on peoples thoughts I would put on a pair of head phones and listen to soothing ocean sounds as I pottered around. Besides, I was busy with all my other creations and had decreed that if anyone needed me for anything, all he had to do was call me or offer up some sort of an offering. The smell of burnt meat always was an attention grabber and I would come running, so I can't be blamed for all that happened behind my back. Eve went behind my back and look what happened to her and poor Adam, as also to Cain. I get really pissed off when I'm not obeyed. I also get mean; very, very mean.

Now, my back was turned for only a few days, as I had gotten busy trying to create a parallel universe in less than 7 days, which as you probably know, was the existing record and I was trying to better it, a lot of time was passing down on earth, hundreds of years in fact, people tend to forget that my days are a bit longer. To put the whole thing in its proper perspective; it takes half a second (my time) for me to blink an eye, during this time 12 of your years have passed. Do the math. Anyways during my absence, there was a huge population explosion down on earth with people begetting like crazy. Not only that, they had become Godless and had forgotten that I even existed. Having failed to create a new universe in less then 7 days I was dejected and in a bit of a bad mood, I needed cheering up, so I decided to check up on Man, and see what he was up to. His antics were always good for a laugh or two.

The stench of burning meat was noticeably absent, which was odd, I distinctly remember that as I slipped through the wormhole and into the space I had created for my attempt to beat the record, the stench of burning meat was distinctly in my nostrils, quite overpowering, in fact I was glad to be able to make a quick getaway. I peeped out from behind a white fluffy cloud, at my people down below. I was shocked, flabbergasted, dumbfounded and outraged beyond words. If Hell had been in existence then, and it wasn't, this is what it would look like. In fact when I finally did get around to designing a place for the ungodly to spend eternity in, I included a lot of the stuff that I saw going on here, but with twists, I didn't want them to enjoy themselves I wanted them to suffer. Boy! Was I mad! There and then I decided to scrap this project and start afresh, no more Mister Nice Guy. As I drew back my arm to deliver a mighty bolt of lightening which would obliterate the entire planet I remembered how long and tedious it had been to create the different species and wondered if I would be able to remember all. What if left a few out? I lowered my hand and mulled over this dilemma. While mulling, the familiar odor of burning meat wafted gently upwards and thin slivers of the fragrant smoke bumped into my fluffy cloud, a slender tendril lodged itself up my nostril. I peered down again to see who in this ungodly world was remembering me and saw that it was Noah son of Lamech, and his three sons, Shem, Ham and Japheth. This cheered me up no end, I couldn't kill these guys they were sending up burnt offerings, a quick DNA scan told me that they had descended directly from Adam. My Adam! So I nixed on the thunderbolt idea and reverted to Plan B. I would save Noah and his clan, but I would drown the rest of mankind like rats. The idea of drowning the world appealed mightily to me as it was much slower and thus they would suffer longer. I chuckled slyly into my beard and took an enormous lungful of the smoke which more and more began to resemble the fragrances yet to be created by the Houses of Dior and Channel rather than that of burning meat.

So, there and then, I formulated my plan, which included plenty of thunder, lightning and of course rain. Plenty of rain, I would fill up the oceans till they overflowed and rivers would flood, I would open up the fountains under the sea bed and let water gush out and all the time it would rain until the highest mountain would be submerged and man would have no place else to run. At first I wanted acid rain, that would really show 'em but I reconsidered; the collateral damage would be enormous, so I stuck with good 'ol H2O.

I called Noah aside and told him of my plan, I gave him a rough sketch of the Ark that I wanted him to build with the length, breadth and height clearly marked out with water resistant magic marker. (150m X 25m X 15m) It would have 3 decks and a window high up on the top deck. I could tell that Noah was wondering about the size of it, but when I filled him in about his passenger manifest, his face cleared up and he got to work. I gave the details of his fellow passengers, two each (a male and a female) of every creature that walked, flew or crawled. I was not going down that road again. Once I had destroyed all living things I would use these creatures to repopulate the earth again and there would be no need for me to reinvent the wheel as it were, always wondering if I had left out any of my wondrous creations, for truly they were wondrous and I would hate to think that I was the cause of their becoming extinct. What if I had left out Bees or *phylum apius* as Eve now called them.

(Which reminds me,) I remember once seeing Adam jumping up and down and howling for Eve and I; he had just been stung by some bees while raiding a beehive for its honey. I got there before she could as she was still naming stuff; Adam was moaning in pain and wondering why I created such horrible creatures in my garden. As I picked the stings out of his swollen face, and gently applied Oil of Olay, I had told him about the wonders of apian society "One day Adam," I concluded "the properties of fiber optics will be discovered, and geographical societies will insert fiber optic cameras deep inside these very same beehives to study their way of life and marvel at my meticulousness and brilliance." But Adam, who had the attention span of a seven year old, heard not a word; he had smeared Oil of Olay on a cracker and was munching contentedly on it. I snatched the jar from his hand and took off. My hurried goodbye was unheard by Adam; he was busy hurling the contents of his stomach into the bushes.)

Anyways I was not taking any chances; I had told Noah what to do; now if any were destroyed I could always blame Noah and his sons for it. I deliberately kept the blueprint of the Ark simple knowing that Noah's workforce and tools were limited. I specified the wood of the Cypress tree as it was available in plenty in the forest nearby. Noah took his time but at last the last barrel of pitch had been poured into the gaps effectively waterproofing the whole boat, and the animals began trooping in two by two, this would take time as the extent of my creativeness was truly awesome, and I, in order to save some of that time, began to amass the thunderclouds, I amassed nimbus upon cumulonimbus and cumulonimbus upon cumulonimbus in such huge stacks that they reached into the ionosphere and blocked out the sun totally but still the queues stretched behind the ark for miles. I was getting impatient now but Noah took his time and ignored my bolts of lightning and the odd showers that I had sent down in order to speed things up. Finally the last Zebra was in and Noah and his clan also climbed aboard. If I had known that they were going in alphabetically I would have zapped my entire creation then and there including Noah, I don't care if he was 600 yrs old. Didn't he know I was in a mighty rage? I had started 2 parallel universes using The Big Bang procedure while I waited, merely because it gave me a way to vent out my pent up rage. Anyway Noah was ready and I could see him lighting a fire on the top deck in order to send up one more burnt offering to me as a signal that he was ready. What was he trying to do? Burn the whole ark down? Anyway I got the message and squirted a stream of water in through the window that I had thoughtfully included, effectively dousing the fire and thereby averting a catastrophe of Titanic proportions. He should have tooted his ram's horn or something. With great relish I pointed my index finger at a nearby stack of cumulonimbus clouds and fired a shot of silver chloride into its heart and watched the rain begin to fall. No soft pitter patter of raindrops on the rooftops with this one. The rain just came down in torrents. Highly pleased with my handiwork I fired off several more shots of silver chloride in random directions and then it really began to pour. Bolts of lightning, thunderclaps, it was getting too noisy for me, with one last glance to see if all was well within the ark I scooted off before I got drenched.

Well I let it rain and rain and rain, the water pretty much covered the entire land mass, from afar it looked totally blue and very pretty, only the ark bobbed about on the surface of this vast ocean like a cork.

Finally, after 40 days of nonstop rain, every single living, air breathing thing that I had created had been destroyed and I must confess to a fleeting moment of doubt; had I done the right thing? Was it fair to destroy every living thing just because of a few rotten apples? Is the sky blue? I brushed them aside, I was God! I AM WHO I AM! I couldn't be wrong I'm never wrong but still when Noah and his crew disembarked after having done his raven and dove routine, I drew him aside and made some small talk about his stay, the food and how they amused themselves on board, sort of leading up to what I really wanted to say "Noah" I said in my most business-like manner, and using my most solemn voice "Never again will I destroy the entire world just because of Man's stupid mistakes"

Noah said nothing but looked at me sceptically " I mean it" I said, getting annoyed at his look offlagrant disbelief, I itched to give him a hot foot then and there just to knock that look from his face, you can't look sceptical when you are jumping up and down on one foot. I controlled the urge and continued "As a token of my sincerity I will make a pact with you and with all the generations who will come after you, never again will I destroy the world so totally. This I solemnly swear" By this time his children had joined our little tête-à-tête and I distinctly heard Ham snigger, he tried to hide it by coughing and clearing his throat but

I wasn't born yesterday. Noah scowled at him and Ham sheepishly hung his head in shame, but now instead of one man looking at me in disbelief, there were four. I could tell they were not going to take my word for it and they needed something more concrete as proof of my sincerity, but what? Did they want something in writing? No way was I not going to fall for that one! I had to think fast. Luckily for me at that very moment a beautiful rainbow was appearing in the clouds and I pointed to it and said "See that? THAT is my covenant with the world. Whenever it is cloudy and rain is imminent or has fallen my rainbow will appear in the clouds to remind you of my promise that I will never again destroy the world with water." This suitably impressed every one and within no time at all the air was thick with the smell of burnt offerings and it smelled good pretty darned good...

THE TOWER OF BABEL

In the good old days men didn't have a clue as to how vast space really was; they had no idea about stars and constellations and naively thought that I had put them there for their amusement. At night, after dinner, they would lie back under the open sky and play connect the stars, a game that gradually bestowed on mankind the 12 signs of the Zodiac and came to be known as Astrology. They also thought that the earth was flat and that Heaven was a little higher than the highest cloud. If only they could fly maybe they could sneak up on me when I was having forty winks and see me in all my glory. Not a good idea; Ham sneaked up on a half-naked Noah, as he lay in his tent thoroughly sozzled, and saw him in all his glory and look at what happened to him. I must agree with Noah on this one though, who would want to peek at their 700-year-old father's testimonials? A pervert that's who!

Anyways the family divided and sub divided and then sub sub divided and divided some more and they were diverse in most things except for one common thread that linked them all together; they all spoke one language and this was the thread that united them and made them feel special. As the population exploded people moved further and further east until they came to southern Iraq or the land of Shinar as it was known then and decided to settle in a valley here. So far so good. An idle mind is the Devils Workshop I always say and that's exactly what happened. Instead of getting down on their knees and thanking and worshipping me for all the prosperity I had brought them they decided come up and visit with me.

"We will build a tower to heaven" they told the populace "We are wise and strong and speak in one voice; we must build some awesome monument to our greatness and unity. It should pierce the gates of Heaven. Let us see for ourselves if the gates of heaven are made of gold or silver or brass or just plain old iron. Why should He have the upper world and we the lower world? It's not fair!" I of course didn't have a clue as to what was going on and had no idea about their shenanigans as I was far too busy with this and that and continued merrily on my way.

Also unknown to me was the logic they used to motivate the people. "Every 1656 years Heavens foundations start to totter and when that happens all the water in heaven sloshes over and causes a deluge down here. Remember the last time? Now it is almost due again. Before we are drowned like rats we should build several mighty towers that will prop up Heaven's foundations and thereby avert another flood."

So they began work, they used bricks for stones and clay for mortar. Whole forests were cut down and the wood was used to fire the bricks. Neighbouring nations were duly enslaved to enhance the workforce. The entire population was put to work making bricks and building the tower. So fanatical were they in their pursuit of the mission that no time was spared for lunch breaks or dinner breaks or any other sort of break. Brief timeouts were called for sex I presume but only at their place of work, and in between the passage of the bricks as they wended their way up the tower, higher and higher. Women who got knocked up were forced to deliver the child on the job, at the building site itself and got back to work pronto carrying the infant in a cloth thoughtfully provided by the construction agency.

You can imagine my surprise the next time I peeked down at earth from behind my favourite fluffy white cloud. The damned tower almost took my eye out and nearly went up my left nostril in the bargain. It was huge and monstrous and rose from the earth like a huge phallus, only more so. It towered over the countryside and seemed to at mock me. "See!" it seemed to say "See how great we have become! Who needs Abraham or the God of Abraham! What a Loser he was! We have a new God now, and when this tower is complete we will install his temple at the very top. Every night a new virgin will sleep in his room which shall be of the purest gold and we will prosper even more."

Without stopping to think about the consequences or to admire the aesthetics of the tower I just let 'em have it. I huffed and I puffed and then I huffed some more. And blew the arrogant bastards away and the tower came tumbling down as well. I cursed their unilingual heritage and vowed that they would never speak in one voice again. So, I mixed up their tongues real good and had them speaking languages of countries that had not been discovered as yet. I sent down hurricanes and twisters and blew every single one of them to the far four corners of the earth so that could speak in the languages I had invented.

For centuries they roamed around, hopping from country to country trying to find the one country which spoke the only language they could speak. I must have set mankind back by a good two thousand years at least. Recently they did it again, this time an even taller structure was erected, two of them in fact and ironically it was built by a multi lingual work force. I knocked them both down also. The irony was not lost on me. Now they are Godless once more, and Abraham has again been forgotten so also for that matter has been David, but I don't mind but what is really pissing me off is that they have forgotten my son and his supreme sacrifice. I will never forgive them for this, I will set them back another five thousand years maybe more, I will send them back to the ice age.   Michael   agrees with me and figures that since man has now ventured into the realms of space it should be something from the realms of space that should destroy them. He has been harassing me for the go ahead, conjuring up on his laptop all manner of space monster disguises that he proposes to assume; keenly asking for my opinion and advice on the types of havoc and destruction each one is capable of wrecking. I wave him away; I have something much better planned for them. "Michael!" I command as he backs away from me "Go into the inner most reaches of frozen space" "Yes my lord" he says his face lighting up in anticipation "What would you have me do there?" "Bring me the biggest rock you can find, smoothen out the rough edges and round off the surfaces, its diameter should measure in excess of twice the height of the Towers I so recently destroyed and its radius not more than the third that also fell." Michael gave me a really blank look and began counting on his fingers "Oh Michael" I said impatiently "Go and find me a really big rock!"

THE STORY OF GIDEON

I chose Gideon for the task at hand because he was an ordinary sort of guy, from an ordinary family of an even more ordinary tribe. My people were at it again and I was at the end of my patience. After Deborah's victory at Canaan there followed an era of peace, but after forty years of it, they grew restless and started worshipping idols again forgetting all about me in the bargain. What's with this Baal chap anyway, he is depicted as a big fat bull and instead of offering him up to me as a nice juicy sacrifice my people chose to offer young virgins to him. Of course, the defloration is not done by the bull but by the many high priests who hovered around waiting for just these sorts of rituals and whom I'm pretty certain initiated them in the first place. During these ceremonies there was a lot of intermingling between the species which is repugnant to me. I have very rigid views on this sort of degenerate behaviour and I decided that it was time for me to exert myself a bit. So,I let the Israelites be conquered and thrashed by the Midianites and the Amalekites. My people in true fashion and in order to save their skins hightailed it up into the mountains leaving all their crops and cattle behind. They began living in the numerous caves that pockmarked the mountainsides.

The Midianites camped in the valley and destroyed or robbed them of their harvest and robbed them of their sheep and oxen too. Whenever the Israelites tried their hand at farming or rearing livestock it would be snatched away and the Midianites cattle and camels which accompanied them ate up all the grass. Finally, when they were totally impoverished and starving, they suddenly remembered Me and they cried out to me for help and deliverance. I would deliver them but I would do it My Way. I had let them stew seven long years and when it became obvious to them that their stupid idols were not going to help them, I decided to rescue them in such a manner that they would know for sure that it was my handiwork that freed them. So I chose Gideon –"Because he's ordinary Michael" I said in reply to my Arch Angel-in-chief's quizzical look. "I have to prove that it is I who is behind this victory" But first I had to convince Gideon to accept the job and this was not going to be easy.

I had Michael send an angel disguised as a prophet to Gideon's house to boost his ego and self-esteem which was low. Gideon had his doubts about his suitability to lead the people of Israel against the Midianites but the angel finally convinced him with a spectacular display of pyrotechnics. The Angel had referred to Gideon several times as Mighty Man of Valour, Destroyer and other such glorious titles which I think Gideon took with a pinch of salt. I decided to speak to Gideon one on one.

After Gideon had destroyed the altar of Baal on the angel's instructions, all hell broke loose and the Midianites and Amalekites gathered together their armies to wage war against the Israelites. It was time for me to take charge.

Now Gideon, perhaps emboldened by all the titles that the angel had bestowed on him blew his trumpet and assembled his people behind him. He sent messengers throughout the land to rally the tribes and formed a mighty army, but he still had his doubts about his own suitability as the leader so he put it to me straight. "If I am really chosen by you give me a sign, I will put this fleece on the threshing floor, tomorrow morning if there is dew only on the fleece and the floor is dry then I will know that I am the one chosen by you." Piece of cake and the next morning the fleece was sopping wet and the floor was bone dry. But the idiot was still not convinced that I had selected him even after wringing out a bowl of water from the fleece and he tells me again "Don't be angry Lord but let me test you just once more; this time let the fleece be dry and the ground wet. If it happens like that I will know for sure that I am chosen truly by you for Israel's deliverance." I must admit that I was pretty cheesed off with all these tests and was all for calling it off and letting my people go back into slavery again. It seems that only when they are miserable and suffering that they find the time to remember me. But Michael soothed my breast with an off key off colour song and I laughed so hard that I decided to go ahead and humour Gideon. The next day Gideon inspected the fleece and saw that it was dry though the ground was like a marsh and agreed to lead the men into battle. I swear that if he had asked me for one more sign I would have zapped him then and there. With Gideon on board it was time to plot strategy.

For starters there were too many men; their numbers almost matched those of the enemy. In case of any battle that was won, the victory would not be attributed to me but they would claim it as their own and take all the credit for it. Some pruning was needed "Get rid of all those who are afraid" I told Gideon and two thirds of the army skedaddled happily back home, that left about 10,000 which was still too much. "Take them to the river and have them drink water" I told Gideon "Observe how they drink. Separate those who lap the water using their tongues like dogs from those who get down on their knees to drink" There were three hundred lappers, just about right for what I had in mind. So, Gideon sent the rest home and using sound and light most effectively caused great confusion in the enemy camp so much so that they fought against themselves and slew each other in great numbers. It was a great victory and Gideon got a bit carried away and chased the two Midianite kings and murdered them in cold blood.

After the battle was over the men came to Gideon and asked him to rule over them for he had delivered them from the Midian's "You and after you, your sons and their sons as well" they requested but Gideon bless his heart refused saying "God rules over you" I must admit I was touched, that was a truly sweet thing to say and Michael got all misty eyed and said "Awwwww!" Having refused to rule Gideon made one request; he asked each man to give him one earring from their loot and plunder and each man willingly tossed an earring onto the cloth laid out on the ground. With this gold Gideon made an ephod and sent it to his hometown unfortunately it became a symbol of temptation and it was not long before my chosen people were up to their old tricks and I was forgotten again. I don't know why I even bother.

Gideon lived out his life in peace and harmony. He had numerous wives who bore him seventy children. In spite of this large harem Gideon also had a concubine who bore him a son called Abimelech which means 'My father is king' Gideon died at a ripe old age and my chosen people went back to their ungodly ways and began worshipping that Baal again. In due course they totally forgot about me and I really did abandon them. I allowed them to be enslaved again and this time shut my ears to their pleas for mercy. Let them suffer! To Hell with them!

HEAVEN CAN'T WAIT

I was pottering around in my garden one fine sunny day, at peace with all my universes in general, galaxies collided as scheduled and black holes mopped up the debris, on a lesser scale; birds were twittering and gaily coloured butterflies zoomed in and around me, fuzzy bees also buzzed about my head and I smiled benevolently at the little chaps, thanking my stars that they weren't those pesky little wasps. I hate those critters and I don't know what I was thinking about when I created them. They are small, needy and nasty little pieces of work with no respect for my age or stature. I got stung on the nose by one a while back and it hurt like hell, so when I saw that the angels were looking elsewhere I had swatted the blighter right into a parallel universe Any way the smell of burnt flesh was everywhere and there's nothing that perks up ones spirits more than the knowledge that one's people love and adore one more and more every day and are burning meat by the tonne in my honour. Of course, I felt bad for all the bullocks and sheep and lamb that were being knocked off in my honour but what was one to do? These were time honoured traditions and I wasn't going to meddle there.

I sprayed some insecticide on my prize azaleas and did some mandatory weeding and then put away my trowel and headed back to my hammock for a lazy afternoon on my back, also, I was eager to get back to my mystery novel which had reached a most interesting stage, in the next few pages the author was about to reveal the actual murderer or murderess; the suspense was killing me and I couldn't wait to find out who the culprit was.

Alas it was not to be, I had barely stashed my trowel when my headset suddenly sprang into life with a series of buzzes, loud chimes and polyphonic ringtones, colouredLeds flashed like a spastic rainbow. The buzzing and Leds were installed by Michael my Arch angel in chief, who ran the CMC (Crisis Management Centre) he knew my allergy to all things technical and had made it impossible for me to ignore the wretched gadget on the grounds that I had not heard it or that I had left it somewhere and couldn't find it. This thing made more noise than the second coming we had planned for mankind in the near future.

I had handed over the day to day running of the CMC to him and it was his job to keep an eye on all my creations notably 'mankind' and though mankind was just one of my creations they were turning out to be the most troublesome of them all; one couldn't take one's eyes off them for even a moment without them finding some new way to piss me off. We had hosts of angels deployed and were still unable to keep track of man's various sins, misdemeanour's and other follies that included a lot of blasphemy.

Knowing Michaels propensity to over react to the simplest provocation from the other side, I had forbidden him from dispensing what I called his style of 'vigilante justice'. Normally it involved asteroids crashing down on to the offender's house or city or Tsunamis washing out large swathes of the offender's neighbourhood/country. He was to bring it to my notice at our weekly conference and together we would try to make things right in a manner that did not involve so much collateral damage although in his favour my way did not give the same feel good feeling that his way did. Michael didn't always agree with my methods and often I would hear him mutter behind his hand to an adoring seraph something that sounded a lot like "Sissy" but when I questioned him once about this he merely said   he was agreeing with my decisions in Spanish which he says he was trying to learn.

Anyway, back to my crackling headset I found the mute button and said "Yes Michael" "Hey Big Guy" was Michaels cheerful response "I think we have a problem" "and what might that be Michael?" I asked patiently, for with Michael it could be anything from a train accident he wanted to prevent to a train accident he wanted to cause because the bad guys were on it. "It's strategic" said Michael simply and I was dumbstruck, for Michael to use a word like 'strategic' must mean it was really serious.

Normally I was the strategist and tactician and Michael was the Fist. For him to be using words like this meant it was really serious and I acted accordingly; I was by his side in the centre in the blink of an eye, literally. Michael was in the conference room waiting for me. "What's the problem this time Michael?" I asked. Michael had prepared a power point presentation and without a word dimmed the lights and began his presentation.

For once his presentation was short and to the point, the gist was that more and more people were selling their souls to the devil! In fact, they were selling their souls in droves. But I was not convinced. "People are wicked Michael" I said philosophically "it's only natural more of them will go to Hell. But how many people are there who will risk an eternity of fire and brimstone for a few measly years of fun and frolic?" "That's just the point "said Michael excitedly "He's given Hell a makeover it's much cooler now! They have installed huge air conditioners everywhere, plenty of cooling streams for the panting hart and its always night there and plenty of nightlife. Wicked night life like in LA." I wondered how Michael knew so much about LA nightlife. I might have to send a few seraphim of my own to check up on him after this crisis blows over.

"These people are our people. They are good people who have gone over, I sent a couple of seraphim under cover and have their report; it appears that Satan is offering them a whole lot of freebies in the afterlife. Hell is no more a place of fire and brimstone. They have reorganized and restructured and now its eternal cruises to islands and never-ending parties. Plenty of girls and no wives around to spoil things, pious people who have never strayed from your path for an instant are now going over in droves and taking others with them. Plus, Satan is saying that heaven is a boring place with nothing to do but sing your praises all day long for eternity, in hell you don't have to sing any ones praise just party and get drunk and in hell there are no hangovers. It's their USP. "I was puzzled "but what about the smell of burnt meat in the air? Surely that comes from all the sacrifices being made all the time in my honour?". "I'm afraid not "said Michael, "Satan has invented a practice called the Bar-B-Queue it involves cooking meat over a charcoal grill and basting it with a spicy marinade and serving it to one's friends with chilled beer and onion rings "said Michael licking his chops nostalgically, "I went down undercover for a week and tried some. It's great" "so what do we do?" I asked Michael "well I managed to trace a couple asteroids about 30 km wide headed towards Jupiter, I could nudge them so that Earths' and their paths intersected in a week or so. It will make an awesome impact smack in the middle of the BBQ belt, guaranteed to wipe out large BBQing populations, that should shake them up a bit and at least those who were considering to cross over but not yet crossed over will be forced to come back to us; it's still a sizable proportion of the population."

Michael and his asteroids! "Let me think about this one" I said and was back in my garden before Michael could come up with another of his hare-brained schemes. I brooded, and then I brooded some more.

The more I thought about it the more I Liked the idea of enticing devotees. Maybe that SOB was onto something here. If they could be enticed to sign away their eternity for a few years of pleasure and wealth and power they could also being enticed into signing up for my eternal adoration albeit, with a few stops along the way.

Why not! I would beat that little prick at his own game. I was back with Michael in a flash. "Here's the plan" I began. It took me awhile to explain the whole concept to Michael but I persevered and soon his brow was less furrowed and I as I continued to explain the furrows disappeared, every single one, and when the awesomeness of the plan finally dawned on him, the look on his face, as with the Mastercard ad, was priceless.

Basically, Michael and a host of his angels were to swoop down from heaven and disperse and mingle amongst the masses, once they were well acquainted with sin and vice they were to mingle and use its attraction to tempt man away from that Prick. I figured that once we had their souls bonded to us in an ironclad contract signed in their blood, Satan would soon lose all interest and pack up his circus and vacate the premises. Am I a genius or what? Basically, my plan allowed for a person to sell his soul to me in exchange for a series of discretions and indiscretions for a finite period of time. All these discretions and indiscretions were negotiable as also the period of time, Money and Power could be given but I insisted that a clause be inserted that it would all vanish if it were used for evil, I was informed by my sources that the Prick allowed for a period of time of up to 300 years but since man was a dope he invariably settled for 20 to 30 years. I wanted these clauses well-hidden as well and agreed upon only if the mark threatened to go over to the other side. Heaven too would be given a makeover and my praises were to be mandatorily sung for only a half an hour in the morning and half an hour in the evening. (Little did they know that I could also stop time) Fetes and bingo parties were to be regular features and exciting prizes could be won. Excursions to wondrous lands would be arranged and even perhaps a meal at the high table if so desired. Only those who came to me first were to be considered and I would have no truck with those went to him first, lucked out, and then came here hoping to get a better deal. Here Michael disagreed with me. He was all for enticing back even those who had already sold out to the rat fink or were about to, he said now was not the time to have an ego trip and did I want them back or not? He reminded me that letting them rot in hell was no longer such a bad thing and that we would punish them once they were safely in our clutches in Heaven. Sometimes Michael makes sense. I would immediately introduce a few fire and brimstone lakes and rivers in Heaven!

I wanted a publicity blitz, angels were to fan out and appear in dreams to as many preachers as possible with visions of the new heaven calling it the New Jerusalem emphasizing the fun stuff and the excursion tours and the Bingo evenings and the afternoon fetes and high tea in the tea tents. Michael suggested that perhaps I could look in at these events but I gave him such a look that he had the good sense to immediately retract his words and instead suggested Moses or Elijah for the job. They spent way too much time roaming around in the wilderness anyway, I told him to draw up a roster of all the prophets and we could persuade them to attend these functions in the interests of heavenly peace and domination.

Michael had my legal department working overtime on a water tight document that would irrevocably bind their souls to me once and for all. I had told them to throw in plenty of 'whereas', 'hither-to-fores' and 'aforesaids' also make it plenty longwinded so that it would drain the ratfinks blood quite a bit and would take him a month to recover before he could start his partying plus it must stand up in ecclesiastic court which was headed by Solomon. Solomon was a cantankerous old coot if I ever saw one, he was such a stickler for rules and regulations that he was quite capable of finding for the defendant if there any lacunae in the document and later they wanted to wriggle out of it. He was nothing like his father. Having done all that I popped off back to my book leaving Michael to carry out the plan.

So that's how I put one over that arrogant bastard, I had beaten him at his own game. The exodus to hell slowed down to a trickle. Man finally had an alternative and he need not have to sell his soul to that SOB just for a few years of pleasure, lust, power and luxury when if he sold his soul to me instead in return for a few years of pious living on earth he would be rewarded with an eternity of bingo parties, fetes and high teas, maybe a few with Moses or Elijah in the Tea tent. It's the suspense that would make it so exciting.

GAME OF STONES

Remember all that stone pelting and stone throwing business that happened in the valley not so long ago? And remember how the actions of one courageous officer ended it with one simple ingenuous idea? And do you also remember all that fuss about how the Council was being funded from across the border and the hunt for certain businessmen cum money launderers? Well I'm not saying that I had anything to do with that but I'm not going to deny it either. The stupid Official Secrets Act prevents me from admitting anything substantial so I will try and give you the gist of it without going into specifics. Just fill in the blanks and feel free to make any assumptions that you may wish to make, you won't be wrong by much I guarantee that.

I was sitting in Q's fake office not so long ago, waiting for him to summon me, I had had one horrible experience, when I had gone down to his office uninvited; my ears are still ringing from the bollocking I got, not to mention the field day his goons had as they manhandled me out of the room. No Sir! Never again! From now onwards I go only when I'm called. After an hour or so the light blinked green feverishly and I did the routine with the loo. For those of you in the loop this is the time to refill your drink or light a cigarette or something for the newbies not yet in the loop I will explain, this routine involves me diving into the loo sitting on the commode (seat down) and pulling the chain. This action ensures that I go whooshing 80 feet down a slide at a speed of Mach2 or Mach 3 and into the belly of the beast and landing on air pillows or something of an equally billowy nature. Once you retrieve you heart from your mouth you are good to go. Easy Peasy!

Q and his goons were having a chat over a cup of tea (Earl Grey) I presumed since he only drank that slop, and laughing raucously at some stupid joke one of the goons had cracked. I assumed of course that the joke was stupid, since one of the goons had cracked it; they were all 6 ½' Jats from where ever, what else would you expect? Droll humour? Satire? Any way, they all charged out on seeing me enter, sniggering amongst themselves and nudging each other slyly. I ignored them and flashed a pearly white smile in Q's direction but I missed him, he had ducked suddenly under his desk but he came up a second later holding a rock, he was hefting it in his hand and fuming, silently, thank God "Catch" he said as he lobbed it in my direction, my lightening like reflexes came into play instinctively, I dived to the right stretching out my hand, if it weren't for those damned heavy brass planters that Q scatters randomly around his office I would have executed a tight somersault coming up neatly holding the rock aloft like King Arthur with Excalibur. But that was not to be so I merely held the rock and examined it like an avid student of Geology examining a specimen from the NeoProterozoic Era. I hefted it from hand to hand, thoughtfully, sniffed it and even licked it tentatively; I got nothing so I gave him my intelligent look and asked "what about it?" This, young man, was thrown at me by those juvenile delinquents up in the valley, I almost got hit on the nose!" I took a moment to admire the courage of the young stone pelter, Q's nose was decidedly bulbous and made quite an easy target, but if you take in to account, the size of the rock (small to medium) and the distance (50 to 75 metres) plus wind velocity etc etc clearly it would take a practiced hand to hurl the projectile across the no man's land, a hand I would have liked to shake someday "they call themselves 'Sangbazi' growled Q " they should all be in school instead of pelting stones at me and the army. I blame their parents and those separatist bastards." "Separatist Bastards" I echoed sternly, still not sure of where I fitted into all of this.

"Anyway" he continued "I want you to go to the valley and do some investigative work for the agency" he tossed a manila envelope at me, "it's all in there I want you to find how these bastards are being funded. We know it's coming from across the border but how, who are the launderers? I want account numbers names and code names and passwords I want addresses and all the dirt on those leeches, Sone, Malik, Yakut, Khattab and all the rest of them, their mistresses their bootleggers the whole enchilada. Got that? "I stuck my chest out and bellowed "Sir!Yes Sir!" and I was off.

The valley is really a beautiful place, a honeymooner's paradise an ideal place for a romantic rendezvous aboard those cute houseboats ideal, for secret lovers and families of course with their screaming kids running around generally making mayhem, in short, a bit of something for everyone.

My first visit took me just south of the LOC, to a quaint little village which shall have to remain unnamed. I had confided to my guide and informer Ashraf, in broad strokes about my mission and he in turn had filled me in in great detail about these guys. A bit about Ashraf, I always like to mention my informers' names in my chronicles, 'cos even though the names I use are not their real names each individual knows who I'm talking about. It makes them feel special and wanted. Ashraf is a young enthusiastic guy who freely admits to being a sangbazi or stone pelter himself and collecting a cool 5000/- per month from Khattab. He also collects Rs 3000/- per month from Malik and 7000/- a month and from Sone as petrol allowance for Molotov cocktails, which he swears that he never threw at any of our brave hearts in uniform but instead he used it for gassing up his Pulsar, which he uses to ferry his sweetheart Fatima around town and to secluded locations away from prying eyes. His enthusiasm made me feel old. When I had told him my mission, he was all for it and hit the bullseye first shot. "Sir these old buggers all have girlfriends, who the press thinks are their daughters, nieces or granddaughters, but they are in fact mistresses and run their (old fart's) households like tyrants, all the wives having been bundled off to UK or Germany with their children, where they would be safe from all this unrest and turmoil that they themselves were sowing. Ashraf hated them would do anything to see them being sent off across the border to be with their masters." I am on very intimate terms with most of the mistresses," he confided proudly "What about Fatima? "I asked "Oh! She was the last and I swore to her that no more mistresses from now onwards I will love only her" he said with finality.

Fatima, Ashraf explained, was Khattab's mistress, a position that she took very seriously, being Senior Mistress gave her an elevated status among the other mistresses and they all listened to her.

Khattab would give her huge amounts of money and In return she made him feel good, for 5 minutes or less, if you know what I mean.

It was to her house that Ashraf brought me, a secluded little cottage on the outskirts of the village. Fatima met us at the door and cautiously ushered us in.

She had on a burqa and sat modestly on the sofa, her hands in her lap while Ashraf explained to her what he wanted her to do. Then he asked me to go into the vegetable garden at the back and pluck a few brinjals and tomatoes for lunch, as he wanted to seal the deal so to speak. I caught on in a flash and was out the door even faster. It took him 45 long minutes to seal the deal; maybe she was a good negotiator but when I went back in she was sitting serenely on the sofa while Ashraf, looking dishevelled said "She wants to show you something" and he looked at her meaningfully. She got up and went into the bedroom and came out again dragging a tin trunk which she put in front of me then she stooped down and opened it and stepped back it was half filled with packets and packets of new 2k notes "She is very thrifty" Ashraf said proudly "Once its full we will get married buy a house and have half a dozen kids and live in peace I picked up a packet and leafed through the notes. I examined one carefully, "These are fake" I said dramatically and then regretted it immediately. She blew her top, because, apparently, there were quite a few dozen packets of these notes stashed away in her little tin box. I promised to replace every packet with real ones, but I needed her help in a couple of things

Once all the dust had settled, we sat down and planned our next course of action. Fatima was still fuming and clenched her fists repeatedly but it wasn't us that made the plan it was Fatima and she spoke rapidly to Ashraf for five minutes continuously. Ashraf, translated paraphrasing along the way, finished the translation in 3 minutes, as he had left out all the curse words.

My original plan was to get Fatima to get me details of Khattab's accounts and passbooks and contacts etcetera. This info when passed onto Q would keep me in his good books for weeks on end.

But she was offering all the accounts names passwords and contacts of every member of the council how would she accomplish this? By rounding up all the mistresses and telling them what these guys were doing after that there would be no need for ordering them to do the dirty work for it is said that hell hath no rage greater than a woman scorned and these were truly scorned women. It turns out that all these mistresses had a network amongst themselves and when they found out that they were being paid with fake money and that I was going to make good all that fake currency, they were furious and ready to rat on them, it wasn't long before I had met each one and coaxed them into getting me the information I needed. I had distributed a dozen or so cheap Chinese smartphones after showing them how to use the camera and how to send pictures via WhatsApp. I also showed them how to delete said pictures afterwards. Of course, coaxing meant a lot of cuddling and smooching and whatnot. It turns out that these guys only go for the 'whatnot'; they craved for the other stuff and couldn't get enough of it and since Ashraf, having sworn fidelity to only Fatima, refused to help I was stuck with the job. Country before Self was and is my motto so I persevered on. I was back at the airfield 4 days later, totally exhausted but with the storage space on my iPhone almost crammed to capacity with pictures of every possible account passbook, code books and address books.

It was a coup of sorts and I knew Q would use this info well. I delayed my return wanting to relax in the officers' mess and recoup my energies.

I was in the bar one evening when this group of officers barged in all talking at once; from my corner of the bar all I could make out that these guys had been stone pelted, again, for the umpteenth time this week. Most of them were on election duty and were tasked to escort the Election Commission staff to and from the polling booths and secure the EVMs as well. It was like the running of the bulls in Pamplona, except in reverse, the stone pelters were without fear knowing that the army would not, could not fire at them because there were so many children amongst the mob. If the army returned fire or retaliated in any way countless kids would have been killed or injured, so the army held their fire. The council was betting that they would, all they could do was duck and take shelter as best they could.

One of the young Captains, he must have been about my age, came up to the bar and hoisted himself on to the stool, he had a wicked gash on his face, the bleeding had stopped but he held a blood soaked kerchief to his face. He looked in my direction and sensing a fellow sufferer remarked "Hurriyat Bastards! They are using kids to fight us! Can you imagine? Some of them couldn't be more than 10 years old." There was nothing I could say, so I sipped my drink and nodded in compassion " I wish we could give them a taste of their own medicine without hurting them" he said passionately "if only there was a way!" In order to cheer him up I tried to make to joke about it "Why don't you tie one of thosepelters to your jeep?" I said flippantly "maybe that will deter them from pelting the convoys' he looked at me "are you serious?" "Sure" I said "it's what I would do if I was the convoy commander" he gulped down the remainder of his drink "Thanks pal, I think I will take off now and get this wound dressed at the MI Room and go and speak to my CO about what happened to day" and he slid off the stool and walked out of the Mess. I didn't think further about the matter and could only concentrate on the sweet thing who was waiting for me on a houseboat on the Dal lake, courtesy Ashraf, No! No! I swear she was not one of Khattab's or Malik's harem, she worked on one of the floating houseboats of pleasure and Ashraf swore that she was a trainee without much experience, Any way all's well that ends well. And I returned to Q with a pen drive chock full of the juiciest details of the councils financial information.

Q made good use of it and forwarded it to the ED and just to prevent a cover up, which the government was quite capable of, to one or two of the loudest and nosiest TV channels, the channel with that loud bossy guy who calls people for interviews and then doesn't let anyone speak, for once it was a pleasure to see him waving a sheaf of papers in the air and shouting down bearded surrogates of the council.

Of the young Captain I didn't hear off again, but that Major from the East certainly must have heeded whatever the young man passed on for he was at first demeaned and criticised and brought up on all sorts of charges for inappropriate conduct but later honoured and felicitated and given a medal. Even Q, whom I met much later, had nothing but the highest praise for the Major's ingenuity and for his ability to think out of the box.

I personally was on cloud nine for about 2 days and then it was back to normal and Q would still shout and curse me and his goons would continue to manhandle me whenever they got the chance or whenever they were ordered to or when they thought no one was looking. Life was good.

KUNG FU PANDEY

In the universe of Spy versus Spy, we, (spies) are all alone. Each one of us, we are individual specks revolving around a single entity. In my case, like the Hydrogen atom, I am the lone electron orbiting around Q's nucleus, never coming into contact with any other specks for fear of setting of an uncontrollable chain reaction, at least that's what we were told. We have no colleagues nor friends nor partners. Our sole contact within this universe is through our handlers; in my case, my boss Q is my handler, never have I met any other specks. "There is no one else" he would tell me gruffly, whenever I asked "you are the only one" but in my heart of hearts I knew that he was lying (his beady eyes always got that shifty look in them whenever he was lying, and since he lies to me almost on a daily basis, I could tell) however I have always believed that there were others and that maybe one day I would get to meet at least one of them. That happened sooner than I thought.

I was fooling around in Q's fake office a couple of weeks ago; Q didn't know I was there, thinking that I was still on my much needed vacation on a tea plantation high up in the Nilgiris, My last assignment at the Vatican, had gone off superbly and we had our PIO where we wanted him. While I was snooping around the palace, I did manage to run into the Pontiff, who unfortunately was just coming out of his bath, he thought I was his page and asked me to hand him his bathrobe. Now his usual page was probably used to this but the little swine was goofing off somewhere, probably smoking a stolen cigarette. I was just a novice with no experience in such situations at all so I picked up the fluffy bathrobe lying neatly laid out on the bed and tossed it over to him shouting "Catch!", the pontiff turned around to catch the robe from me and I got a glimpse of his alabaster white body and his junk. I think we both screamed together; I like a wood nymph surprised by the hunter while bathing in a cooling stream and he like said hunter, who has just discovered that he is about to become a man-eating Bengal tiger's breakfast. Before he could even say "Madre Dios" or "Mama Mia" (what do pontiffs say when surprised? Maybe one of those two, I seriously doubt if WTF was in his vocabulary) I was out of there in a flash for the benefit of CNN /BBC viewers, the dour expression on the Pontiff's face during that famous photo – op session recently, had nothing to do with the person standing beside him. However, I can't comment on the dour expression on face of the person standing beside him. I think it was the orange guy with the funny hair. In my report I omitted to include this little nugget of information, so Q was happy. And that's what counts.

My little vacation in the Nilgiris had been going along well, I had called in a favour with the manager of a tea plantation (I had gotten him out of a sticky situation not so long ago. And he owed me big-time) and he had very graciously lent me the use of his bungalow in the garden itself and had very thoughtfully arranged for me to try my hand at plucking tea shoots. I had managed to convince the supervisor to replace the 80-year-old tutor that he had selected for me, with a couple of cute twenty-year-old things, to teach me all they knew about the art of tea plucking and more. During the day I would immerse myself in learning about tea tables, maintenance foliage and tipping. And during the long evenings that followed, they would bathe my numerous scratches and scrapes with tea oil and other aromatics all the while murmuring" Muttal, Muttal" and giggling. I must look up the meaning of this word; I'm sure it means handsome virile lover or something like that. However due to an unfortunate concatenation of events and misunderstandings with the indigenous population, who by the way, are a petty, narrow-minded and suspicious lot, would you believe, that they refused to believe my explanation as to why I was cavorting with 2 semi naked tea maidens in my bedroom. Has the term National Security lost its sanctity? Anyway, not being one to linger and argue with these ingrates, I was out of a nearby window and using the tea bushes strategically I was able to scoot to safety. Halfway through my little vacation, I was forced to beat a hasty retreat from the pristine surroundings of the Nilgiris, to the hot, crowded polluted and dusty   place that is our capitol.

So, there I was, in Q's office and thinking of things to do and having thought, got the idea to pay him a surprise visit. In retrospect it was a bad idea, a very, very bad idea. As a rule, it is forbidden to enter the underground labyrinth that is Q's lair, without being called and buzzed in, but I figured, with my special status and all, I could cut a few corners. So, I went into the Loo, sat on the seat and pulled the chain, by the way, if you go to the loo and put up the seat as one would normally do, and then pull the chain it will flush, as loos are wont to do. As I plummeted down, I thought of how pleased the old man would be to see me. I dusted myself off and I could hear Q on the phone "He is one best operative I tell you, he is exceedingly intelligent resourceful and well skilled in all weaponry and can shoot a pea off the nose of a prime minster or president for that matter" I blushed, Q was really building me up, I never realized he thought so highly of me "Yes he knows all the martial arts and is an expert in Kung Fu" Q was really spreading it on thick. I knew a bit of judo and karate, yellow belt level I suppose, but me an expert? No way! "Of course, he is fluent in several languages including Mandarin, the MSS want him" Q continued. I heard '*Missus*' and thought that Q had taken it a bit far, taking his wife's advice. In any case I thought she was dead; did he really think I knew Chinese? Something was not right. Anyway, after this build up there was no way he would yell at me for barging in like this. So, I stuck my chest out and swaggered down the corridor and into Q's office, and guess what? He yelled at me "what are you doing down here you moron?" he hollered (Hollered is a better word than Yelled; more appropriate) "you little piece of shit, are you spying on me?" he began jabbing a button on the underside of his desk. Uh Oh! I knew that button it was used to summon the goon squad whenever he wanted to throw me out of his office. From past experience I knew that I had 15 seconds to take in the scene. Q was not alone, opposite him sat a young man my age, height and weight brown hair and eyes that belied an oriental background. He was smoking one of those long cigarettes (smoking in front of Q???) and eying me with a quizzical expression on his face. Some would even call him good looking. I guess, if you liked the Bruce Lee look. So, there was at least one other I thought as I felt my self being lifted up from under my armpits and whisked off by two of his goons "bring him back in an hour" was Q's parting shot.

The goons hauled me off to a small waiting room and bundled me inside. I was cursing their combined ancestry with a great deal of vim and vigour hoping to salvage some of my pride in case there were onlookers but I didn't see any. I took in my surroundings; it was a bleak room with a bright light dangling from the ceiling, 2 upright chairs and a plain wooden table was the only furniture in the room. I sprawled into the chair and hoisted my feet onto the table defiantly and thought about what I saw. Who was this oriental dude? Could he be Q's son? Maybe, he did have a sort of *Pahadi*look and Q I knew was a Pahadi, but I had my doubts. Or maybe someone from RAW but I dismissed that thought immediately, RAW didn't even know we existed, So, that left an obvious conclusion – he was another electron like me! Were there actually two electrons revolving around Q? was there more chemistry involved than what met the eye? Was Q actually a Helium atom? Did Q have more protons than he was showing me? I filed all these questions away in my mind; to be pondered over at my leisure. Q's goons came back and tried to lift up out of my chair from the armpits again but I slithered around them and scooted back to Q's office where Q was waiting for me. Alone.

"Who was that?" I asked jealously "None of your business" he replied gruffly "Why are you here? What happened in the tea garden?" "You told me I was the only one" I said bitterly ignoring his segue "You lied to me" "Calm down" he said mildly "I lie to you almost every day, it's nothing new" he motioned for me to sit and spoke into the intercom "two coffees please" Wow! Q was finally treating me like a grown up!

"Shut Up and listen" he said gruffly. So, I listened; Q rumbled and growled for 15 minutes. I must have dozed off in between, I just caught that this guy was a Chink from Chinatown in Kolkata, Q used him in black ops in the eastern hemisphere just as he used me in the western. In a very rare moment of cooperation the Chinese MSS (Ministry of State Security) had passed on some extremely important information regarding our great friend Pakistan's nuclear programme and their proliferation activities vis a vis North Korea. All I know that South Korea, the MSS and the ISI were involved, I'm also including the CIA, on a hunch, since it is very unusual in a case like this, for them not to be.

Now although China and Pakistan are as thick as thieves most of the time, China did not approve of the Pakistanis sharing their nuclear know how with the North Koreans, especially their ICBM technology. Given that N Korea has been ruled by a series of unstable dictators, the Chinese feared greatly that there was no knowing when little 'Rocket Man' would get it into his head to turn those pointy missiles of his at Beijing instead of Washington. The Pakis, being perpetually broke were just doing it for the money. We cooperated for the same reason; if those ICBMs could target Beijing, they could target Delhi as well. After many launch failures some reported and some not, a final draft blueprint prepared by Dr Khans laboratories, had reached the Pakistan High Commission in Delhi from Islamabad and would be handed over to the North Koreans at their embassy near Saket in 3- or 4-days' time by an ISI operative. I knew what was coming next so I jumped in "you want me to break in to the paki high commission and steal the blue print" I blurted out eagerly like an overly zealous student proudly anticipating his teacher's approval. Luckily for me 'Q's desk was broad and wide or I would have gotten one his famous jabs across the ear, "No you moron! Why do you think I brought in Bruce Lin? (Wow!

That was really racist of Q) Since you have broken into the high commission repeatedly your job is to get him inside the High Commissioner's office, it will be heavily guarded, leave the rest to Lin. Spend the next two days with him, get to know each other and don't give up any strategic information in order to impress him, I know what a little show off you are. Today is Tuesday you will go in on Friday night, now get out, you little turd, if you fuck this up don't bother to show your face around here."

Lin met me in the parking lot and introduced himself, his name was Rakesh Pandey and he spoke with a heavy Bong (Bengali) accent. He excelled in martial arts and was a marksman, wielded a mean blade "Which one " I asked excitedly, hoping it was a KA-BAR or a Bowie (both are Zombie Killer Knives and I was dying to see one) "Kukri is my preferred blade " he said "but I can kill you with a butter knife" he boasted. He was probably right there. . We spent the afternoon getting to know each other. He told me his story which was remarkably similar to that of my favourite character in RED, no not Bruce Willis, Han Cho someone, and I told him mine which went along the lines similar to that of James Bond. Since we both loved girls and tequila shots & partying we could really bond. I never had a friend my age before and I really enjoyed his company. We were coming back from a disco in Gurgaon and were in the parking lot, Pandey was in a very good mood having had a gazillion tequila shots and was trying to sing Kung Fu Fighting in a reedy offkey voice and doing all those poses so typical of Bruce Lee. I was dancing around him like a puppy having had quite a few shots myself when all of a sudden, we were accosted by a group of 7 hefty Jats who wanted to borrow my car for two hours or so. I was all for handing over the keys and taking an OLA cab home But Pandey wouldn't have it, he took the keys out of my hand and slipped them into his jacket pocket, then he held both his arms out and dared them to take the keys of him. In typical Jat bully style they rushed him together with a roar of abuse and flailing fists. Pandey was Han Cho in the flesh, he delivered a series of kicks and fists to all and sundry and in a minute, all was quiet in the parking lot. That was the first time I saw him fight and he was awesome. From that moment onwards, he became "Kung Fu Pandey and I never referred to him as anyone else.

Friday morning we went over the plan which was pretty simple come to think of it; scale the wall - easy peasy, enter through side door of left wing, - no problem there, as I had a master key, courtesy 'Q' from a previous mission inside, race across the vast central hall beneath the blue dome, while I circumvented the hall scurrying like a mouse along the wall, Pandey crossed in seconds by executing a series of somersaults and landing like a cat in the corridor that lead to the high commissioner's office. I caught up with him. All huffing and puffing and pointed "first corridor to the left, the office is right in front. Be careful there may be guards" he nodded "wait here" but I followed him like an inquisitive puppy. What I saw astounded me, 'Q' hadn't been lying about his Kung Fu skills, I had seen a sample in the parking lot but what he displayed here was awesome. There were 6 armed guards at the door and they didn't stand a chance. He was a blur of fists and legs and chops and kicks they were out cold in 20 seconds. Having gotten rid of the guards he took out what looked like an Allen key and jiggered the lock a bit and the door opened noiselessly. He was inside for precisely for five minutes then he came out, joined me and we went back precisely as we had come in. I was still in awe of his amazing Kung Fu skills and begged him to teach me a few tricks but he just smiled inscrutably and handed me a fat manila envelope "give this to your boss, it should get you a good posting, tell him to act on it fast. Thanks for all your help you are very good, without you I could never have completed my mission" he had hailed a passing autorickshaw and jumped in. "but what was your mission?" I asked as the driver slammed down the meter with a loud clang "you will read about it in a month or so" and with a friendly wave he went out of my life and I never saw him again

The next day being a Saturday meant that 'Q' would be playing golf all day so I hung around in my room, called a few friends over and we went to a night club close by where we had quite a good time but my heart wasn't in it, I was still thinking of my friend and wondered where he was. On my eighth tequila shot I decided that the two guys who looked like bouncers, who were sitting quietly in a darkened corner of the club, minding their own business, looked remarkably like two of the thugs Q kept hanging around his office just for the sole purpose of throwing me out whenever he said so and I decided to conduct further enquiries and if not satisfied I would have to take matters into my own hands Kung Fu Pandey style, I confronted the duo with traditional fighting talk by referring to their mothers' private parts (*Teri Maa ki* .....) I had hardly uttered these words when I felt myself being hefted up and slung over a shoulder, before I knew it I was sprawled out on the sidewalk outside the club. I knew that heft! definitely it was familiar, I had experienced it a hundred times before ,every time Q threw me out of his office I had found myself on my butt in the parking lot, courtesy a very similar heft. I would take this up with Q later at a convenient time.

Monday saw me bright and early in 'Q's office, back to my old exuberant self, clutching the manila envelope close to my chest. 'Q' bounced in a little later and gave me a jovial "Hello dumbass! How did your little break-in go? I hope you didn't fuck it up. Did you fuck it up?" he asked querulously, suddenly worried about the scandal and the diplomatic storm it would cause if I had "No Sir, au contraire" I remarked very much like 007 would have replied to a similar query by 'M'. I slid the envelope across his desk, he grabbed it in the manner of a ravenous tiger pouncing on its breakfast coolie "what's this he asked as he began ripping the cover open "see for yourself" I replied, unwilling to let on that I had no idea whatsoever "So what happened inside? Tell me all" he asked absentmindedly, thoroughly engrossed by what he was reading. So I began my spiel, heavily embellishing most of it but for the dust up by Kung Fu Pandey which needed no embellishment "why this is a list of ISI operatives in Delhi & this is a complete record of payment made to various NGOs, individuals and complete Hurriyat Council, those bastards won't know what hit them, and here are WhatsApp numbers of more than 1500 people" 'Q' was like a little boy opening his presents at Christmas he looked up at me suspiciously "how did you get your hands on this? I hope this is not one those ISI scams to fool us" "No, No, Sir! It's the real thing straight from the High Commissioner's Office, Pandey himself gave it to me" "Who is this Pandey you keep referring to?" "Lin! Sir, Lin! but I call him Pandey because of what Lin means here. His full name is Kung Fu Pandey, to me he will always be Kung Fu Pandey.

Two months later I finally learnt what Kung Fu Pandey's real mission was, not to steal the missile plans but to alter them so that the launch was bound to end in failure.

Headline in National Daily

North Korea launches missile but test ends in failure ICBM explodes over own city injuring dozens Unsuccessful test fire in eastern coastal city comes hours before US vice-president is due to arrive in Seoul

I guess Kung Fu Pandey had a successful mission after all.

PARAGON HOUSING SOCIETY

I had just returned from a highly successful mission in the East, you know the one I'm talking about,, the one with the hot khasi chicks and the careless G1, and was now in the nation's financial capital eager to begin some hard earned R&R, as had been promised by my boss, let's just call him Q, as whenever he was in conversation with me he would use that letter (Kyon? Q?) a lot, to be fair he also used the word 'NO' as often, but we can't go around calling him NO can we? Unless he was a doctor, then I guess it would be alright.

In order to legalize everything and make it look official, I was ostensibly posted as a Station Staff Officer (SSO) in the Station HQ, but I had been seconded to the General's office nearby. It sounded very important and officious but in reality I had nothing to do except sit around in the office all day (till 1 PM) and think up ways and means to meet up with all the hot young starlets who flocked daily to the city from all corners of the country, in the hopes of landing 'the role of a lifetime' which would make them famous overnight. At least that was Q had said, but he has been known to be economical with the truth before as well. I was forced to take him at his word as you can't very well look to further your career and go around calling your boss a bally liar at the same time, can you?

"Your job is to look after me" said my General Officer Commanding (GOC) as I stood rigidly at *savdhan* (attention) in front of him "you will come in before I do and leave after I leave" said the grizzled old SOB, "I want my tea on time and if I don't get my Macvities (digestive biscuits) at 11 am

I will chew your balls" He raised his hoary head , looked at me and showed me all his teeth in a grimace, as if he had just cracked the funniest joke EVER. I would have laughed raucously as is my wont whenever a general crack a joke, even a bad one, but since I was being introduced to him for the first time, I merely allowed my upper lip to twitch "Sir yes SIR" I bellowed back at him. "Relax son, have a seat, I won't really eat them, I will tell Lisa to brief you about how we operate around here."

'Here' was the entire first floor of this imposing Victorian era granite 3 storied block building, the remaining floors were for the rest of his HQ but the general's secretariat occupied the complete first floor and was quite lavish, even my office once had an oceanic view but some unscrupulous builder had built a high rise 1BHK apartment complex in front, so now they had my view and all I could see from my window was their laundry.

Lisa was the general's PA and was as old as he was or maybe even older, it was hard to tell, but what was obvious to anyone with half a brain was that she was in love with him and couldn't take her eyes of his sagging tushy but the old coot was unaware of her pash as he was too busy ogling the pretty young would-be starlets from his first floor office window, as they strutted up and down the promenade which passed below his office window. Now I'm all for office romances as they always give me the upper hand, but before I gave this one my full endorsement I would have to check out the Generals wife, if she was bitchy, tyrannical and a shrew then I was all for the old man getting a little loving in the office. It turned out that she was all three of those adjectives so I thoroughly encouraged Lisa to go for it and promised to build her up to the old man every chance I got.

By the end of my first month as unofficial aide-de-camp (ADC) to the general I had settled into a nice little routine. It went something like this; reach office by 9 am, have coffee and discuss various parts of the generals anatomy with Lisa, meet the general in the portico below as he arrives at 930 am and escort him up to his office on the first floor, have more coffee with the old man and make notes of whatever he wanted me to do for the day, remind him about his appointments, screen visitors, make new appointments and help Lisa out around the office, check his correspondencefor typos and grammatical errors before he signed them , screen his 'First Sight Dak' folder (official mail) into what he should see and what was unimportant and could be fobbed off onto his other staff officers. The latter category formed the bulk of it and I ensured that only very few letters actually reached his desk for him to read and then finally see the old bugger off for lunch by about 1 PM. In a nutshell I controlled what he saw, whom he saw and when he should see them. That in a nutshell is the ADC's real job.

I was free after that, to pursue my stated goal of trying to hook up with would-be starlets. I was having no luck at all mainly because I did not seem to resemble the stereotype of what a producer or director should look like by any standard, even when I wore designer shades, a golf cap, loud bush shirts and puffed vigorously on a stinky cigar.

One morning as I was scanning the FSD folder, I came across a letter from a housing society asking some favour from the general, like a true staff officer I fobbed it off to Q Branch, without batting an eyelid, as they dealt with these matters, and thought nothing more about it. Later that afternoon the Col Q rang me in my room and told me to fix him up with an appointment for the next day. It was to discuss the PARAGON HOUSING SOCIETY's request to add additional floors or something like that.

The Col Q arrived on time for his appointment but instead of going in to meet the old man, he instead, proceeded to brief me about the case and tell me what a good thing he was onto and if cards were played right, all of us (him, me and the GOC) could land up with a flat each in a posh area of the city, and at a throw away price to boot. All the GOC had to do was to give his sanction as the building was in an army area. Now, frankly, I smelled a fish not one but a whole school of them, and by the looks of it not a very fresh school at that. He instructed me to sell the idea to the 'old man' and that he would return tomorrow to discuss the case with him, after I had softened him up. I dislike tall thin supercilious looking colonels giving me orders, even though they had every right to do so by virtue of the fact that they were senior, besides this guy would be more at home in Hitler's army and certainly looked the part, if anyone was casting for the role of Himmler or Goebbels they would choose him at once, in a nutshell I didn't trust him specially since only the old man's name and signature would be there on the documents and nobody else's.

I checked out the builders, it turns out they were the same guys who had built the one BHK block of apartments that was blocking my view of the ocean. Not cool.

So, when the old man came the next day, I briefed him and told him that something was fishy about the whole thing and that he should have nothing to do with it. I then ushered in the Col Q, after winking at him conspiratorially, shortly afterward and I heard the old man giving him a good bollicking inside, later on when he came out he was fuming and told me that the old man was an idiot and who did he think he was, Mahatma Gandhi or something? I was full of commiserations "what to do sir, and it was for Kargill war widows too." "Yeah," said the Col Q "that was a good idea of yours including the Kargill angle, how could he refuse Kargill war widows? Has he no shame? Anyway, I'm keeping this file; he will be gone in a couple of months, maybe the next GOC will have some brains and will listen to me. This is a golden opportunity; these old timers don't understand how to survive in the modern world. What will he do with his 'honesty and imandari"? Can he eat it?" He huffed and puffed some more then glanced at his Rolex looking watch, "ok kid I have to go, come to my house in the evening, some filmi people will be there, cute things, also that famous director of HAHK , I forget his name. Anyway, be there round about eightish, you can man the bar if you like." Wow. Maybe the Col Q wasn't such a bad guy after all. A starlet was a starlet and if she saw me chatting with a famous director who knows how the night could end up. I had done my good turn for the day so I figured one good turn deserves another. I resolved to be there at seven and check the place out. Long story short, I got lucky that night and it seems my general got luckier as well.

A decade later I see every TV channel running the story of the latest scam to hit the army and I figure wow that was close, same builder again, how many more yet to be uncovered. Paragon housing society has not yet been named, but the other one is really making headlines. They had also used the Kargill war widows' angle as well!

It won't be long before some plucky reporter makes the connection. God bless the 24x7 news concept. Their never-ending hunger for headlines ensures that out of 100 news items, 99 may be petty and frivolous stories but the one, it will be huge and a lot of heads will roll. I scan the list I see many army generals' names also but I'm happy to see that my GOC's name is not there and I'm thankful for that. Underneath my hard veneer I guess I'm just a big ol' softy at heart.

RUNAWAY PLANE

In the first place, don't be misled by the title, my mission, at least in the beginning, didn't have anything to do with planes or runways or runaway planes. It was a covert operation ordered by my boss 'Q'.

Now for the newbie's and latecomers, let me digress a little bit and tell you something about my boss 'Q and why he is called so. If I were to be asked for a one word description of the man it would have to be 'Meansonofabitch', two words 'Meansonofabitch, Meansonofabitch' three words, but I think you must have gotten my drift by now, he calls himself 'Q' because he says he is the 17th incumbent as head of this organization. The previous sixteen are now referred to with the prefix 'Late'. Only A,D,G,H &M died peacefully in their sleep or in old age homes set up by the Govt for precisely such contingencies; that they might somehow survive and live to a ripe old age, he once mused, the rest were taken out by violent means and of F they could find nary a trace, the reddish blob that was found on the parquet floor of the lobby of Hotel Kanishka, after extensive DNA mapping, research scientists offered a 70% chance that the mess was solely that of F. But and there was always a But, they couldn't be sure and needed more time and samples from his Kin and since he had none the file was closed and buried deep in the archival section pertaining to the East India Company. 'Q' in our trysts favoured trench coats of the type worn by pre-war British agents & the cold war, smoked a fat, stinky cigar (half smoked and half chewed) of the type favoured by Churchill but he wore a stylish golf cap of the type favoured by Tiger Woods and he favoured moods of the type favoured by bad tempered bull dogs who think that their favourite pork chop is about to be snatched away.

My take on why he is called 'Q' is because his favourite word whenever he is in conversation with me is "Kyon" Hindi word for "Why" and pronounced 'Q' whenever we met our conversations would go along these lines

Self" "Sir, may I have your permission to speak?"

Q "Kyon"

"Sir, I have to go on leave for a few days"

"Kyon"

"Sir, my grandmother just passed"

"Kyon"

"Sir, she was ailing and bed ridden"

"Kyon"

"Sir, last week she tripped and broke her Hip"

"Kyon"

"Sir, she was going to the toilet"

"Kyon"

"Sir, she had to pee"

"Kyon"

"Sir, she has diabetes and she takes Lasix"

"Kyon"

"Sir, Lasix is a diuretic it helps diabetics to pee"

On that occasion he won, he wore me down and I settled for two days and one extra shift on a Saturday, My grandma had passed a good 5 years ago and I only needed one day to entertain and seduce this eager young chick who thought I was really a successful business man, my cover at that time. So it was a win win for everybody I guess, except that the eager young chick suddenly developed cold feet and in spite of my very generous offer of making her Head of PR as soon as I got back from Tokyo, she was stricken with a head ache and disappeared. I think it was my youthfulness and boyish charm that threw her, most of these chicks have 'Daddy issues" anyway, or she may have read my latest ATM withdrawal slip which I had carelessly left lying around. I think it was the "Daddy" thing. I have digressed enough about 'Q', now let me steer you back to my latest adventure.

I was sitting in 'Q's upper office waiting for him to summon me into the dungeons below which is where his real office is, when who should walk in but my old pal, the G1 from my days in Divisional HQ, the Orbat scam remember? He was no more G1 now; he had risen through the ranks and was now festooned in ribbons, brass, and gaudy lanyards. Christmas trees looked less flashy. It took him a moment or two to recognize me and then his face dropped "What are you doing here young man? Do you know whose office this is?" I was sent by MS branch Sir "I said not letting on that I knew anything of what was going on. "Well be careful you don't say anything stupid to anyone. I remember how you were always saying stupid things in the Div HQ and pissing everyone off. Where is General Basnett?" He asked in a calmer voice. "I have no idea" I replied "who is he?"" You are sitting in the man's office and you don't know who he is? What sort of an officer are you? You must always know your seniors' names. Why, I can recite for you all the names of the officers who are senior to me in my directorate" he droned on but I was still pondering this latest revelation about 'Q' BASNETT? BASNETT!! Q's name was Basnet! He was a 'Kancha'!!!That explained his being so short stocky & stubborn and the fierce scowl!

The G1 had finished reciting the names of all those senior to him (and there were dozens) so I asked him what he was doing here and he said that that he (Basnett) was being promoted to head his directorate and that he wanted to be the first to congratulate him, typical lickspittle tactics but very effective if one was on one's way to the top.

He looked around and then at his watch " I have to run, My boss has gone for lunch and is due back any moment so I better hurry back or he is likely to chew my balls if I am not there when he arrives" he said winking conspiratorially at me, at his open use of the B word. Only very senior officers were allowed to use the B word without inviting retribution and his use of it was to demonstrate to me his rapid ascension up the ladder. Tell him, when he comes back, that I was here"

I sank back into my seat and contemplated my discovery and how to use this to my advantage but I had barely struck my contemplative pose when my chair began vibrating vigorously and before I knew it I was plunging down, down, down into the murky maw of darkness that was the lair of 'Q' below. The SOB had renovated and installed this free fall device in lieu of the antiquated lift in the toilet. I had left my stomach back in the upper office, I had to wait a few seconds for it to catch up with the rest of me, but I recovered rapidly and it was quite the suave agent who stepped off the dais and into 'Q's presence. "Who the hell were you were talking to in my office?" he growled doing his bulldog thing but also desperately trying to hide his Jell-O thing which he seemed to have been doing immediately before his bulldog routine "just a Chamcha (spoon/ lickspittle) Sir, but he was looking for some Bassinet so I told him that the crèches are in the East wing and that he would find plenty over there" "Why was he looking for me" he said ignoring my rather clever jibe and relighting his stinky cigar which had gone out, He said you were going over to his directorate and he wanted to welcome you. Are you posted out sir I asked trying to keep the exultation out of my voice, is their going to be an 'R'?? I can't--wait to meet my new boss of course I will miss you terribly sir I said trying to sound sad and heartbroken but failing quite miserably at this herculean task. I took out my silk monogrammed handkerchief as if to wipe away a tear and blow my nose softly as befits a young officer in mourning at the loss of a dear friend and beloved boss. This charade was swiftly put to rest when it turned out that the silk monogrammed handkerchief was actually a silk monogrammed panty of the pretty young thing from the night before, hastily stuffed by me into my uniform pocket, as I hurriedly dressed to keep my appointment with 'Q'. Q spotted it and pounced, " Pervert! I knew there was something twisted about you, I'm never wrong. Whose panties are these? He asked ferociously I replied quite calmly "Sir these belong to the wife of the Defence Secretary, she wanted me to get her pair or several pairs from Victoria's Secret, next time I go abroad since I knew nothing of panties except that they sometimes play spoilsport I asked her for a sample and she gave me this. I feel hurt and pained that you could think so low of me." He ignored my little speech and remarked" you may be going abroad sooner than you think" he said squinting at me through his foul smoke "I have a job for you" Abroad! My whole body was aquiver "Where sir?" I asked excitedly, praying fervently that it was to some place exotic. "New York" he said, his face deadpan "you are to go to New York as part of the PM's delegation. Once there you will meet Major Aziz who is also part of the Paki PM's delegation. you will give him this file" he said tossing a card board covered file across his desk " and in return he will give you a similar file, which you will bring to me soon as you return" "New York I mumbled blankly I hate New York , Why can't we exchange files with a Paki delegation in Paris or Vienna? What's so great about New York?" this outburst seemed to exasperate Q no end "Why it's the greatest city in the world he bellowed "what do you know? you're a dumbass, there a tiny place in Manhattan which serves the best chicken tikka ever and if you go down South Avenue, past those fancy shops in an alley between the Burlington Coat Factory and Supreme Chocolatiers is an antique shop where you can buy and sell exquisite Chinese jade ornaments" I glanced at the small jade statuette of a smiling Buddha, squatting on his desk he continued "you are a cultureless idiot, *Bandar kyajaaneaadhrak ka swad!" (what does a monkey know about the taste of ginger)* You are going to New York and I don't want to hear any more rot about Paris or Vienna or even Rome. It's New York for you and no more of your backchat."

There was not much more to tell, everything went as Q had planned, I joined the delegation and although we were in the 'PM's" delegation I never saw much of him. I handed over the file to Brig Aziz and he handed over his file to me. Although our countries were at daggers drawn back home, at the UN it was quite different. In fact, he was quite a friendly sort and after the exchange of files he invited me over for a drink at the Delegates Dining Room in the United Nations building. After several of them we parted on quite a pally basis.

The next day, we were already seated at the UN summit for peace keeping hosted by POTUS no less, I was hovering somewhere behind the PM's chair trying to retrieve a piece of paper that had drifted off the table, when the Paki delegation trooped in, I straightened up, saw Aziz and waved out to my new found friend excitedly, the Paki PM thinking that his counterpart had waved out to him waved and smiled at his counterpart, his counterpart thinking that the Paki PM had waved out to him waved back and smiled. This caused quite a bit of excitement back home with the media making a big thing about the two PMs waving and smiling at each other.

I slunk out and back to my hotel room in the Waldorf. We were to leave a few hours later and so I wandered around hoping to meet a few young chicks, I had heard that American dames really dug our smooth copper coloured skins and I was hoping to enamour at least one before my flight went. I wandered past the Chicken Tikka place and munched on the juiciest, spiciest and most awesome tikkas I had ever eaten, they just melted in your mouth. Ii even found the little antique store and picked up an amber statuette of the statue of liberty for Q. it was as I was coming out from the alley that I caught a suspicious movement from the corner of my eye. Looking into a plate glass window I saw that a seedy unshaven bum was following me, he was trying to be unobtrusive but to my trained, eagle eye I could tell at once that he was a paki agent, he was wearing a hoodie and his hands were in his pocket, just like that guy, Usher.

Now let me explain why I was being followed; the file that I was carrying had explosive contents, Aziz was Q's very own mole high up in the Paki spying apparatus and had handed over a file that had the complete network & organization names and contact numbers and codes for online communications, for example the top boss was 'babe' and their handlers were called 'dogs' a pistol was CD and rifle DVD; a whole roster of agents called 'bhai' 'black beauty' 'cobra' 'chikna' etc were also included.

Q had very categorically told me that I must guard that file with my life if necessary, on no account was I to let it out of my sight so I had the file on my person when we went for the summit and I had it on me now, it looked as though the Pakis were had discovered the leak and had probably 'interrogated 'Aziz' mercilessly. This scenario had all the makings of something out of a John Le Carre novel and while I admired JLC's works I would much prefer if I was reading about them on a cold winter's evening, by the fireside with a hot toddy within easy reach rather than being the main protagonist.

My life on suddenly becoming endangered spurred me to heights of self-preservation hitherto unknown to me and I did what all good agents are trained to do; I scooted, I hailed a cab and tried to get lost. My pursuer did the same (Both our spy schools have a common origin, Vauxhall Cross in London, the chase was on. I was unarmed and hence crouched low on the floorboard, in the back of the cab. The cabbie was an Indian from Punjab, I told him I was an army officer and that we needed to ditch the cab that was following us, and then hit JFK airport. The cabbie looked doubtfully at me, as if unsure that a person of my youthful appearance, could be a major, but a shot fired from a silenced Mauser pinging off his hubcap convinced him of my credentials and he dived back into the cab and gunned the motor. "Don't worry Saar he said cheerfully I know that driver; he is Madrasi, recently arrived from India, these Madrasi's have no sense of direction, they don't know the city as I do, I know a shortcut through the tunnel. True enough, we were on the outskirts of JFK within 40 minutes, traffic being slow.

I threw a wad of one dollar bills over the seat and jumped out, I rolled across the road and found myself in a field, the perimeter of the airport was a chain link fence about 500 metres away, which I scaled effortlessly, silently blessing Q for his insistence that I do all the physical endurance tests that he regularly sends me on. Huge airliners were taking off and landing regularly on the multiple runways as I made my way towards the concourse. JFK being such a busy terminal with baggage trains criss crossing and passenger shuttles weaving in between, I had no trouble in hitching a ride on one of the baggage trains and was enjoying my ride all the while thinking of my next move, I didn't have to think for long our train was slowly approaching an air bus 380 which was hissing impatiently on the tarmac, its jetway still deployed. I hopped off the baggage train and headed for the aircraft, too my delight it was our national airline, delayed as usual because there was technical problem, in reality they were probably waiting for a prominent politician, I crouched in the shadow of the baggage train and waited and waited, time was running out, the Paki's must have figured out where I was headed and were probably already inside the perimeter. The plane was about 100 meters away but I still had to wait for the politician and his entourage to arrive so that I could slip in. once on board, being our national carrier, I figured I would have no problem in finding a vacant seat for myself. I could see the headlights of two fast approaching vehicles the pakis had probably called in a few favours from their American friends and were barely 200 yards away, I cursed our tardy politicians and prepared for the sprint of my life. Just then the stewards atop the jetway sprang to life and I saw our tubby neta waddling hurriedly up the stair case, in his wake followed his family and in their wake the bureaucrats, bringing up the rear was a couple of lowly dep secs struggling with the all the neta's hand baggage. I sprinted towards them; I swear at that moment, if he had been there, I would have beaten Bolt by a mile. Anyway, I reached them and grabbed a couple of bags from a sweaty dep sec, who was only too glad to hand them over to me and headed up the Jetway.

I sank into a seat and looked out, the vehicles had screeched to stop and five or six bearded blokes jumped out, but the door was closed and the pilot revved his engines, or whatever it is that pilots rev when they are about to take off.

It was only when we were airborne and the seat belt signs went off that I truly relaxed and accepted the cute airhostess's proffered drink and gratefully helped myself to several Jack Daniels' one peg bottles put my feet up & closed my eyes.

If 'Q' was exuberant, elated or even excited at my success, he hid it very well. He hates to shower praise on me, he says it's bad for my ego, and that I would get a swollen head if he did as it is he thought I was insufferable and could not bear to imagine the side of my head if he should s p on me. This did not bother me a bit; I was almost skipping as I followed Q into his office, a sort of little lamb to his dour Mary. Even as we spoke paki agents were being picked up in droves. The TV channels were told that these were people who had overstayed their visas, and that was that. Of course ,they were never seen or heard of again.

Q looked at as if he was in great pain, "I have a job for you, you miserable turd and I don't want any back chat from you.

You are to meet the Indian ambassador to Austria and hand over this envelope to him he will in return hand over a package to you. Guard it with your life and if you lose it don't even bother to return, just apply for asylum there itself." Austria" I almost cooed "that's more like it. I can almost smell hot pizza in the oven and Risotto bubbling in its pot all thick and gooey, the swish of the sleek gondolas as they streak through the water and the love songs of the Gondoliers as they glide down the canal. O Sole Mio" Q shut me up with a terse "That's Venice you idiot. You're going to Vienna Can't you get anything right? Now listen....."

THE ARMS DROP

In September 2014, the visiting Indian PM presented his Australian counterpart with 2 antique Shiva idols pertaining to the Chola Dynasty, a 900 year old bronze of Nataraja (Lord Shiva in a dancing pose) and a 1100 year o[d sculpture of Ardhanariswara (Lord Shiva as fusion of male and female forms).

Not many people are aware that this gesture by the Indian government, almost never took place, were it not for the intrepid actions of a CE agent who prefers (was forced) to be nameless and allow his superior officers to hog all the glory and limelight.

This is his story......

I was fooling around in the billiards room of our Divisional HQ Officer's mess; I was playing against the 'marker' as all the other officers were out on our annual exercise somewhere on the Gangetic plain. Why was I not with them, you may ask and what was I, your favourite young & intrepid counter espionage agent doing in the Billiard Room in the Officers Mess of an Infantry Division? To this I would have replied that they were all out on a divisional exercise that involved the air force and jumping out of planes and what not. Now I was no mean jumper out of planes myself& had been looking forward to this exercise, but since I had been detailed on a refresher course by my real boss, 'Q' I had no option but to go. 'Q'was the one person who was immune to my boyish charm, cherubic good looks and disarming smile, in fact the 'refresher' course he had sent me on was in fact one of the toughest courses in the army. How tough you ask? Think of the dreaded Para Commando course, which lasts for about 6 weeks, encapsulate that into 10 working days without any changes to the syllabus and you have my 'refresher course'. I was not clear as to what exactly was being refreshed, suffice to say I felt drained and totally fagged out at the end of it. The whole divisional campus was empty except for a few JCO's & OR's left behind as rear parties of Div HQ and a few other units that shared the campus. The marker who was also officiating as barman, had gone to fix me my usual afternoon drink, of freshly squeezed orange juice, crushed ice, all nicely blended with a couple of ounces of vodka, the sprig of mint was optional as was the lemon slice on the rim. (Sadly, neither was available). But this was a field area and one has been trained to bear such hardships with a stiff upper lip.

I was practicing my potting whilst I waited for him to return and above the sound made by the clacking of billiard balls caroming of one another as they were dispatched to their respective pockets I could hear the strident sound of the telephone ringing in the ante room. This episode took place during the good ol' days, before the advent of musical caller tunes and what not, when a telephone rang, everybody knew that it rang. I would have sent the 'marker' to answer it but since he was out on an errand of mercy on my behalf, I decided to answer the bally thing myself thereby breaking one of about a dozen cardinal rules for young officers in the field – NEVER EVER VOLUNTEER EITHER KNOWINGLY OR UNKNOWINGLY FOR ANY TASK WHEN THERE IS NO REQUIREMENT TO DO SO, AND THERE ARE NO SENIOR OFFICERS AROUND TO APPRECIATE IT. Had I let the bally thing carry on ringing or told the marker to see who that was, I would never have found myself plunged into the murky depths of arms and rare artefacts smuggling, shady foreigners, secret agencies including ours, theirs and the CIA, who always seemed to be around.

It was the ADC to the GOC or rather I should say officiating ADC to the GOC, since I was the real ADC. He was a supercilious snob who wanted my job and would do anything in his power to get it. And the only reason he didn't have it was because my boss Q decided that I should be inserted into the area to sniff out a spy ring, which I did by the way, and as a reward I was waiting for my posting orders, probably to a place with golden beaches, swaying coconut palms & dozens of nubile, willing wenches. Well at least one. I had written down my standard reward criteria, and handed it over to 'Q' at one of our rare meetings, in a disused parking lot this time. If I didn't know better I could have sworn that he deliberately chose these locations on the odd chance that I might get mugged by any one of the numerous gangs that plague the streets of our capitol these days "It doesn't always have to be abroad Sir; as long as the criteria are met it can be in India as well." He had grunted handed me my next mission, puffed a cloud of stinky cigar smoke into my face and then turned and disappeared into the shadows of the deserted parking lot but not before I heard him snigger and my keen hearing distinctly picked up the sound of paper being crumpled up into a ball. I presumed he had an eidetic memory and had committed the contents to said memory, and was now destroying the evidence. All of us agents are trained to do this sort of thing all the time but if you have an eidetic memory it helps. Anyway, to get back to my tale of woe; This ADC informed me that the GOC had left his briefcase containing data vital to our operational role, in his hut and wanted it at his location ASAP. I told him that there were no other officers available and that I was the only one in the mess, he told me to hold while he informed the GOC of this and I knew what was coming before he said it; "Old man says for you to bring it and reach here before last light" He further informed me that a vehicle had been dispatched to pick me up. "What's it about? I asked nervously, I was nervous because my posting orders were due any time, I was lying low after I had completed my refresher course and intended to hightail it out of there as soon as it came, which could be any day now, any diversion now would surely result in 'Q' cancelling my cushy posting and posting me to some arid desert outpost or worse, he may convert my present assignment to a regular posting and I would be stuck here for another 2 years.'Q' was quite capable of that

I knew for a fact that the GOC had requested that my services be extended indefinitely. While he may have been clueless about my true role in the service of our motherland he was well aware of my great social skills; my ability to organize fantastic & fabulous meals and parties in the Officer's Mess was legendary. It was these skills that the old man wanted to harness. "I'm sure I don't know" said the jerk. His days as ADC were numbered if he really didn't know any ADC worth his salt would have known, and been able to offer an opinion to boot. Maybe he wasn't telling me because he wanted me to look bad in front of the old man so that I would get booted out and he, slimy snake that he is, could slither in to my place. I, however was too much of the optimist to brood for long I figured; 8 hours' drive to out to our op location, 10 minutes to hand over the briefcase. 20 minutes for a quick bite and then 8 hours later back to base. I could still make I in time to intercept the next day's Dak. No problems! So I hurried over to the GOC's Hut, which was a stone's throw away from the mess, in fact, after a couple, he often threw stones at the mess, whenever he wanted to draw their attention, sahayaks had been told to ensure that there was always a pile of smooth rocks handy. When I said HUT, I was speaking metaphorically, some 'hut' it had a huge ante room with bar, an equally large dining room, three bedrooms, for the wife and kids when they visited, a conference hall that seated 25, a study, 3 bathrooms and a kitchen which would put quite a few of the better hotels' to shame. Anyway, I picked up the bulky briefcase from his safe, whose secret combination happened to be his son's birthday! The ADC had omitted to tell it to me hoping that I would screw up this simple task I suppose, thus paving the way for his permanent appointment. He had not counted on my safe blowing abilities however. I didn't need to blow the piece of junk since it had a ridiculously easy combination and is one of the first things they teach you in spy school.

I was driving the Jonga and since I was in a hurry I really put the pedal to the metal. The driver was understandably nervous and hung on for dear life. In fact, it took me a mere 6 ½ hours for me to reach our op location and I was immediately to escorted to the old man's caravan where I submitted the briefcase and turned to go, I had almost reached the entrance when he called me back. So close!

"Just where do you think you are going?" growled the GOC as he perused the a bulky file from the briefcase I had brought him, "Back to the Rear "I replied with forced cheerfulness "That's what you think, I have a job for you"

I slumped visibly causing him to remark"Cheer up, you can get your gear and jump out of a plane, there's one due to take off in 30 minutes, don't be late, those air force cowboys don't wait for any one, not even for me. You like jumping out of planes, don't you? When you've finished your jumps come back to me, I have a big job for you?" with that he turned his broad back to me and once more immersed himself in the file.

Two hours later I was back at his office cum residence, waiting for him, the ADC had ushered me in earlier and informed me that the GOC was finishing his bath and making himself presentable, I sniggered "that gives us about 3 hours" I ignored the ADC's horrified gasp and sat down on a nearby sofa and leafed through a weekly. The ADC hovered around the door like a mother hen, stage whispering to the horde of sahayaks that were scurrying around like blind mice, to bring ice, glasses, snacks and soda, chop chop, and where the f*** was that new bottle of Jack Daniels? "So how are things with you" I asked attempting to make some small talk to pass the time. "How did you open the safe?" he asked glaring at me "I never gave you the combination, did you break it open? Old man will be furious if you did, he will chew your balls!!" Some things never change; a hundred years down the line, if India and Pakistan have not blown each other up by then, some crusty old general would be threatening some newly inducted Subaltern, that if he didn't do some stupid thing or the other, he would CHEW HIS BALLS! "Relax pal, I never busted it open, I didn't have to, it was already open." This caused the jerk to go all pale and bloodless; after all he was responsible for the GOC's files and valuables. Anyway, the GOC finally appeared and we including the horde of sahayaks, all sprang to 'Savdhan' (Attention) "Good Evening Sir" we chorused "where's my drink "he replied as he flung himself onto a nearby sofa, his beady eyes scanned the room till they settled on me. The room went deathly quiet, "Son, come and sit next to me" he said, in a voice that I presumed he meant to be soft and affectionate but came out like a low rumble of thunder, "the rest of you fuck off!" "Even me Sir? Asked the ADC timidly "especially you" rasped the old man, winking at me, as he shifted his weight sideways to accommodate me on the couch. "That runt thinks he will become my ADC after you" he grunted "what a hope! He's a moron and an imbecile to boot." He took a huge gulp from his glass and turned to me " I have a job for you, son" Son? Son! Six months I worked for the SOB and not once did he ever call me son, Idiot, Dumbass and Shithead are just a few of the names he did call me but never son, even once. This is serious I thought to myself, old man must really want something. I waited for him to continue, "Are you familiar with the Chola Dynasty and their culture? I looked at him blankly "Chhole Sir? I asked remembering the oily but spicy lunch I had had only two days ago, "with Baturas or puris Sir?" I asked him vacuously, sticking strictly to my cover of dumb ass Captain. The GOC sighed " you're useless" he snarled, dropping his doting father act like a brick and reverting to his usual grizzly bear with a hangover voice" I'm talking about the Chola Empire that ruled southern India during the 12th& 13th centuries AD, famous for their art, their culture, their temples, their architecture and specially their bronze sculptures. Nothing remains now except a few temples and their bronze sculptures. A number of these sculptures are dotted around the world, a few in museums donated or presented to the government concerned but a majority are in the collections of unscrupulous private collectors, who spend vast amounts of money to acquire these priceless artefacts. Our local intelligence unit has intercepted a message from notorious international antique smuggler Mr. Gopal Das Bhattacharya alias 'Murthy' apparently Murthy has a gallery in New York and a workshop in Mumbai where he manufactures dozens of copies of each antique which are then exported, along with the originals concealed amongst them, to his gallery in New York; the fakes are then sold as cheap souvenirs while the originals are sold to discerning collectors who have either pre ordered them or buy them in secret auctions. "

This sounded like a mission fraught with real danger and I went into a funk. Surely this was a task more for our Para Commandos who can barge into clandestine meetings, guns blazing at the drop of a hat. They have no fear, I've seen them eat glass for god's sake "what do you want me to do Sir?" I asked timidly hoping that the tremor in my voice was not discernible. "We want you to intercept the package" he said simply "Murthy's agent in this area is a rogue police sub inspector named Bhowmik, he is unaware about the message intercept and is waiting for Murthy's courier to take delivery of the idols. The code word for the pickup is *kala pathar* (Black Stone). "where do I start sir I asked, you will be air dropped by an Antonov AN 26 aircraft over Jhalda town in Purulia District of West Bengal he saidfrom there you will make your way to Shilphore hillock where there is a state inspection bungalow. Go to room number 3 knock and give the password. the door will be opened by Bhowmik who will hand over a package to you in return you will give him this; and the old man pulled out an envelope from the briefcase and handed it over to me. What's in inside sir"I asked as I slipped the envelope into an inner pocket of my Para jacket. "It's the pay off, a cheque for 50 lakhs INR giving account number and other details. Hand that over to him pick up the package which weighs about 20 kg btw and head back to the drop zone where you will be picked up by Cheetah helicopter and dropped off at Siliguri airfield, you will be met by that shit head of an ADC, give him the package and fuck off! I never want to see you again. Here is your posting order and your movement order to Goa, though why MS Branch would want to post you there is beyond my comprehension. He threw a slim packet at me; "this is for your expenses" he growled.

I was elated! GOA!! With all the naked beeches and foreign chicks, I was off to paradise, with a slight detour to Purulia via Siliguri, nonetheless GOA! I patted my jacket pocket as I said goodbye to the ADC who was sulking in the adjacent waiting room "see you in Siliguri shit head and fairly skipped back to the hangar where a dark gloomy AN 32 was waiting along with an equally gloomy crew. I climbed aboard and sat down in one of the canvas bucket seats and felt around for my seat belt, there wasn't any, and I wasn't expecting any, I leaned back and braced myself for take-off. I had travelled in shittier aircraft before, most recently on our national carrier, so the lack of creature comforts didn't faze me. "Don't get too comfy" said the cowboy at the controls, shouting to be heard above the roar of the twin engine plane "We will be over the DZ in 25 minutes and we can't afford to circle so we are flying straight over, you will have to guide yourself towards the red flare, the flare guy is also your guide. "Okeydokey "I said happily.

On schedule, I jumped out of the Antonov, in bright moonlight, a flock of geese honked raucously at me as they flapped by, quite peeved about this intruder in their domain, I free fell for about 2000 feet and then using the steering lines glided towards the red flare which was rapidly growing in size as I drifted towards it. Suddenly I felt myself being yanked upwards and backwards, my girlish shriek was drowned out by the roar of approaching aircraft engines. It was another Antonov, and I had got caught in its backwash. For a moment I thought our cowboys had lost their bearings and were circling around hoping to ask a passing goose for directions, I suppose. On closer scrutiny I saw that I had wronged them, it was an AN 26, an earlier version of the AN 32 and it was heading straight over our makeshift DZ. it circled our DZ thrice, then veered off in a nor' nor' easterly direction, when it was about 2 KM away a string of parachutes mushroomed out behind the aircraft, like eggs from a fish. There didn't appear to be any personnel jumping out, only boxes and crates. Two green flares were winking in the wilderness below. I soft landed and rolled and unhooked my harness and made my way to towards the flare, it was spluttering and flickering and was out by the time my guide met me with hands folded, he spoke passable English, he introduced himself" Saar, myself Chandra Babu, myself special informer to SI Bhowmik and I will lead you to him" I looked around bewildered" but what about all this?" I asked, "This is not our concern saar! Second plane pilot make mistake, he see my flare and circle, and He want green flare about 50 miles from here. Come I have to take you to Bhowmik saar, he is waiting and drinking and drinking and waiting, if he drink too much he will make me dance by shooting bullets at my feet" As We trudged towards the town the stillness was shattered by the sound of low flying choppers crackling through the night, flashing lights and sirens added to the cacophony of sound that was gradually building up to a crescendo as they drew nearer, we melted into the darkness in the direction of Shilphore hillock, which thankfully was in the opposite direction. As we began the climb up the hillock, we saw someone bending and running uphill, then another and another they were all running uphill in the direction of the inspection bungalow "Ssshhh! "He pulled me down to the ground "Naxals!" he whispered "Naxals?" I echoed in horror, imagining a band of peasants in loin clothes with sickles brandished high above their heads. The image was not incorrect, however, instead of loin clothes they had substituted cut off designer jeans, Instead of sickles they had AK – 47's and instead of brandishing them high above their heads they held them very professionally to their sides as they moved forward and upward towards the inspection bungalow. The sound of small arms fire and ricocheting bullets split the air as the Naxals opened fire at the bungalow, there was no return fire as the occupants had bolted. We crested the hill in time to see two Naxals kicking down a door and spraying the room with automatic fire. They then planted explosives all around the bungalow and blew the building up. By the time we reached, the building was just a pile of smoking rubble, of Bhowmik there was no sign, room number 3 now had almost no walls but the door was still hanging on by a rusty hinge. We entered gingerly looking for bodies, thankfully there were none, but I noticed a brown paper parcel covered in dust, wedged between the bricks, I picked it up, dusted it then hefted it, about 20 kg or so I thought, fits the description. What will you do now Chandra I asked not really caring but eager to get back to the DZ. "I will drop you off at DZ and go find Bhowmik Saar." This reminded me, I pulled out the slim package the old man had flung at me, and handed it over to him "for your trouble" I said and I trotted after him holding the parcel close to my chest.

The next day the media was awash with speculation about the drop, apparently not being satisfied with one drop the AN 26 had attempted another one in the same area and was intercepted by our air force but that's another story

I had been picked up from the DZ by helicopter and dropped off at Siliguri airfield, on the tarmac, but that didn't bother me I wandered over to the commercial area and into the departure lounge where I saw the ADC waiting impatiently for me at the coffee shop. "Here's your package" I said and thrust it at his chest give it to the old man with my love and give him this too" I said, handing him the manila envelope" tell him to buy himself something pretty.

THE HOLE IN ONE

On one occasion I was posted to a Divisional HQ as a Staff Officer to the General Officer Commanding (GOC). Now although my rank was considerably higher I was perforce, because of my youthful and cherubic looks and age, compelled to pose and act as a junior Captain. In other words, I was to display no knowledge of my profession nor display any hint that I knew anything more than today's date or of what was going on around me either operationally or in general.

Since I was the junior most I was also expected to be present in the Divisional Officers' Mess every afternoon and every evening, and preside over, in a sort of 'Major Domo' capacity. I would arrive before the more 'senior' officers arrived and see that their gimlets were made properly and that the bitters angostura, being a rationed item, was used only for the General's Gimlet and nobody else's. I was also expected to be the 'fourth' in the foursome for a rubber of Bridge if no one else was available and lastly if the great man (GOC) so desired, caddy for him around our very own 18-hole golf course and in his absence for the deputy GOC and so on down the line. This tradition has long since been abolished and not a moment too soon I might add. Not that I minded it. I loved the game and caddying for senior officers gave me a chance to assess them out of the office, after all, anyone of them could be the traitor. Traitor? Oh didn't I tell you? I'm usually sent in by Q to check out leakages of information at the very highest level. Usually very senior commanders or aides to very senior Commanders. Since all the areas of operation are in non-family stations these guys are very vulnerable to the oldest trick in the little black book of the spy master – the Honey trap! My job was to prevent all this hanky panky and keep our country's secrets safe.

I also gave valuable advice and tips to whomsoever I caddied for. Needless to say said advice was never heeded because I was just a stupid Captain who knew nothing. So even if my advice to use the Sand Wedge instead of the 9 iron to get out of the sand trap and onto the green proved to be spot on, it was taken to be a mere 'fluke 'After all, how much can a dumb ass Captain know.

Before I proceed further I think I may have omitted to tell you about my mission and why I was posted there in the first place and in such a demeaning role at that. Firstly the only occasions where I will let myself be demeaned is if my country demands said demeaning. Secondly ,I would consider being demeaned if my real boss promised me a really cool posting on my accomplishing said mission and thirdly I wouldn't mind said demeaning if the chicks were hot and I had a more than 7 ¾ % chance of scoring with them, all of them or any one of them.

Since in this case all three factors had come into play I figured I could be demeaned down to a 2nd Lieutenant's rank for all I cared. But being a Captain again was also cool.

The area of my operations was notorious not only for its highly porous borders but also for its super-hot women who had only one obsession; to snare an army guy for a husband. I was told of this fact by none other than my dear old grandmother, now deceased, who gave me numerous examples of the fate of fine upstanding lads whom she knew, who fell for their feminine wiles and who never returned from this particular area, when I told her of where I would be going for the next 2 years, she proceeded to outline for me their modus operandi and all the pitfalls and traps I should beware of. I forget her exact words, as she can be even more long winded than I can be, and I had tuned out, but I know it involved these hot chicks inviting unsuspecting army guy home and slipping something into his food or drink and then getting pregnant or something equally sinister. I was all for it and smacked my lips in anticipation.

Coming back to my mission; our listening units had picked up signals and coded messages regarding smuggling of drugs and weapons from across the border. Sensitive information was being supplied in exchange for heroin, SA missile launchers and AK-47's. What was worrying the top brass in Army HQ was that given the high value of the shipments that had been intercepted, millions of dollars said my boss expansively he was not known to exaggerate, what would be the quality of the information being supplied? One could only guess but it had to be super sensitive and the leak could only emanate from the top or very close to the top. That's where I came in; to plug the leak and expose the bounder for the entire world to see or at least for my world to see.

So here I was, posing as a vacuous Captain posted as a Grade III Staff Officer in the Intelligence branch of a Divisional HQ or G3 Int or G3 Intelligence, an oxymoron I once said in an aside to the G2 Intelligence, but he didn't even crack a smile, probably didn't know the meaning of the word I thought, I mean I laughed at all his insipid jokes.

Apart from my duties in the Mess, the most arduous task that I had to perform in the office was to man the shredder and to keep a record of all shredded documents. I also coordinated the deployment of vehicles for various officers' comings and goings and detailed sahayaks for every officer in the HQ *sans me*! Apparently, I was too junior to merit a sahayak of my own, it would lower the morale of the troops if they were made to do such menial jobs I was told this in confidence by the G1, who took great pleasure in reminding me of my lowly status. According to him I was supposed to earn my right to a sahayak and maybe one day I would merit one or if I ever reached the dizzying heights of being posted as a G1 or even a Col Adm in Divisional HQ like him, maybe even two. But he looked doubtful as he said it and there was no conviction in his words.

My boss, the G1 was sharp, ambitious and humourless. I'm pretty sure he didn't like me at all but since the GOC did he had to pretend that he did too. He was a slogger if ever there was one and read every file twice before he would reply to it. His replies were always long winded and he brought his work to his basha daily in a vain effort to catch up with yesterday's backlog.

An uneventful three months passed. Mission wise that is, otherwise I was doing pretty well. I was everything you could dream of in a young Captain, although clueless about the office I kept the mess running like clockwork, since this was a field area and the GOC did dine there our mess got the best free rations ever and our cook was a treat. His meals were awesome; meat at every meal, bacon eggs and OJ for breakfast. I also ensured that everyone got a few drops of bitters in their gimlets and not just the GOC, no mean achievement I might add since Bitters was an extremely rare commodity and prized by all messes. I laughed raucously at the GOC's jokes, slapping my thigh quite often, loudly at the Deputy GOC's (no slap) and politely at the G1's though most of his were not funny at all. In my spare time I also kept trying to get snared by the pretty young khasi girls who seemed to be everywhere but whenever I came across them in the town or in the marketplace, they used to giggle and point at me and then run off. My grandmother couldn't have been more wrong. God know where she got her information from. She wouldn't have lasted a day in the intelligence gathering business.

One of the major drawbacks of this mission was that there was no way I could contact my boss in Delhi. Mobile phones had not yet been invented and the only way was through official channels which meant a whole string of army exchanges. So, either I took some leave and went to Delhi to meet my boss or I should resolve to stick it out on my own and wait for my boss to contact me.

One day I was required to be the fourth for a couple of rubbers of bridge. The GOC was playing so "no wise cracks" I was warned by the Col Adm, he was another PSO of the GOC, very pretentious and a real pain in the ass. "and don't get excited and overbid like you did the last time, you were lucky you made that hand." He was just worried because I was partnering him again and didn't want to lose too much, I had already decided to overbid every chance I got. This would endear me further to the GOC and the G1 who was his partner. Whenever the GOC played he picked the best player available and that was that. No 'cut for partners after every rubber' crap. That way he never lost. I was a good player but since I was undercover I was forced to play like a dummy, and very often ended up being the dummy even when the call was mine. Very often, during breaks for dealing or while snacks and drinks were being served the GOC would bring up some work-related problem and would discuss it with his two principal advisors. I would pretend to listen intently all the time thinking of some cute khasi girl who had looked at me and giggled, did that mean she liked me or did it mean she would only go out with me if I gave her two blankets and a kilo of sugar? But today my ears really picked up when I heard them mentioning words and phrases like "change of Orbat" "and operational role being revised." He also told the two PSO's to give him ideas of how to spend his Training Grant financial allotment which was in excess of five lacs of rupees. (peanuts today but a huge amount in those days)

It was almost 8 pm by now and the game of bridge had deteriorated into a mini conference as the three began to discuss the revised operational role of the formation. I was sent to the G1's basha to get his briefcase which contained the top-secret letters defining our new role.

The basha was in darkness except for the bedroom which was brightly lit, I could see someone moving around, probably one of his sahayaks I thought and was about to call out to him to fetch the briefcase when I noticed a bright flash coming from inside, I crept up to the door silently and was taken aback by what I saw. One of the sahayaks, a Nepali guy called Vir Bahadur had carefully laid out the contents of the briefcase onto the bed and was carefully photographing each sheet with a Kodak Pocket Instamatic 60 using a flash cube. That was the flash I saw. I knew these pocket instamatics as I had used them myself for similar jobs many times. From the number of burnt out cubes on the bed it seemed that his work was almost over and he carefully began putting them back into the briefcase. I had found my leak. It took me but a moment to pounce on the blighter and de camera him. I called for help at the top of my voice as I tied the amateur photographer's hands behind his back, just as we had been taught in Intelligence school, with the G1's regimental lanyard, it was a flashy orange Brigade of the Guards thing and the G1 used to spare no effort to remind me of the greatness of his regiment and the insignificance of mine, I told a couple of sahayaks who had wandered in from other bashas to call the G1 here and to tell Col Adm to call the Military Police. The G1 was in a funk and the GOC was understandably, furious. Then the big boys took over.

Under intense interrogation, an euphemism for the third degree, Vir Bahadur confessed that he had been recruited 9 months ago when he had been first assigned to the G1 as his Sahayak, it was a typical honey trap operation, the cute young khasi girl who had promised to marry him if he did as they told him, was actually in her 30's, already married and with quite a few children of her own. Thanks to this guy, the movement had received a heap of stuff from across the border including a steady stream of arms and ammunition for their struggle for an independent homeland, plus the drugs they sold enabled them to pay their cadres who were reluctant to struggle unless they got paid.

A total of eight men and two women were arrested from the surrounding villages, a huge cache of arms ammunition rocket launchers and about three kilos of pure quality heroin was found during one of the many raids, each raid led to more round ups and each round up led to more raids.

More importantly from my bosses' point of view I was a hero of sorts because I was instrumental in busting a spy ring that had spread its tentacles far and wide. In fact, it turns out that the leak was from a sister division in the plains and they rounded up quite a few locals who had infiltrated the division as sahayaks and mess staff. If the contents of the G1's briefcase landed up in enemy's hand the consequences would have been catastrophic and a lot of heads would have rolled, including the GOC's. All for a little bit of nooky. Once again I was thankful for the great restraint and will power, I had demonstrated while fighting off the hordes of Khasi hotties who were trying to entrap me. At least that's what I'm going to say in my report.

A few days later while I was caddying for the GOC, I was still undercover and awaiting my cool posting, he noticed that I was limping a bit as I hefted both his and my golf bags from one shoulder to the other as we trudged along towards the eighteenth hole. I was part of the playing quartet this time but still had the honour of carrying the GOC's bags "What's the matter, Son?" he enquired gruffly "tired already?" and I saw him look mischievously at the Col Adm who was partnering him, "Sir" I replied "What we need are a few silent reconnaissance vehicles for missions beyond and behind enemy lines" "what are you talking about? " asked the new G1 who was my partner "Don't talk nonsense to the General you idiot" but the GOC remained silent as he putted in his last shot, a birdie to finish up top of the leader board with a score of 6 under par, miles ahead of the rest of us, and that was how it would stay as long as he was GOC, he was silent till he saw his jeep driving up, he turned to me and asked "are they expensive because we can really use a few" "about fifty thousand per piece or thereabouts" I replied "put up a statement of case(SOC) for about five" said the general to the Col Adm as he signalled for his jeep driver to get out "come with me son" said the general as he sat behind the wheel and the driver dove into the backseat. I hefted both our golf bags into the vehicle and was about to get in when the Col Adm caught me by the elbow and asked "what was that again? Silent what?" "A silent reconnaissance vehicle, required for missions beyond and behind enemy lines." I replied as the general gunned the engine of the jeep and headed for the Officers' Mess for a cup of hot tea with cucumber sandwiches.

That is how our golf course got its battery powered golf carts, but not before we had to pass on a couple of them to the Army golf course along with a copy of the SOC, which I am given to understand was used verbatim by them when they projected *their* requirement for *Silent Reconnaissance Vehicles for Missions Beyond and Behind Enemy Lines.* That also explains why they got into all that trouble later.

THE INVITATION

Now that it's all over, I can safely include this little episode amongst the shinier jewels in my memoirs, what's more, I, I can narrate it without fear of reprisals or injury to reputation or even of governmental denial for that matter.

Aren't I a little too young to be writing 'memoirs' you may be tempted to ask, maybe you're right, after all, I am under 25, it's just that the very nature of my job coupled with my passionate love of country and my boundless zeal and willingness to risk my life at the drop of a hat, makes it likelier and likelier that every mission my heartless boss 'Q' sends me out on could very well be my last and I just want to keep the record straight. If I were to get neutralized during a 'black op' I would officially not have existed at all except in a file stored in an anonymous cupboard in a basement somewhere in Kashmir House. This way, by putting pen to paper, in a manner of speaking I would at least be alive between these few pages. In the end, is it not *that* what every man is striving for, to leave something behind for posterity? Now back to my tale;

Firstly, when they declared that the ceremony at the Abbey was attended by 1900 invitees, I would like to mention that only 1899 turned up also the reception, planned for 630 but only 629 could attend and the little intimate affair for 300 close friends, only 299 could make it. How do I know these statistics? 'Coz I was the missing invitee on all three occasions. Thanks to my Boss Q who craved anonymity and insisted that all his agents do the same. He saw himself as a faceless shadow while I, on the other hand, saw myself to be modelled more on the lines of the 007 variety. You see, I had unknowingly saved the best man's life a few years ago and had not given the matter any further thought, I didn't know who he was until much later. I only knew him as 'Red'

It was in Jun 2007 and I had just completed an eventful week in Ottawa with the CNSC (Canadian Nuclear Safety Committee,) and since I had a bit of spare time on my hands I thought I would drop in on an old school friend of mine who had relocated to Canada (a country attached to North America, at the top) after doing his basic medicine over here; he went there and became a neurotic or neuro psychiatrist or something that had neuro in it. It's something that the Canucks can't get enough of apparently, and my friend is in tremendous demand there and he makes pots of money.

We kind of drifted apart and lost contact during the dark ages (before Internet) and then one fine day he just rings me up out of the blue, and invites me over for a re union and a bit of sky diving.

There were four of us in this re union, my friend, let's call him Shabby, 'cos although it's only a fake name it sort of describes him to a Tee. Then there was Giddy (Govind), Dizzy (Dasrath) and me. Lifelong buddies, we were linked by imperishable memories having all done a stretch together at the good old 'Alma Mater' when striplings. Though separated by time, distance and profession, no closer friends could there have been except maybe for the three musketeers and if so, then by maybe a whisker.

We all happened to share a love of jumping out of airplanes, they, for the sport of it and because it allows them to de-stress, and self because sometimes in my line of work it becomes necessary in order to stay alive.

We were over South-eastern Alberta flying over an area called Medicine Hat; Shabby and Giddy had already jumped and no doubt were opening cans of Fosters and Dizzy was making his final preparations which invariably consisted of praying fervently to his maker and making all sorts of extravagant promises, of treading on the straight and narrow if only just this once, his parachute opened when it should. We had been earlier informed by the club that we had a sky shark in our area (the Canadian Army was there), but just for basic jumps, which was about 5000 ft below the height we were jumping from.

I looked around as there were a good 90 seconds before my jump. The pilot had suddenly veered towards the left a manoeuvre not called for at this time as it took us towards the Canadian DZ. While I took all this in I saw that a stick parachutists were floating down towards the DZ, the Canadian aircraft, a CC-115 Buffalo, cargo/transport aircraft, was in the process of discharging its last parachutist , had begun to turn Nor' Nor' East and the last jumper was falling his mandatory free fall before his chute opened. I could see all this since I was above him at a height of 15000 and heading South South West'. I thought I would jump as soon as his chute opened so I waited... and waited suddenly it became clear to me that the last jumper's chute was not going to open and that the poor soldier was in big trouble. Without thinking I catapulted myself from the Cessna towards the hapless guy who was spinning uncontrollably like a starfish, I pressed my arms to my sides and rocketed towards him like an arrow and shouted at him not to panic within seconds I was hovering above him and In a deft manoeuvre which I had practiced before, caught the poor unfortunate in a firm clasp and stopped his tailspin. I quickly opened my own chute and we drifted down towards the Canadian DZ. Once we were firmly on good old terra firma he thanked me profusely, there were tears in his eyes I think "thanks mate, yer saved me life thass for sure" "my pleasure" I mumbled feeling totally embarrassed by the fuss the rest of the blokes were making of me. My hair was ruffled and I was thumped on the back countless times till I thought I would surely cough up a lung or two. Tankards of beer appeared as if by magic and quite a fuss was made of me.

A vehicle was standing by, courtesy the Canadian Army to take me to my mates who must have seen the amazing rescue first hand and I couldn't wait to get back and gloat. As I got into the left-hand drive Jeep my 'rescuee' came to see me off. He thanked me once again and I was amazed that he spoke the language so well cos' normally it's very difficult to understand the English used by the Brits, this guy spoke it almost as well as we did, and we exchanged names and mobile numbers, I told him mine and he said his mates all called him 'Red' cos of his red hair and that since they were in training he did not have a mobile. Now that his helmet was removed I could see that the sobriquet was justly deserved.

We shook hands and I drove off to be re united with my friends where I was soundly criticized for not having landed in our own DZ, and secondly for not having free fallen the full distance. At least another 2500 feet before you pulled the chord I was advised by them. We then sat in the afternoon sun waiting for our own club vehicle to pick us up. It was not due for another 20 minutes. Enough time for a can of Fosters and another bash at 'Hallelujah' in the style of Leonard Cohen, I thought no more about that incident till now. The papers were full of the engagement and of course the 'best man' got a mention too. He looked familiar but I couldn't precisely say why.

Imagine the buzz when the Three Royal Invitations were received three years later, I was forced to admit that I did not know anyone in the royal household leave alone the best man and that maybe there had been a royal goof up, my boss rang MI-6 at Vauxhall Cross and asked his counterpart to ask around. But MI-6 knew the reason and my boss listened for a couple of minutes and then hung up. "The British Government is grateful to you and Her Majesty wants to make you a Knight. When you were in Canada you just happened to have saved the best man's life, why was this not in your report? I" "I saved a guy named Red "I shot back "how was I to know who he really was. Nobody told me. "This is great I better get started with packing and apply for visas "I said bravely but my boss was already wearing his 'we all make sacrifices for the motherland' face; "there's a problem" he said gravely "we can't let you go" And that was that.

My boss was adamant that I should not go and he had hundreds of reasons ; it would blow my cover, my real reason for being in Canada was geo political and if it were known that I had been there at that particular time, spy masters all over the world would soon put two and two together and figure out the reason for the Canadian Governments amazing U-turn in supplying nuclear fuel to our country at the same time that our neighbours' nuclear chief was exposed to the west for proliferation as being a bit too coincidental.

So as usual I bargained for another cushy posting and we settled on a city known for its culture and love for life. Actually, *lust* for life my boss whispered as he signed my posting order with a flourish in his signature alphabet and his signature green. But that's another yarn...

THE LITTLE DRUMMER BOY

I was sitting just 2 rows behind the President and the Chief Guest, I can't say who he was but he was the leader of the second largest democracy in the world. The occasion was the Beating Retreat held every year, three days after our nations Republic Day Parade was held. In my humble opinion this ceremony is far more poignant than the RD Parade; I can watch the entire RD parade without my eyes getting even moist but when it comes to the Retreat and the playing of the Last Post and the playing of "Abide with Me" from the ramparts of North Block, the chimes from the tubular bells echoing across the vast concourse that was Vijay Chowk, always manages to get a lump firmly lodged in my throat and no matter how hard I try to appear as a manly man, the waterworks flow freely and I'm not ashamed to admit it. It's not a crime to love one's country is it? At least not for now but with the way things are going I'm not too sanguine about the future. For me it has always been the flag first and everything else next. Anyway, back to my narrative and please don't go wandering off again for I promise you this one's a real doozy.

I surveyed the enclosure and the tight security cordon guarding our VVIP's, I was not a VVIP or a VIP or even an IP I was just a P and was here courtesy my Boss Q, as my so called reward for my role in thwarting a major calamity with catastrophic consequences, actually I was there as a filler, the idea being to show the cameras and the world that our president and his guest did not need bullet proof glass partitions, when they were in public. Every one of us in the rows behind them had a security clearance higher than a Deputy Secretary so there was no threat there. Everyone knew that Depsecs and higher were all wusses. A point of interest here for the curious, how do we stand in the number of declared VVIPs? Well America has 242, UK has 140, France has 113, China has 442, Russia has 412 & our nation has a mere 5, 42,501 or so I'm told!

I was sure that no one not even the President had any idea of just how close they had come to being blown up by the jihadis, had they any inkling I would be sitting between them. I watched the ceremony it was drawing to a close, the bands were marching up to the podium and all the Kettle Drummers were detaching themselves from their respective bands and merging into a single line, aligned height wise, shortest in the middle and it was in this area I that I concentrated on, then I saw him, all decked up in the ceremonial uniform of his regiment, it was hard to believe by just looking at him the mayhem he was capable of unleashing or the cold blooded cruelty he was capable of. I had had a glimpse of both these aspects of him not so long ago. In fact, it was because of him that a major calamity was averted and the Republic Day celebrations could go on. I spotted him right in the centre of the line-up, resplendent in his dark green tartan kilt; Gurkha cap at a jaunty angle, the kettle drum hung from his belt and seemed to almost touch the ground, his face stoical and emotionless, eyes staring straight ahead, as if looking at me directly. He was, and having caught my eye, he looked at his drum which he was whacking pretty heartily, he caught my eye again looked down again at the drum and winked slyly at me, then he was staring ahead again his face stoical as before.

It took me awhile to figure out the reason for his Mona Lisa like smirk but I whittled them down one by one until there was only one possibility left; I was horrified, dumbstruck and flabbergasted all at once, was it even possible? Now my own cherubic exterior hides a streak of ruthlessness and cruelty that is second to none and the hall mark of every remorseless assassin but it pales in comparison to those displayed by Thapa, and when he requested that he be allowed to interrogate the terrorist we had captured, I almost, but didn't (thank goodness), declined his request. But I digress, back to my story.

His name was Raj Bahadur Singh, from one of the most feared regiments in our army. He was a loner and those in the unit who knew him, feared him and left him alone those, that didn't know him, learned the hard way to leave him alone. There are at least two one eared and one, one- eyed Havildars (now posted out) who found out the hard way, it seems that they each developed amorous inclinations towards him and had approached him after Rum Parade. He was known as Thapa (a sort of generic name used in the army to describe all peoples of his facial appearance) and had grown up in the mountains around Batalik. As a youngster he was a hunter and could stalk, kill and skin a fox in under 10 minutes flat, he had developed a flair for skinning wild animals and his expertise was invariable called in on "Meat days" Now, while every Gurkha worth his name could decapitate a sheep with a single stroke hardly anyone could skin the animal as expertly as Thapa and his beloved chakmak could. When not on duty Thapa spent his waking hours honing the blade of his Kukri and chakmak, he used a Karda for sharpening the blade of his kukri and the chakmak for skinning and doing jobs for which the 14-inch blade could not do. The Chakmak was a much smaller blade, about 4 inches long and this he wielded with great dexterity.

I knew him because he had been detailed to my squad by Q who had assembled a reconnaissance team to verify some disturbing signal chatter that had been picked up by our wireless surveillance section in the Batalik sector. Our friendly neighbours, who were still smarting from the thrashing we gave them last August in the Kargill sector, was up to something and they were looking to exact revenge of some kind, the question was what sort of revenge and more importantly when and where?

Thapa knew this sector like the back of his hand and eagerly volunteered to be scout. There were two signalmen who could decipher most codes and could pick out a pin dropping in a thunder storm. Of course, there was muscle, 4 super commandos and I was the squad leader. We were embedded with an LRP (long Range Patrol) and were to report back to base in fifteen days. We were back in three.

The patrol had reached Batalik the first night and set up makeshift camp, Thapa who knew this area backwards requested permission to scout ahead up to Jubar also known as Pt 4279. My two signalmen set up their gear which included a VHF radio scanner; it was rumoured that the jihadi's were using a new technology for communication called YSMS, which basically paired smart phones with VHF Radio sets. YSMS was a new technology which both sides were still experimenting with and basically allowed line of sight encrypted mobile communications without mobile towers, very hard to hack but the guys in R&D had prepared this sliding frequency gizmo to try out.

so one the first night Thapa was out, my two signalmen were hunched over their equipment sweeping the range bandwidth, trying to find a bandwidth to pair the Samsung smartphone with. I strolled over to where the super Commandos were sitting sharing a bottle of what seemed to be very expensive whiskey. The days when they drank rum and chewed glasses were long gone I guess. But the other aspects had not changed, they were horsing around and arm wrestling one another. They called out to me to join them and as I sat down, I was immediately challenged to a duel by one of the beefier ones. This was not the first time that I had been challenged because of my slim, athletic physique, but I decided to cut this short and as he stretched out his heavily tattooed hand I grabbed it and applied the Wuxi Finger Hold I learnt this courtesy my friend Kung Fu Pandey, and within seconds he was out, presumably somewhere in the spirit realm where he would stay for a couple of hours. The others cooled down rapidly and sat down around me and offered me a drink. Whaddyouknow! Inside the fancy bottle was indeed good old fashioned XXX rum! I was content, another peg or two and probably that nice bottle would have been nicely chewed and spat out in neat piles. About mid night the fire had begun to wane and the super commandos were all tuckered out and snug in their sleeping bags when I was shaken awake by one of the signalmen "Sir, we have intercepted a message from YSMS channel. Since it was a text message he had noted it down and thrust the sheet of paper under my nose. It read

Wedding date has been set. Aka has given consent chhoti bacchii has been collected from school. Give plenty of cds to guests Cdscvs and all dried fruit with chhotibacchis father.

226

Venue is known to you. Make sure you reach in time to greet guests May Allah bless the couple. God is great,

I think the Pakis are slipping up, so confident were they in this paired end to end encryption technology of theirs and buoyed by the fact that our media had made such a fuss about our inability to decipher any intercepts on these frequencies they hardly made any effort to actually encrypt the text, this code was ridiculously easy to crack but what was not so easy were the details, it was obvious that a terror attack was being planned but the where when & who needed definition. I WhatsApped the message to Q and went to sleep.(btw WhatsApp also uses end to end encryption that only the sender and receiver can read)

Thapa came back at about noon the next morning, hot, sweaty and panting from exertion "there are 10 of them and will be here by 4 pm; they probably use the ravines to infiltrate, we can cut them off there.

And that's how it happened we killed 8 of them (they killed themselves actually as soon as they realized they were being ambushed but, in the report, that I would submit, we killed them) Thapa managed to knock out one of them before he could bite down on his cyanide pellet. Turns out he was the leader, Abu Khaled or something; these guys all have impossible names. The 10th man got away. The countdown had begun. We needed to know who when where and how and there was no way this guy was going to talk if we asked him politely but I tried anyway. But it was no use every time I asked him a question he would yell out something in Arabic and then demand in English that he be treated as per Geneva Conventions! Some nerve these guys have got. Any way after asking him politely 10 to 15 times I signalled to my squad of super commandoes to give it a try. They were only too happy to have a go at him. First they almost drowned the guy by waterboarding him, then they tried torture, breaking fingers and toes at random, extracting some teeth with pliers and finally they tried to brand him with hot iron spikes, that was when Thapa intervened and begged me to let him have a go, but we had to let him be alone with him, no one was allowed to be present not even I. the clock was ticking. I figured what the hell! "Don't kill him if he doesn't talk we'll need to take him back to HQ for more intense interrogation."

I left one of the super commando's outside an abandoned sheep herder's hut which was about 100 metres away, with instructions not to go in no matter what. We came back to our temporary base

I tried to radio base camp for a chopper to take our precious cargo back pretending all the time not to notice the screams which were audible even at this distance away. After about 10 minutes a white faced shaken super commando appeared "Sir" he croaked "he is asking for salt and red chilli powder" I nodded "Check Murli's knapsack, these thumbis always have some with them" the commando ruffled through the knapsack grabbed the condiments and scooted out of the tent still shaking. The screams resumed with increased intensity and then stopped, the silence was eerie. Shortly the commando appeared once again this time grinning from ear to ear "he broke him, we got every single detail" this was indeed good news, we could move on. I had finally gotten through to Q and he was sending a chopper in an hour. I strolled over to the hut and met Thapa standing outside "don't go inside sir, please" so I stood outside "how is he?" I asked "dead" he replied and that was that.

The strike was planned for the 28th of January during the Beating of Retreat. The explosives were planted inside the VIP sofas, first three rows; the timers were preset to detonate during the fly past or if earlier by remote by the 10th man who was to be present under the guise of being a waiter from the presidential palace. His documents were impeccable and able to withstand the rigid scrutiny of our law enforcement agencies. In fact, he had been allotted the role of serving the chief guests the customary juice/soft drink of choice. In fact, even if the 10th man had not made it, the timers on the detonators would have ensured that none of the attendees in that VVIP pavilion would have come out alive. The rest of the squad were to randomly spray the crowds with automatic fire. The Pakis would have had their revenge. But thanks to our little drummer boy this tragedy had been averted. The drummers having performed their drum routines were moving back to their respective bands, Thapa's band was closest to us and I saw him for the last time smartly beating out a tattoo on his drum with its newly replaced drum skin.

Next day I received a picture from Thapa on WhatsApp. It showed Thapa looking as fierce as ever, in his ceremonial outfit complete with drum. The caption read "Me and Abu Khaled."

THE RAVEN

Okay, so I'm not really an ADC, I simply tell everyone that I am, "ADC to some prick general" sounds much better than "Junior Staff Officer to some prick general" doesn't it? If I were to write my memoirs, "Confessions of an Aide de Campe (ADC)" surely reads better than "Confessions of a Junior Staff Officer"

A Junior Staff Officer who I might add, was forced to be nameless and to go undercover and perform incredible feats of bravery, violence, and sacrifice. The icing on the cake was that all this was to be done anonymously. Considering all that I have done, in any other nation this would warrant a ton of medals and at least two invitations to dine with our supreme commander. But here? All I get is verbal abuse from a crusty old fart who doesn't seem to have an iota sympathy or compassion in him. But I love my job however and wouldn't trade places with anyone for it, neither with Bill Gates nor with the King of England nor anyone else, okay maybe with Baba Ramdev! He's so cool!

Actually, most of the time I did play the role of a junior Staff Officer or SO, which does not sound all that glamorous. My boss Q, I will come back to him later, had in the past, tried to insert me as an ADC into the various trouble spots, whenever he thought something fishy was going on. But my reputation as an unmasker of the corrupt and traitorous seemed to precede me and hoary old generals threatened him with stay orders from the highest courts of the land if he tried any funny stuff. In the old days, mused 'Q', these guys would have been lined up and shot summarily, Q being of the old school himself, yearned for the return of those days and sometimes when he thought no one was around he was known to hum that old Joan Baez favourite "Those were the days my friend" under his breath. Now, he continued to muse, it was all about welfare and pensions and extended service. Q's view on pensions and retirement was not unique "we fed them clothed them and paid them for 30 years " he would fume " they should have saved up their money instead of buying cars, motor bikes, eating in fancy restaurants and buying duplex houses" this view was similar to that of many senior bureaucrats in the government today; when a man had gotten too old to ride a horse, the kindest thing one can do for him was a quick shot to the head, not to stick him behind a desk and constantly find ways and means to keep him busy besides it meant a leaner, meaner, and most importantly, an almost non-existent pension bill. Sadly, such noble traditions were discontinued after Aurangzeb. To this day our generals are molly coddled and our pension bill consumes almost the entire defence budget leaving us just enough left to buy a couple of boxes of ammunition and a few hand grenades.

So, I had to compromise and allow myself to be placed in humiliating appointments such as GSO3 or G3 for short or Camp Commandant with instructions to go nowhere near the Camp. Now some of you guys in the know may well ask, why, for crying out loud, how was it that someone such as I, could not be accommodated in a more senior/glamorous appointment such as a G2 or even G1 for that matter. The problem lies in my looks; I look too young; having been cursed with eternal cherubically good looks, boyish charm and a disarming smile, this was my Achilles Heel. And while this may work to my advantage in the field, it was a huge disaster when it came to promotions and awards. The promotion committees invariably consisted of a group of fogeys who looked as if they had joined the army during the days of the Great Sepoy Mutiny, and anyone who did not look to be at least a hundred or in the region thereof, didn't deserve consideration. Q, I know for a fact used to invariably attach 8x10 colour glossies of myself to my dossier, thus whenever it was pulled for consideration the vetting clerk would take one look at my profile and mutter "No way! Too young, too young" under his breath" let's promote that bald guy instead, he looks to be a sprightly sixty-five at least" and throw my dossier out before it even reached the first round. When Q would then call me to break the sad news about my being looked over, again, he would make clucking noises and say "Too bad son, I really thought you would make it this time, I gave you very high scores." Sometimes he would throw in a cool posting to one of the great metropolises to soften the blow and cheer me up. Except for the one time that he forgot, he cancelled every one before the ink was even dry on the order.

I was in Paris as the new millennium dawned; I had been shanghaied by my boss 'Q' the previous week from my cosy little nest anchored off the banks of the river Adyaar where I was playing 'house' in a houseboat with a cute young Madrasi girl who was teaching me a thing or two about kathakali and I was teaching her a thing or two about interrogation techniques and how to not betray her country's secrets even though she was being ravished repeatedly by a dashing young counter espionage officer (me) She didn't have much resistance I must say, and due to my relentless interrogatorial techniques, she had already revealed the fake nuclear weapons' location, the fake nuclear codes and identities of three of our agents across the border, I was halfway through my next interrogation regarding the fake locations of our Armoured Divisions when Q's idiotic goons barged in and with nary a thought about my delicate position, whisked me back to HQ

Apparently, our bellicose neighbour, you know whom I'm talking about, was acting up again, Q began his briefing without preamble, after the attack on our parliament, things had hotted up exponentially and had almost reached boiling point, troops were being massed by each side along the border and daily ceasefire violations were too numerous to count. Something had to be done and public posturing aside, an honourable means to defuse the situation, without loss of face on either side, had to be arrived at. The Americans, the Brits, the Frogs, all sponsors of the other guy I might add and of course our only friend in this pack the Ruskies had all wearied themselves out from repeatedly asking the both of us to stand down. Back channel diplomacy and dirty tricks were the last resort. That's where I came in.

The current dictator was a pompous ass, and his ego would allow his nation to be destroyed rather than back down from the inevitable confrontation that was looming on the horizon. Q's counterpart Aziz, had contacted him and made a deal; the thug, who had promoted himself to President along the way, had sent his immediate family, consisting of his wife, son & daughter to Paris ostensibly for attending a symposium honouring the father of their nation, but everyone knew it was to get them out of the way in case we bombed the hell out of their presidential palace. At this point I felt that I had to ask 'Q' an intelligent question; well I thought it to be so "Sir" I asked brightly "if both our countries have the same mother, doesn't being the father of their nation make him the uncle of our nation?" fortunately I had a reflexes like quicksilver and I had anticipated his reaction so I leapt like a Thompsons gazelle being chased by a couple of lionesses, high and to the left while his knuckle whizzed by, low and to the right. Like the proverbial arrow that was shot into the air, I descended to terra firma I knew not where, actually it was onto a coffee table (Q has so much junk scattered around his office) and I bruised my shin causing me to hop around on one leg. Once order was restored Q continued his briefing. "Do you know what a Raven is?" he asked me like a schoolmaster questioning an errant student. This one I knew, I could hit it for a six, right out of the stadium "Sir it's a large black crow with glossy black plumage" I answered confidently "you are an ass" growled Q "didn't you even read any of the books prescribed at Spy school?" I looked suitably chastised and hung my head in shame, assuming the duffer position that is guaranteed to induce remorse and sympathy in the hardest of hearts, and it worked, Q explained it to me in a fatherly manner something akin to a father explaining to his mentally challenged teenage son about the birds and the bees. Apparently, a raven was a male f*emme fatale* who seduces females in order to gain intelligence for his country. WOW! I had not heard beyond the phrase 'seduces females' & 'country' nothing else registered. "you are to make friends with this girl he said showing me a postcard sized photograph of a girl, who, for want of a better word looked like a dog, a schnauzer to be precise, minus the long scraggly beard. "Who is she?" I gasped "Never you mind who she is", said Q "you are doing this for your country.

Now, as the saying goes, is the time for all good men to come to the aid of the country" he said smugly, clearly enjoying himself "what is my mission Sir" I asked fearing the worst "Why young man you are to woo her!" Woo her? Woo her?? Who even says the word woo now days? "Woo who?" I asked querulously sounding like quite the nervous owl, "You woo Lyla, she is the daughter of that blow hard from across the border, who is at the moment is amassing his troops on our borders. Thousands of lives will be lost if this lunatic is not contained. By the way we are working with our counterparts from across the border, on this one. It is essential that you do your part for the plan to succeed, so get her to love you, which considering what a little turd you are, is a pretty tall order. You must do whatever you can or whatever it takes. Buy her flowers, trinkets, French perfume, lingerie, take her to shadowy candle lit, bistros, walks along the Seine show her the Left Bank, Right Bank the Louvre, show her that you can be sensitive take her to the top of the Eiffel tower and deep down into the catacombs and whisper sweet nothings into her ear, win her heart." "Then what?" I asked "just follow instructions, I will be contacting you from time to time, each time I will give you your further instructions. Paris is the city of lovers so I want you to do a lot of snuggling, cuddling and smooching, no one is going to bother you. There are no Anti Romeo Squads in Paris "Smooching?" I interjected "have you seen her? She's a dog! What will my friends say, I will be ruined, and no more parties with beautiful models and starlets for me. I beg you Sir, release me from this cruel game; I will do anything you want. Do you want me to 'Off' the Vice chief?" I knew that Q had a running feud with him for a number of years "I will do it in a jiffy, wait here, I've got my Glock with me, it will only take a few minutes, I'll be right back" but Q was relentless "You're not going anywhere you moron, Do you think that if I wanted to off that SOB I would trust a blabbermouth like you to do it? I Might as well off him on national TV. Anyway, that's not the point. You will smooch, cuddle and snuggle and like it, that's an order, do you understand? I'm getting fed up with all this whingeing and whining of yours. Man up, you are a soldier for God's sake. Suck it up you miserable worm. It's for your country Do it or else.... Once he had calmed down he continued " You are to accompany the Military Secretary and his family to Paris, he is attending a conference and his wife wants to do some shopping, you will be posing as his son Aayan who is sick and in the military hospital here, so please don't go gallivanting around the left bank like a drunken maniac as is your wont when not under my close scrutiny, Aayan is a very well behaved and conservative kid, quite the Mama's boy if you ask me, if you get caught by the gendarmes or the DPSD (French equivalent of our organization) you will bring shame and disgrace to the Military Secretary, and he is front runner for Chief next year. So, God help you if you screw this up. He will chew your balls." "Sir No Sir" I shouted, elated at this opportunity to score with a French chick in my spare time, (number three on my bucket list) I suddenly remembered my house guest back on a house boat on the Adyaar, I couldn't remember if those goons had untied her from the bed post or not, such was the rush, to get me onto the next flight to Delhi. I just hoped for the best.

I reported to the MS and his wife in the wee hours of a late December night at the international airport. "Sir,

Ma'am I am your son sir" I said in a loud clear voice that rang out across the concourse "Sssshhh! Hissed the MS glaring at me, "I know who you are you idiot!" His wife, a plump homely lady placed a pudgy hand on her husband's arm and said softly "now dear he is just a boy, you are scaring him." Then she turned towards me, grabbed my arm and yanked me towards her bosom "come here son, don't mind him he is just a big bully" her pudgy arms smashed me into her ample breasts and held me there, I realized that if I didn't come up for air soon I was likely to asphyxiate, with a mighty heave I surfaced "Hi Mom!" I said gasping for air. As I disentangled myself I heard a disembodied, girlish snigger "my mommy likes you my mommy likes you!" It said, I broke free from her clutches and found myself face to face with a cute snubbed nose girl of indeterminate age, though probably in her mid-teens, judging by the development of her protruding chest. "Who are you?" I gasped "I thought I was an only child" I looked accusingly towards the general, "She is youngest daughter of my late sister's husband's youngest brother" "we call her Priyanka and she calls me mommy, she is just visiting" interjected mom helpfully "I've heard about you" warned the general, wagging a stubby finger in my direction "so no funny stuff. If I have even the slightest doubt that your intentions towards her are not honourable I will chew your ba... er.. Ears off" he said grumpily remembering just in time that his wife and Priyanka were listening in eagerly. I hung my head and let my eyes tear up; I was immediately engulfed by a tsunami of warm soft fragrant flesh, YSL I mused, remembering the slim nubile French Martinique chick I had sniffed on my way back from the buffet table during a luncheon thrown by the RM for the visiting French delegation, who were hoping for a huge order for their Dassault Rafale. "Leave him alone "she snarled at him, like a plump tigress protecting her unbelievably handsome cub.

The flight itself was uneventful, though I must admit that the air hostesses paid me an undue amount of attention, maybe they found me irresistible and wanted to bask in the warmth and sensuousness that I seemed to exude, or maybe it was because the brat Priyanka, who was sitting beside me was pressing the overhead button an undue amount of times. I prefer to believe the former.

Charles de Gaulle airport was nothing like the one we had left back home, chalk and *paneer*, apples and *karelas*. (Italicized words referring to the one we had left back home) it was all concourses and mezzanines and *boutiques hors taxes* (Duty Free Shops) We hung around the VIP lounge waiting for the Charge de affairs to sort out our documentation and then whisk us off in a limousine to our five starred hotels. I tried my best to catch the eye of the French air hostesses, who were clacking to and fro in their stiletto heels but to no avail, it's as if I was invisible. So, I gave up, in any case French air hostesses were known to be frigid so maybe I had dodged a bullet there; So far so good, I was sitting in the lap of luxury and everybody from the embassy bowed and scraped in front of us.

The hotel was a totally different kettle of fish. It was owned and staffed almost exclusively by the French with hardly the ubiquitous Malayali or Bihari to be seen, though I did spot a Mallu steward in one of the dining rooms but he avoided our little group like the plague. When I asked him later, why he did not want to greet a fellow country man of his, he told me that our countrymen are the worst tippers ever, they convert every foreign currency into Rupees and then tip accordingly, in Rupees, and if the rest of the staff found out about his connection, he would be saddled with us for the entire duration of our stay without hope of any monetary gratuity. He had a point, so I tipped him with a Ten Rupee coin I had found in my pocket and went on my way. I would be damned if I were to be the only one to be different.

The frogs treat every guest like crap and I'm happy to report that there was no discrimination on grounds that the frog government was footing the bill for our stay, we were treated no different, the concierge sneered at us as he directed the bellhop to carry our luggage to our rooms, I had a suite courtesy my AMEX Platinum Card and the MS had two but thankfully on a different floor. The bell hop glowered at us accusingly as if reprimanding us for interrupting his cigarette break and the lift attendant yawned in our faces as he punched the appropriate buttons. Liberty equality and I forget the rest, I guess.

Q contacted me the next day. "Listen carefully" he whispered "I am going to say this only once" he began "Allo! Allo" I bellowed into my iPhone, borrowing the word from the frogs that used it frequently when in telecommunication with each other "Allo! Who is speaking? "It's me you idiot! Now listen carefully" "Allo! I can't hear you, Say again, Over!" "I said listen carefully you moron, this is an unsecured line so I am going to say this only once you imbecile, and stop bellowing like that, I know you can hear me perfectly" he seemed to be foaming at the mouth but since I was 7000 km away from his left hooks and right jabs I felt safe and secure "Bonjour Monsieur!Comment allez-vous?" I said reading from the phrase book I had swiped from a stout German couple at the breakfast buffet, who had gone for a second helping of Knockwurst, Bratwurst or was it Buckhurst? Who knows with these Krauts?

Anyway, Q continued "it's all been arranged she is having breakfast at the Bivouac Café, where you will accidently bump into her at the buffet, then do your thing. Don't fuck this up a lot of lives are at stake here; it makes me slightly nauseous to think that we are all dependant on a turd like you; but the die has been cast and I will have to live with this decision of mine forever."

That was quite a speech and I could catch the desperation in his voice so I tried to cheer him up with a speech of my own "don't worry sir, have I ever let you down?" then continued on hurriedly before Q could begin listing out the many occasions when I had "I will have her in bed before the week is out. I give you my solemn promise" Q merely grunted and then hung up the phone.

I stepped out of my suite and into a cloud of Chanel Number 5. Her name was Amandine and she was gorgeous, she occupied the adjacent suite, and she was on her way for some breakfast downstairs. I gave her my disarming smile as we walked towards the elevator we exchanged pleasantries and cards, hers read "Amandine Fleur, Personal Consultant" mine read " S R Khan, Super Star" in the elevator she leaned into me and breathed into my ear "cherchez - vous un bon moment?"

My high school French is a bit rusty, "Oui! Oui!" I wanted to reply but it's difficult to do so when one is trying to staunch the flow of blood from a sharp bite on the ear lobe and a simultaneous pat on my tushy. Wow! Here was a chance of ticking off number 3 on that Bucket List of mine, then I remembered Q and the billions (1.25 to be exact) waiting back home for me; forget them I reasoned this was a French chick! They would understand, wouldn't they? Wouldn't you? As I went in pursuit behind her, we had entered the lobby which was draped in flags of the world, they surrounded us and then I got a glimpse of the good old Tricolour, that was drooping morosely wedged in between the flags of Ireland and Italy, they too were drooping as if wondering how they had come to be with a third world country. and I wavered, she was at the entrance to the dining room and I was about to follow her in when I was jostled aside by a fellow guest who was also headed towards the dining room as if eager to reach before they closed up shop. It was an enormous Sardar with his wife and three kids in tow, "Aphasosa Ji, para assijaldivichhai" a fellow countrymen! He continued huffing and puffing "Assinaste la der nalarahe ham" loosely translated it meant that they were in a hurry and that they were late for breakfast, she had disappeared by now and I considered the omens, 2 of them, the tricolour and the Sardar, would the poor chap even have a country left to go back to? So, I changed course and headed out of the huge glass doors and hurriedly hailed a cab, even though the Napoleon Hotel was within walking distance; if I was to keep my tryst with destiny, I didn't want to be late.

I made my way to the café and sat down facing the entrance and in due time she entered with her body guards. They were both supposedly Aziz's men so I winked at the burly duo as if to say Hi Bro! Whassup? They ignored me and led her to a cubicle along the side of large plate glass window and then sat down at a table where she was clearly in sight. Very professional and I nodded my approval at them, quite wasted of course since they could not see me. I concentrated on my prey! She looked more of a dog than in her picture and I steeled myself for the encounter reminding myself that I was doing this for my country. I moved towards the breakfast buffet, by the way frenchies have lousy breakfasts; croissants, coffee and fruit, no idlis or dosas or even an omelette station! I grabbed a plate and did the rounds, the French waiters here as well could not parlez vous anything but French. From the corner of my eye I could see that Lyla had reached the buffet table and was diving into the fruit bowl, like one of the dolphins at Waterworld. I did my thing and we were chatting about this and that in no time at all. Mainly about what lousy breakfasts the French have. By the time I had escorted her back to her table we were reminiscing about *Choley Baturays and Alu Parathas* and in no time at all she had agreed to go on a sightseeing trip with me "But they have to come" she said eyeing the two gorillas who were pretending, to be invisible and failing quite miserably at the job "I wouldn't have it any other way" I said, at my chivalrous best.

All the tourist agencies boast of 'Paris in 24 hours, but we did it in four. We had fun, and for a moment I forgot that she was the daughter of the man who would destroy my country in a snap, if he could. The gorillas were following us in a black Citroen looking quite frazzled with the pace we were setting. We leaned back in the taxi, headed for the Louvre and I was eager to see it especially their most famous painting, I told her that I was eager to see if I could figure out the reason for the smirk or something equally inane and she laughed and I pushed my hand onto hers and gave it a squeeze but she slapped it away so hard that it stung. Maybe later, after I had softened her up a bit more, but I was unnerved I tell you, upset that my magic was not working, we whizzed through the Louvre, stopping only to admire the mystery woman, sadly the glass pyramid was 'under maintenance' so were out in record time. "Where to now" I asked "I want coffee" she said petulantly about to stamp her foot impatiently as if she were in her presidential palace and ordering an attendant Colonel to get her one. Paki officers are notoriously subservient to their current dictators' family needs. So, I looked around for a bistro but nary was a one in sight, Paris supposed to be crawling with them. We got back into the taxi and she ordered it back to the Hotel.

Once at the hotel we went back to the Bivouac and ordered coffees, hers was a latte and mine Irish and I went back into my role of Romeo with gusto, had there been any Anti Romeo Squads roaming around it was most likely that I would have been thrashed to within an inch of my life, but since there were none I went at it with great verve and passion. You know, somehow, I was not getting the response I expected and I felt as if I was swimming against the current. She was resisting me quite fiercely and I figured that if I continued along these lines she was likely to make a scene, she had already delivered a few sharp kicks to my shins below the table and slapped my wrists till they were red above the table. I really felt as if I was barking up the wrong tree. How could she resist me for long? Was I losing my touch? Then I thought of something and I excused myself and walked towards the exit, giving the two gorillas thumbs up as I passed their table. I fumbled for Amandine's card and called her. It was a brief call and I was back to our table in a jiffy. This time I kept my hands and legs to myself like a gentleman. We chatted about this and that for some time and I could see that she was getting bored. I tried one more time "why don't we take this party to your room " I said softly "Why" she asked suspiciously, sounding a bit like Q "So that the three of us can have some fun" I said patiently "Three? But there are only two of us" "NonMon Cherie, now we are three" as if on cue Amandine glided up and sat down beside Lyla. Lyla was transformed, from a wilted lily to a blooming rose, all in a few seconds. She indicated to the gorillas to pay the bill and scrambled to her feet and together she and Amandine made a beeline for the elevator bank. I had to struggle to keep up but I did stop briefly by the gorillas' table to whisper "Menage et trois" to them and then hurried to catch up fearing that they were likely start without me!

And that's how it happened Lyla scarcely was aware that I was even present as she concentrated all her attentions on Amandine who surprisingly reciprocated quite enthusiastically as she shrugged me off repeatedly and I gave up as both women concentrated on each other. I think *ménage at trois* must mean something else in France. My work was done here the both of them couldn't have been in a more compromising position and I left closing the door gently behind me

It was not hard to figure it out, I thought as I walked briskly back to my hotel, packed my suitcase and made a bee line for CdG airport. Aziz's guys probably had more cameras in her room than Harrods has in their dressing rooms.

I was back in Q's upper office the day after, waiting for the summons and it came PDQ. I sat stiffly in front of him and he beamed at me, he was extremely bucked and switched on the 70" monitor. It was all over the news; Q kept flicking through the channels until he came to the channel with that loud-mouthed guy. He was ranting about what a stunning victory it was for India, and how our military might had forced the enemy back into their cantonments without firing a single shot and how our brave hearts deserved the nations gratitude and that they should be rewarded with a hefty pay hike blah blah blah. The last time we really won a war and lost hundreds of lives, the reigning government cut out allowances under the guise of rationalisation. So, we didn't set much store by what the neta's said, unless we linked our salaries to those of the neta's. Wishful thinking.

Any way Q was mighty pleased with my contribution to the withdrawal and i reminded him of his promise to reward me beyond my wildest dreams and he did just that.

Two of his goons attached themselves to me as I headed to the car park and then they half pushed half dragged me into Q's BMW and simultaneously pulled a black canvas bag over my head. My girlish protestations were drowned as the driver revved the motor and screeched out of the facility. One of the goons snarled into my face "keep still you little punk or we will slit your throat and stuff your balls down your throat" so i kept still cursing Q for this humongous betrayal. I guessed that this was all part of the deal they must have made with the Pakis; we will pull back if you hand over the defiler of our First Daughter!

After about 2 hours we came to a halt and i could hear the sound of waves lapping against the shore. Surajkhund Lake! Were they going to drown me? Anyway, I kept a stiff upper lip as I was pushed/dragged across a rickety plank and aboard some sort of a boat the bag was whisked from my head and i was amazed to see that I was aboard a houseboat! I looked towards the goons who were almost at the car by now and one of them gave me a thumbs up though his thumb looked more like a cucumber and i replied by giving him the traditional finger. I heard the familiar clacking and jingling of payals coming from inside the house boat, I rushed in like a mighty wind and into the arms of my little madrasi dancer. I had to dodge her lunging neck as she assumed the traditional stance. I picked her up and we fell on the bed and the last thing i saw as i closed my eyes in bliss was a shiny set of handcuffs dangling from the bedposts.

WARROOMS HAVE EARS

I was fooling around in Q's so-called office, which by the way, was small, dinghy, dusty and hot. I thought it odd that a man of his high status and stature should be allotted such modest accommodations, was he not whom he purported himself to be? Was I being manipulated by a mere undersecretary level underling? It was as I was mulling on this profound discovery that the man himself bounced in looking pink and chubby and bursting with good health. He turned pale when he saw me or as pale as a man with such a ruddy complexion could go pale. "You" he hissed and I don't care if any number of English Professors say, you can't hiss a word without sibilants, if you're Q, you can and he didn't even have his stinky cigar sticking out from between his yellow teeth. Only his teeth were not yellow instead they were pearly white, as if tobacco hadn't ever touched his lips this was not the Q I knew of the deserted parking lots and darkened allies, this Q was round robust and red. I hardly knew the man "You" he repeated, his toothbrush moustache bristling at me ferociously, then he composed himself and adopted a more conciliatory tone. After all, I thought, noticing his Dr Jekyll and Mr. Hyde act, I was his most successful agent in a long time and a little license was to be allowed for someone with my rare talents plus, did I mention my boyish charm, cherubic good looks and disarming smile?

"So" he said with fake affability" what brings you to the metropolis? I thought you were in Goa, why are you here?" He asked suddenly worried and his brow furrowed, "have you been exiled from that state? What did you do? Did you get some Russian chick knocked up? I told you weren't to fuck around with Russian dames or any dame from the eastern bloc for that matter, or is it the Ukrainians? They run all the drug rings down there. What did you do to piss them off? Has your cover been blown? I'll chew your balls if your cover has been blown?" I had all but wilted under this barrage of questions and took a few seconds to recover,NNNo Sir" I stammered "it's neither the Russians nor the Ukrainians it's the French"

On hearing this he visibly relaxed and flopped into a rickety chair on the other side of the table "So what are the frogs up to then? "he asked good naturedly "have the Germans crossed the Maginot Line again "he chuckled at his witticism "what have we got to do with this?" "Maginot Line? Don't you mean McMahon line?" I queried him, eager to show off my knowledge of military history, many a canister of midnight oil had I burnt, in an unsuccessful effort to clear my promotion exams so that Q would no longer have an excuse for not promoting me and though I had narrowly failed to get the required grade this time, I was glad of a chance to prove that all that oil had not been burnt in vain, to be fair, we were in a field area with no electricity and the oil I had burnt was Kerosene and had been pilfered from the quartermaster stores "You're an idiot" he growled at me "if you have left your post and come all the way to my office with some cockamamie story and without official orders at that, you will be guilty of desertion and I can have you shot for this offence, first thing tomorrow if I can swing it, and believe me I can, so speak up, you worm" I was unfazed, being Q, this was par for the course and I had undergone worse bollockings from him, so I just 'pretended to be petrified, I was good at pretending to be petrified, sometimes I could be petrified with very little effort and I suitably replied in high falsetto "No Sir, they were retired officers and they were talking in French to two suited guys, through an interpreter. I was at the Bar called Red Pigeon with a cute little Slovakian girl so I was not paying much attention but the word Scorpene did crop up frequently as also the words 'Heavy Commission' I tried to pay more attention but the Slovakian girl had her hand on my thigh and her scarlet coated nails were digging into my sensitive flesh. Now my thighs are my prime erogenous zones also I was wearing Capri's so I clean forgot about air force officers, Scorpene and heavy commissions and took the young lady for a walk on the lonely beach in front of the Red Pigeon. It was only after our walk and I had dropped her off at her hotel, while I was having a post walk cigarette that the significance of what I had overheard sank in. I rushed back to the bar but they had already left. The barman, a young goan, who was studying for MBA by day and moonlighting as barkeep by night told me that he didn't know the foreigners but knew the other two by sight. They were ex naval officers who had started their own diving company called Murli Ocean Diving Academy" I finished my story breathlessly and paused to gulp in some sorely needed oxygen "You mean Naval Officers" said Q quietly " you mean you forgot about the naval officers Scorpene and heavy commissions don't you?" "No Sir, the two guys at the bar were naval officers but they mentioned something about assets and I heard the name Wing Commander something Vay crop up" " then what happened?" asked Q, all business now " then she slid her hand right up my thigh Sir and raked her nails all over my skin, it gave me goose bumps, so naturally I took her by the elbow..." "You Moron, I'm not interested in your miserable little sex life. I mean what did you do next?" He bellowed at me interrupting me just as I had reached the part where things had begun to get a bit risqué. "Why sir, I came straight to you"

For a tubby little chap, Q could be quite agile when he wanted to, this he ably demonstrated to me as he leapt up from his chair "follow me "he said cryptically and then dived into what I only could assume was the toilet. I must admit that I hesitated, I mean there are limits to what one could do for a promotion, and in any case, this was hardly the time for an amorous tryst with your boss. What are we Paki officers? "Hurry up you imbecile" said Q, sensing my reluctance, so joined him in the little cubicle. Much to my surprise the door concealed a rickety lift circa 1850's. I half expected to see old man Otis as the attendant but apparently this was one of those do it yourself jobs and Q began punching buttons furiously. With a shudder and a lurch, it began its descent.

I now know that his real office is located 12 storeys below North Block in one of the numerous nuclear bomb shelters dug deep below North Block. Q maintains that they are not nuclear bomb shelters, constructed in case the Pakis decide to take the Indian government out, or worse, if the jihadists get their hands on one or two n devices, after all the Pakis are notoriously slovenly with their nuclear housekeeping protocols, and are quite capable of leaving one or two devices lying around unattended, but just numerous interlinking basements constructed during Lutyens time and that he is merely making efficient use of the extra space for his vast secretariat. Of course, he had a front office on the surface as well, which he used whenever he had appointments with other heads of ministries and ministers but since no one even knew that he existed, it was unused and just afforded him a means of being dramatic Harry Potter style. There was a set of stairs that appeared to be ascending up to the bell tower, but on closer examination actually descended down into the abyss. Quite the Penrose conundrum and typically Q I might add.

He all but pushed me through into his office which btw stood out in stark contrast to his office above. Plush opulent and luxurious are the three adjectives that immediately spring to mind while trying to describe it. The walls were plastered with dozens of monitors and it took me awhile to realize that I was looking into the offices of the HM, RM, PM & leader of the Opposition. A gesture from Q and the screens went blank. "One word of this and I will kill you, you miserable little turd, only my wife knows about this place, and she is dead!" he said nastily. Frankly I was getting a tad fed up with the numerous death threats he had been making all day and I was about to draw myself up to my full height and assert myself vigorously when he sat down in his enormous chair & gestured me to do the same. "What about Scorpene" he asked "I don't know Sir; do you think they wanted to hire one? I prefer the Innova myself. "from the corner o my eye I could see Q's fist beginning to clench so I rapidly changed track "Or is it some sort of code word?" it's a submarine deal with the frogs" he said impatiently "if you weren't so busy trying to get into that Slovakian floozy's pant s we would have more information, we have been after this gang for years. They have moles in the highest echelons of the MOD and god knows where else" he glared at me. I blushed suitably "actually Sir I was trying to get her out of her pants" he didn't let me finish, instead he picked up a remote and flashed it at the bank of monitors; all of a sudden only one monitor remained, it appeared to be some sort of a conference hall with a few uniformed guys fiddling around "that's the Naval War room, today is their strategic defence presentation to the RM. All the services & MOD will be there, the Navy is trying to push for a firm called Thales which manufactures the Scorpene class submarine. But the def secy prefers the British one, those bloody babu's don't know squat about submarines except that their commission is higher. There is talk of huge kickbacks floating around but we don't know for sure." "how can I help" I asked him, ever ready to make some brownie points and further my own interests without getting in to actual danger, I had long ago come to the conclusion that I was more of a virtual danger sort of guy "we have to get you into that conference room" said Q looking quite determined "at all costs you have to find out what is happening and prevent it" prevent what sir?" I asked anxiously "why, any war room leaks of course, it would embarrass the MOD no end, and the RM could end up with egg on his face." He studied the monitor intently "who are those guys" he queried "what are they doing?" "seems to be a couple of waiters Sir" I replied, eager to show how much on the ball I was "I think they are making tea arrangements" "Hmmmm" he said, a nasty glint in his eyes "guess who is going to be serving the RM tea today?" I shied away like a skittish horse "me sir? You want me to demean myself to the rank of a seaman first class? I don't know anything about serving tea to VVIPs, they are all so finicky and fussy, I couldn't tell Earl Grey from Orange Pekoe and what do I know of scones and cucumber sandwiches?" he growled at me like a bad tempered Bull Dog protecting his pork chop " I said the RM not Queen Elizabeth, you moron, you will serve tea, biscuits and samosas to them just like everybody else, now get out and report to Naval HQ, I am sending your clearances and new ID ahead, check your phone to see who you are, then after the conference meet me in the parking lot of the officers' institute at 2100 hours tonight and" he paused dramatically " wear a shirt and tie and not those stupid clown outfits you seem to favour so much these days" then, as if recognizing a good exit line when he heard one, he stomped out of his office. He stomped right back in ten seconds later "Get out" he snarled at me. "this is my office, why should I leave?" I couldn't argue with his impeccable logic plus I could take a hint; I was gone in 60 seconds. It should not have taken even 20 seconds, but I had to make a detour via the upper office to pick up my precious flash drives, all eight of them, I had hidden them under a mouldy cushion, cleverly anticipating what I thought would be one of Q's corny routines that he used on me sometimes, getting me strip searched by two of his Para Commando body guards cum goons. Why did I have seven flash drives with me? you may well ask and I will tell you why because on my way here I had made a detour to the residence of one of the ADCs to the COAS, who had borrowed them more than a week ago and I was nervous that I might not get them back. But I did and they now nestled safely in my pant pocket till I got the idea of what his goons might do, hence the subterfuge However, that didn't happen, the goons must have been busy busting some poor Dep Sec's chops, and then we jumped into the toilet before I had a chance to recover them. Anyway, they now were nestling safely in my pocket as I made my way over to Naval HQ. I truly valued those drives for they contained my entire collection of girl on girl porn with back up and backups backup, you know son father grandfather.

Naval HQ! What a glorious place! All chrome and glass and an atrium as huge as that of the Burj. I sauntered over to the Reception, checked my phone for who I was this time and identified myself as such to the pretty receptionist, who looked as if she would be more at home in a Miss Universe pageant then behind the counter of some naval office. I mean what a waste, we all know that these sea dogs & pups are known to sometimes steer on the wrong side of the road or shipping lane if one wants to be nautical, ask any submariner, I felt sorry for the poor girl and immediately proceeded to rectify that, I flashed her my winning smile, the one that had charmed the pants of that Slovak chippy back in Goa, but I could have been flashing that smile at the statue of liberty for all the good that it did me. She checked out my credentials on her computer and made out a temporary pass for the 3rd floor and handed it over to me, as I turned towards the elevator bank she called out after me "Sir, this came for you" and she handed me a brown paper wrapped package which contained, I surmised, my Seaman First Class uniform. I just hoped that Q had gotten my size right this time; he had screwed up far too many times in the past for it to be 'accidental' as he claimed trying desperately to hide some sort of internal convulsion that seemed to have suddenly taken hold of him and turn his little pot belly into Jell-O.

Thankfully the uniform was a perfect fit and I did look kind of dashing as I admired myself in the bulletproof glass window. I transferred the flash drives to my pocket of my well-fitting trousers and hoped that the bulge in my pants didn't give any of these old fogeys any reason to think that I was happy to see them. The guy detailed with me or rather to oversee me, was a Petty Officer by the name of Shankar Pillai, and boy was he petty, one would think that the Queen of England really was coming to tea rather than a mere RM, who was clueless about any of the etiquettes of High Tea. We split our responsibilities, he would plate and I would serve. We did a couple of trial runs and I finally mastered that we serve from the right and remove dirty plates from the left and I finally managed to not stumble while walking head held high and spine ramrod straight, "Remember" he told me for the fifth time "We bow but never stoop and we say Sir and Your Excellency and not Yes Boss or Roger That." Once he was reasonably satisfied about my ability to perform, he briefed me about the conference. Apparently, he was a regular in the War Room and had attended every conference since Ram Das.

The conference room was sound proofed so we in the pantry had no idea what they were saying. But we could clearly see through the toughened glass partition. Two air vice marshals and a wing commander sitting in the second row, one or two admirals and the RM of course, a sprinkling of OG a lieutenant General and a couple of major generals two fat majors sat in the second row and an assorted helping of bureaucrats, Secretaries, Deputy Secretaries and Under-secretaries where would we be without them? I assumed Q was also watching, the sly dog. The meeting broke up after 45 minutes, everything had gone smoothly, no tea was spilled on anyone, the samosas were highly appreciated and compliments paid to the chef, who was, I later found out, an apprentice from the naval canteen downstairs, the conference dispersed in dribs and drabs, seniority took precedence so all the top brass went first, I hung around in the galley munching on a samosa, they really were scrumptious btw, stuffed with cottage cheese, cashew nuts, raisins and accompanied by a tangy salsa dip.

I glanced through the glass partition, just in time to see Shankar Pillai pull a flash drive out from the computer and lay it on the table alongside it were 7 similar drives, he glanced furtively around him, but not behind him, thank goodness, and carefully inserted a flash drive into the RMs computer and fiddled with the keyboard he placed all the drives on the same silver salver that I had used earlier to serve those scrumptious samosas, Pillai then headed back to the pantry and I had just enough time to leap away from the window like a Thomson's Gazelle with a 200 kg lioness at its heels.

When he entered I was whistling nonchalantly at the kitchen sink, washing out a porcelain cup, it was yellow submarine I think, or maybe lion king, I forget. Pillai glanced at me slyly " you can go" he said placing the salver carefully on the counter and pottered around the overhead cupboards "why don't you go and change" I said "and then I will scoot, you look awfully hot and bothered, we can have a cup of tea before I leave, I would be honoured if you would oblige, I learnt a lot today from you, maybe you could give me a few tips, so that I too can aspire to reach the pinnacle of success, as you have done. In fact, I heard the RM asking about you from Admiral Whatshisname and the Admiral had replied in glowing terms about your efficiency." "Really" asked Pillai breathlessly "what did he say?" "I think they want you in MoD" I replied innocently

"Yes, Yes, Yes" exulted Pillai, sounding very much like that girl from Slovenia, back in Goa "all my efforts have paid off. I will just go and change and then we can have that cup of tea, and maybe I will give you a few pointers, so that you too can achieve the dizzy heights of success as I did" With that he withdrew to the staff toilet. I wasted no time; it was the work of a moment for me to substitute the flash drives with those on the salver and it was with a tear in my eye that I bid farewell to my precious porn collection. No amount of money could ever compensate me for the loss. If only the public could be made aware of the sacrifices that we make in the name of patriotism. I stuffed the drives into my uniform pocket, when Pillai returned I poured him a cup of tea, we were sipping our cups of tea like old friends when suddenly the main door of the conference room burst open and the Wing Commander strode in, cocky as only a flyboy could be, "Pillai" he called out loudly looking at the plate glass window. Pillai jumped up like wood nymph surprised by a huntsman while bathing in a babbling brook " Saar" he said resorting to the patois of his home state, he snatched up his salver lifted the cover and shoved two samosas under it and made for the service door " I will give him samosas" he said "Go GoGo" he whispered at me so I went wentwent.

I met Q in the parking lot, and because it was club night, it was rather crowded. I was smartly dressed in blue blazer, grey trousers, black Oxfords, black socks and regimental tie; his regiment not mine of course.

I handed over the flash drives to Q quite proudly and stood back to receive the shower of praise and accolades I was sure he was about to heap on me but instead he proceeded to give me a bollocking without any preamble, "you're an idiot, do you know what you have done? You allowed one USB to be carried out by that flyboy "Impossible" I said, my voice rising several octaves "I counted 7 and it so happened that I had 7 flash drives on me" you had 7 flash drives on you? What was on them? Your porn collection?" He asked slyly "you forgot the flash driveon the computer you dolt" "you knew about my flash drives?" I asked incredulously "of course I did you moron, I know the colour of your shit. We saw you hiding them from my office so I sent a couple of techies to install locators on each. Some information would have reached the agents and several copies must have been made by now" he said taking stock " but thanks to the locaters in all the drives, we have begun rounding up the spy ring " he handed me an envelope "here's your ticket back to Goa and a little something extra for your efforts, my car will drop you at the airport. Good luck"

He disappeared, this time in the direction of the club house. I stood there dumbfounded for a second, things had moved so fast, then a parked car flashed its lights twice and I headed towards the black BMW with blackened windows. Wow! I thought so this is Q's ride, not bad and no dep sec would warrant a official car of this splendour and magnitude.

I leaned back against the plush cushions in and opened the envelope expecting a wad of high denomination notes along with the ticket which was executive class btw, inside were three photographs of three gorgeous women; I flipped the photo over and saw the mobile numbers of each girl written on the reverse of each in Q's unmistakable handwriting. the SOB must be getting senile I thought happily but what the heck I deserved this.

EPILOGUE

It was not surprising, when Thales Enterprises were awarded the contract worth $3.7 billion for supply and indigenisation of umpteen Scorpene submarines. In spite of their competition releasing details about the submarine nothing of strategic value was exposed. But I guess every cloud has its silver lining; Thales' competitors were treated to some of the finest porn that most of the continents had to offer.

The CBI inquiry that followed and the crackdown on one or two minnows and their accounts seized. All the big fish got away as is so often the case in our country. I felt sorry for Pillai though.

NO ORCHIDS FOR MRS MIRCHANDANI

It all started innocuously enough, I had just returned from a highly successful mission in the valley and was resting on my laurels, so to speak. I would have told you all but I'm forbidden, by stupid and archaic secrecy laws, to speak of my great feats of valour and derring-do, but let it suffice that there is now a barren stretch of land in Nowshera, where previously clusters of paki border posts and LET training camps used to be. Very mysterious their disappearance, it's almost as if they had been 'surgically removed.

Anyway I had gone to the 'Phool Mandi' at RG Bhavan in Connaught Place in order to buy some exotic flowers for my boss Q ,his birthday was coming up sometime this week or maybe the next, but since it was important that I keep the old geezer in good humour, I had decided to give them to him tomorrow itself. Let me explain, for the benefit of my international readers, that 'Phool Mandi' pronounced Fool Mundee and it means 'Flower Market'. Phool means flower and Mandi means market. However, when my boss calls me fool and bloody fool he is not calling me 'flower' by a long shot.

'Q' is a cantankerous old fart, who just happens to head our nation's most secret and covert black operations division. It so secret that even the NIA & RAW doesn't know we exist. Like us, there are several other countries that have similar organizations and all the heads are very chummy except when the politicians interfere and try to rig each other's election, that's when the claws come out.

Anyway, as I was saying when I was in the flower market, I noticed that almost all the stalls were empty, a few were selling marigolds and jasmine and some anaemic gladioli stems but of tulips, roses, carnations orchids and azaleas there was nary a trace. I didn't think much of it at that time and proceeded to the back of the market where the exotic plants were sold. As I approached, Aziz sidled up and beckoned to me conspiratorially, Aziz by the way is one of our informants, and quite an industrious one as well. Thanks to him we have busted several Paki sleeper cells, unearthed at least 3 counterfeit gangs & cracked quite a few heroin smuggling rings. We, in turn, have lavished on him much silver and since flowers were his passion (his family have been growing the poppy flower for generations in the Hindukush Mountains), we set him up as flower trader at the Phool Mandi Stock Exchange, where he was doing pretty well for himself. "Need some orchids Aziz" I whispered in an equally conspiratorial manner, playing along with him, "and I need them fast" "No can do" he whispered back "mine and everyone else's complete consignments have been bought up by Paris I have just diverted a whole shipment to Paris, they will reach in a day or two, have some marigolds or jasmine instead, I can get you some at cost price." I stamped my Gucci clad foot impatiently "if I wanted marigolds I would have asked for them. It's for my boss I need to stay in his good books for a few more days till he issues my posting orders. "I'm sorry but most of the traders have sold their stocks to flower markets in Paris" "how about some Tulips? I asked hopefully "Paris" was his succinct reply, every flower mentioned got the same reply "I have a few artificial orchids if you want" he said slyly "your boss won't even know the difference until it's too late" he dived into his rickety wooden cubicle and reappeared holding a magnificent bouquet of the most glorious orchids (made in China of course) I had ever seen "they have a very complicated scientific name, they are more commonly known as the Lady's Slipper Orchid. I'm sure your boss has got quite a few lady's slippers himself" he smirked. I was not too sure myself but it would have to do.

As I walked briskly to Q's fake office the next day, I had a smile on my cherubic countenance and I might have been whistling, I'm not sure, but I did get many an admiring glance from the other staff in the building. I had this bouquet n my hands and I'm sure many wondered enviously as to who the lucky lady was. If they only knew! I entered his fake office and held the bouquet aloft towards the cameras, like Arthur with Excalibur. A green light flashed impatiently signalling me to come down. If you are new, and have missed out on my earlier chronicles, Q's real office was 80 feet below in a huge bomb shelter built to protect our fearless leaders any time the Paki's decided to do a surgical strike of their own. It was a vast labyrinth of corridors and passage ways and in the initial stages I must admit to surreptitiously using my GPS to get around.

Anyway, I dived into the loo, sat on the toilet seat and pulled the chain; even though I had done this quite a few times before I still felt as if I had left my stomach behind as I whooshed down the chute, easily at Mach 2 or Mach 3. I slammed into the airbags and ricocheted onto a foam mattress which was so soft and downy that I must have sunk at least 3 feet before I was gently raised to the surface. All this while I was still holding the bouquet aloft and it was no worse for the ride, still magnificent still gorgeous.

I popped into 'Q's office all smiles and bonhomie which vanished in about 2.33 seconds.

"Don't grin at me like an idiot, you moron, why are grinning at me like that?" "Happy birthday Sir" I squeaked "Hope you have many more to come and live a long and healthy life" I replied untruthfully, I hurriedly pushed the bouquet at him across his vast desk. As it slid towards him like an incoming missile, he swatted it away with the file he was reading, like professional tennis player, sending it flying across the room and landing it knew not where, actually it was in the far corner of the room, still looking slightly dishevelled but gorgeous never the less. "It's not my birthday you imbecile, what is wrong with you" "it's not your birthday?" I squawked in fake surprise "I thought it was and bought you these rare and expensive flowers as a token of my love and respect for you" "Are you high on smack you worm? I will chew your balls! I will have you court martialled and shot, believe me I can do it". This outburst was par for the course for Q and I countered it with my cute adorable hangdog look of shame and remorse.

"Why are you even here" he growled "Why Sir after that Nowshera business I'm awaiting my posting, you promised to send me to someplace nice" I replied still in remorse mode "I'll give you nice, how does Itanagar Capital of State of Imphal) sound? I think it sounds good maybe you will" I cut him off "I'm banned from that state sir, after that incident with the CM's wife" while 'Q' thought of other nasty places to send me I looked around the room and down at his desk. I noticed a lot of travel brochures scattered across it. Some had pictures of the Eiffel tower others had pictures of the London Eye, there was even one with pictures of the Brandenburg gate but the one that seemed to have caught 'Q's fancy was a brochure with huge roller coasters, Mickey and Minnie mouse and of course Donald Duck, Disneyland??? "Planning a holiday Sir?" I asked coyly "none of your business" he snarled immediately covering the brochures with his forearms like a third grader. "Why are you even here? Oh yes your posting, how does Kabul sound?" he asked nastily "I think as a junior assistant to the Military Attaché you will be quite a hit with all those Pathans over there" "Why can't you send me to Disneyland?" I asked desperately "or Paris or Germany?" "Fat chance" he snorted "we finally have good relations with the Yanks, Frogs and the Krauts if I send you there you are sure to fuck them up. Kabul it is young man now get out." But I was going to give up without a fight "But Sir" I pleaded "Nowshera! Surgical strikes! Training Camps!" I could see that my pleas had struck a chord "OK not Kabul, how about any city in Bangladesh? Your choice. We have quite a few irons in the fire there" the phone rang shrilly and he grabbed it eagerly "Yes "he bellowed into the instrument, gripping the handset so tightly that I immediately felt a wave of sympathy for it. It very could have been my neck that he was squeezing the life out of. Any way he grunted several times like a boar preparing to mount its favourite sow and then slammed the handset down " that was my French counterpart, those bastards have hit Paris again" he fumed "they are always one step ahead of us, if we could just catch a break, just once." To see Q so disillusioned that he was forced to confide in me merely underlined the seriousness of the matter so I, also put on a stern face, eyes like slits my jaw clenched, "those bastards" I said "what can I do? Tell me Sir? Do you want me to go to Paris and do some wet work? I can leave in 40 minutes and be back for dinner." But he was too frustrated to yell at me "if we could just have inkling as to where they are going to strike next we can round up the whole network once and for all." "Yes, Sir I said dutifully and studied the intricate designs of Q's wall hangings behind him. "Nice flowers" he said and I immediately jumped out of my seat and made a bee line for the flowers still lying in their corner, like a prize-winning golden retriever. If I had a tail I would have wagged it "they are fake" I said cheerfully" thrusting them at him "I know" he said irritably "get me a few more, RMs birthday is in a week and then it's the PM's anniversary" "No probs Sir I'll just pop over to Aziz's place this evening and pick up a few. In fact, only artificial ones were available; all the fresh stems had been bought up by Paris markets. Huge demand there" He merely grunted and waved me away

Two evenings later, I was back at the market and it still looked as forlorn as ever. Aziz was playing Candy Crush when I barged in to his cubicle. He hurriedly put away his iPhone and greeted me "Ah, it's007, twice in a week? What an honour" "Shut up Aziz" I shot back "My boss wants real orchids for his boss and the big boss himself, so get me a dozen stems each, two bouquets" Aziz hung his head in mock shame "Sorry sir most flowers have been bought up by Blooming Market in Amsterdam. I sold my stock at a very good price" Bloemenmarkt is the largest flower market in the Netherlands and is the world's only floating flower market. Millions of stems pour in daily to be auctioned off to the highest bidders that throng around the place.

"Don't you have anything?" I asked desperately "I can let you have some artificial one like the one I gave you earlier" he said diving back into his cubicle and re-emerging a second later with two bouquets, triumphantly held aloft like a naked Joan of Arc holding aloft her sword, only He was not naked instead he wore jeans and had hairier arms. "Here, take these, your boss will love them, maybe even post you to nice place this time." Right "I said "He is threatening me with Kabul" "Ah Kabul! Nice place I have lot of relatives and friends there. My cousin sister also she is there. I give you her number you can look her up, she will show you good time" but I was out. I grabbed the flowers and walked hurriedly past the empty stalls.

I reached Q's office next say at noon and found him staring blankly at the TV monitors; they were all showing the same thing, Scenes of horror and carnage some screens showed members of the public laying wreaths and bouquets and candles. The actual site of the blast was a vast ocean of flowers and candles. "They hit Amsterdam this time" sad Q filling me in. on hearing this my ears pricked up "Amsterdam? The Netherlands Amsterdam? It's funny but 3 days ago I went to the flower market to buy you some flowers and all the shipments had all been diverted to Paris and there was a bomb blast at the Le Figaro main building yesterday I went again went to the flower market but all the flowers had been diverted to Amsterdam, and today this blast at the main Metro station. Something's not right" but Q had already made the connection "Set up a meeting with Aziz at Chandni Chowk, tell him to make sure he is not followed, now scram get out and vamoose keep your passport ready and be ready to move at very short notice"

I don't know what transpired at the meeting between Q and Aziz but the next day he was in a far better mood, he tossed a manila envelope at me and said "Go to Bangalore and arrest one Mrs. Mirchandani and bring her back here. No one should know about this. Pretend she is your mother." Bangalore" I yelped "I don't need a passport to go to Bangalore? "No, you don't" was his succinct reply.

I read the dossier on Mrs Mirchandani that Q had hurriedly assembled. She was the wife of a Brigadier and quite the socialite. Unknown to our homegrown intelligence agencies, She was also the owner of a vast international chain of Niche shops under a web of various names and aliases that specialized only in flowers, candles and teddy bears, her shops were all over Europe, the UK and United States. She was also the founder and convener of the Florists' Union of Traders Worldwide Association or FUTWA as they like to call themselves. FUTWA had its Headquarters in Columbia as it was the world's largest supplier of cut flowers and heroin, but not for long she was planning to move the whole shebang closer home, maybe Lahore or Rawalpindi where conditions would be more conducive for business.

She was a sweet old lady, could be anybody's grandmother; that is if anybody's grandmother was a gun toting silver haired old biddy, who dived behind a planter after firing off a volley of shots at us as we barged into her mansion. I hid behind a strategic pillar as our SWAT team shot up the pace and finally overpowered her.

She told me all on the plane ride home.

She had always loved flowers and in her day had quite the green thumb, I glanced down at her hands which were neatly folded in her lap, and her green lacquered carefully manicured nails told me at once that had been quite some time since they held a trowel or any other gardening tool. Anyway...

Ever since ISIS and Al Qaida appeared on the international scene Her business in Europe had flourished. Every time there was a shooting or a suicide bomber blew himself up there would be a massive public out pouring of grief and huge mountains of flowers would be laid at the site, then there were the individual funerals and memorial services. Every time there was a blast or shooting the sales in her chain of florist shops, would sky rocket, and stocks would be sold out within minutes and there wasn't enough time to get some more as each shop couldn't really order huge stocks of flowers and then hope for something tragic to happen. So, she to take matters into her own hands   She went onto the Internet.

"The internet is a beautiful thing" she explained to me, sounding very much like a High School teacher, explaining the wonders of baking soda to a bunch of 8th graders in her Home Science class. "You can search for any and every thing; you just need to know what to ask for" I yawned politely there wasn't much that I hadn't asked for from the internet and I always got fantastic results, this was nothing new "In my opinion" she continued "the crystal ball that the fortune tellers used and so favoured by the ancient soothsayers was probably a desktop monitor hooked up to the web with a Google app or something equally good and probably got wiped out during the dark ages by the plague or some other virus." I nodded my head vigorously "that's what I also thought" I said excitedly "Aliens probably visited and set up the world wide web along with the Pyramids, the Incas and Harappan civilizations." She stroked my arm and murmured "so young and yet still so knowledgeable" I blushed and asked her to carry on

"I searched the web using key words *Al Qaida, ISIS, SUICIDE BOMBER* and *God is great.* You will be surprised at the number of hits I got. I chose my websites carefully filtering out all those sites which gave me instructions on how to make a bomb with contents of ones fridge, kitchen or bathroom, I maneuverer my way through this labyrinth of sites and finally found a chat room and entered calling myself flower girl "fatat alzuhur "in Arabic.

As I entered, I wrote God is great in capital letters and salaam alekum and got several alekum salaams in reply.

I was approached by several members with names like fist of god, death to America.

I then typed in how do I become a suicide bomber and all the messaging stopped, the public board stopped scrolling and a deathly hush descended in the room.

I got a private message asking for my WhatsApp number which I gave immediately. My phone rang and the voice asked what I wanted, I told him that I want to talk with Al Bakri "about what? My caller asked angrily "about a business proposition" she had replied.

One day while she was in Dubai scouting out some new locations, the Middle East was full of potential and it was important to be ready she explained, she was approached by an Armani clad Bedouin who led her to a waiting black limousine "get in" he said in a cultured voice "we have a proposal for you"

"What if "he asked once they were seated and the limo joined the traffic "you were somehow able to know in advance when and where the next attack was to occur, would it help your sales?" "I suppose so "she had replied not realizing the import of what she was hearing "Good he said we control most of the terror organizations today including ISIS and AQ and

Al Shabab. I have a list of towns and dates. Send your entire stock to the cities a day in advance and then sit back and rake in the profits" he pushed a small piece of paper into her hands and ordered the limo to stop. As it pulled up to the curb he added "of course we would want a 60% cut of the profits in cash, half yearly. This is not negotiable We will meet again 6 months from now, and that's how it started beta" Beta! It means Son and I leaned away from her as far as my seat belt would let me. This woman was a monster.

But Q saw her as a sort of Golden Goose, he finally got what he wanted; dates and times of the next attack. Mrs Mirchandani was carefully cultivated like some species of rare flower. Q would inform his counterpart of which ever country was next on the list, and the would-be terrorists or suicide bomber or shooters were invariably on their 'persons of concern' list they would be easily identified and caught and rounded up without the public even knowing about it. Of course, the spurt in sales of FUTWA subsided dramatically and the euphoria only lasted for 6 months. But it was a good 6 months never the less.

You would think that since I was the one who uncovered this deadly cartel I would have been honoured and many plaudits heaped upon me. But no, not when Q is your boss all I got was a surly grunt as I strutted into his office. It is very rare when Q's foul moods and temper can deter me. I snapped him one of my dashing salutes a la Hans Solo and flopped down into one of his super comfy chairs, I crossed my legs and looked at him expectantly "what are you gawking at you moron?" he barked at me "I have just spoken to my counterparts in France and the Netherlands and they have thanked us quite profusely for our inputs. I guess you also played your part and deserve some credit so I am posting you as an assistant to the Assistant Deputy Military Attaché to the Vatican. Let's see how you screw this one up. You are not to fraternize or hit on any of the sisters, nuns or anyone else who has taken the cloth and that includes the Pope. But there are plenty of other diversions, besides there is something brewing in the Vatican and I want to find out what. The papal guard has a few PIOs, see if you can turn a couple, tell them how great we have become, tell them about our surgical strikes, tell the we are building toilets in every house, tell them about GST and Aadhar cards and come back in 3 months" I must say I was expecting worse Vatican City seemed ok plenty of culture. This was too nice for Q I looked at him suspiciously "Do I get full diplomatic immunity?" he nodded "you get full diplomatic immunity" "Do I get the platinum credit card?" he relied "you get the Platinum credit Card" he said patiently "can I rent a Ferrari convertible for sightseeing?" I asked hopefully. I realized I had gone too far as Q pressed a buzzer and two of the ten goons he kept around him bounced in grinning hugely they hoisted me out of my chair, threw me over one of their shoulders and jogged out. At least I would get to see the Pope I thought glumly as I was tossed out into the underground car park.